that ...

"Yes."

"Where is he?"

He shrugged. "Texas. Mexico."

Marie couldn't deny a quick flash of relief as it washed over her. Maybe she wouldn't have to face the marriage issue right away. She and the children could get settled in and...

"For how long?" she asked.

His gaze never left the road. "Can't rightly say. Could be next spring before he gets back."

"Next spring?"

Panic overtook any sense of relief. Her funds were almost gone. The children would starve to death by then, unless... She shivered at the thought, but unfortunately Stafford was her only hope.

Something in his eyes, the way they shimmered, had her mouth going dry, her nerves tingling as though a storm was approaching. Maybe there was another option.

"Who lives at Mr. Wagner's ranch in his absence?"

"

AUTHOR NOTE

Welcome to THE WRONG COWBOY. If any of you have read THE COWBOY WHO CAUGHT HER EYE, Marie was the woman on the train with all the children. From the moment I typed that minor reference I knew I had to write her story.

In doing so, I was also provided with the opportunity to incorporate an inanimate object that used to drive me crazy into one of my books. Our previous home had a wood stove that I could build a fire in blindfolded. Then we moved into *this* house and I encountered the stove from—well, you know… That stove and I battled… I have a scar from when the door mysteriously swung shut, hitting me on the head. Mysteriously because I was the only one at home. I am glad to say that stove never got the better of me—not completely—before we replaced it years ago.

Unfortunately the stove Marie encounters *does* best her—but everything happens for a reason.

I hope you enjoy meeting Marie, Stafford and all the children who eventually provide Marie with the family she's always wanted.

THE WRONG COWBOY

Lauri Robinson

MILLS & BOON

® and TM are trademarks owned and used by the trademark owner and/or its licensee. Trademarks marked with ® are registered with the United Kingdom Patent Office and/or the Office for Harmonisation in the Internal Market and in other countries.

Published in Great Britain 2014
by Mills & Boon, an imprint of Harlequin (UK) Limited,
Eton House, 18-24 Paradise Road, Richmond, Surrey, TW9 1SR

© 2014 Lauri Robinson

ISBN: 978-0-263-90996-8

Harlequin (UK) Limited's policy is to use papers that are natural, renewable and recyclable products and made from wood grown in sustainable forests. The logging and manufacturing processes conform to the legal environmental regulations of the country of origin.

Printed and bound in Spain
by Blackprint CPI, Barcelona

Lauri Robinson's chosen genre to write is Western historical romance. When asked why, she says, 'Because I know I wasn't the only girl who wanted to grow up and marry Little Joe Cartwright.'

With a degree in early childhood education, Lauri has spent decades working in the non-profit field and claims once-upon-a-time and happily-ever-after romance novels have always been a form of stress relief. When her husband suggested she write one she took the challenge, and has loved every minute of the journey.

Lauri lives in rural Minnesota, where she and her husband spend every spare moment with their three grown sons and four grandchildren. She works part-time, volunteers for several organisations, and is a diehard Elvis and NASCAR fan. Her favourite getaway location is the woods of northern Minnesota, on the land homesteaded by her great-grandfather.

Previous novels by Lauri Robinson:

HIS CHRISTMAS WISH
  (part of *All a Cowboy Wants for Christmas*)
UNCLAIMED BRIDE
INHERITING A BRIDE
THE COWBOY WHO CAUGHT HER EYE
CHRISTMAS WITH HER COWBOY
  (part of *Christmas Cowboy Kisses*)
THE MAJOR'S WIFE

Also available in Mills & Boon® Historical *Undone!* eBooks:

WEDDING NIGHT WITH THE RANGER
HER MIDNIGHT COWBOY
NIGHTS WITH THE OUTLAW
DISOBEYING THE MARSHAL
TESTING THE LAWMAN'S HONOUR
THE SHERIFF'S LAST GAMBLE
WHAT A COWBOY WANTS
HIS WILD WEST WIFE
DANCE WITH THE RANCHER
RESCUED BY THE RANGER
SNOWBOUND WITH THE SHERIFF
NEVER TEMPT A LAWMAN

**Did you know that some of these novels
are also available as eBooks?
Visit www.millsandboon.co.uk**

DEDICATION

To my wonderful friend Jean.

Thanks for the lunch dates, the brainstorming,
and the research trips.

Chapter One

August, 1884, Dakota Territory

Stafford Burleson prided himself on a few things—he wasn't a quitter, his cooking wasn't all bad, he was a mighty fine carpenter and he was quick on his feet. His wits were good, too. He was known for coming up with a plan at a dead run, yet right now he found himself dumbfounded. "What?"

"Mick's mail-order bride is waiting for him at the hotel in Huron." Walt Darter's scratchy voice repeating exactly what he'd said a moment ago made about as much sense the second time around as it had the first.

This time Stafford added a few more words to his question. "What are you talking about?" He set his cup down and dug his fingers into hair that sorely needed a good cutting. His scalp had started to tingle and he scratched at it. Eerily. "Mick didn't order a bride."

"That's not what she says." Walt couldn't have looked more stone-cold serious if he'd been standing before a judge and jury.

"Who?"

"Miss Marie Hall." The old man's face was sunburned from years of riding in the summer sun, and as he said her name a grin formed and his chest puffed with pride as if he'd just announced he'd found a goose that laid golden eggs.

The woman's name was completely unknown and Stafford pondered that. No one from Huron had been out this way for several months. Not that it was expected. The little town of Merryville had sprung up around the people who chose to stay behind when the railroad camp packed up to follow the tracks westward. There weren't too many businesses there yet, but he and Mick now bought their supplies in Merryville. It was only a few miles north of their land, and the railroad company had promised that, when the line was done, a depot would be built in the settlement, which meant cattle could be shipped and received there. It was what he and Mick had predicted would happen when they settled on their tracts of land and formed a partnership for the Dakota Cattle Company.

Their plan, to build one of the largest cattle

operations in the north, was falling into place more smoothly than the railroad line. Although Stafford would be the first to admit—and he often did—they still had plenty of work to do before they could sit back and savor the rewards of what they'd sowed.

Right now, they were still driving in herds every year, consisting of various breeds to ensure nothing would wipe them out. Not weather or disease. He'd brought in a hearty line of Herefords out of Texas this spring, and Mick had left a few weeks ago to go farther south, into Mexico, to purchase some of the Spanish cattle he'd read about.

A grin tugged at Stafford's lips. Mick must have stopped in Huron, let it be known he was heading south. "You almost had me on that one, Walt," Stafford said, letting out a sigh. In the five years since they'd settled out here and claimed hefty shares of glorious land from the government, Mick had talked about finding a wife, especially during the long cold winters. Stafford, having had his fill of women before he left Mississippi, told Mick countless times what a bad idea that would be. He went so far as to suggest Mick heat up a rock on the cookstove if his bed was that cold, had even hauled home a few good-size stones now and again, just to keep the teasing going. Practical jokes were never far apart

between the two of them. Mick was like that—
a jokester.

Half the men in the territory, including Walt,
had heard Mick spout off about finding a wife,
and the old jigger must be trying to carry on the
joking. "So, what's your real reason for being
here?" Stafford asked, picking his cup up again.
"No one rides a day and a half just to say hello."

The deep wrinkles in Walt's face remained
as the merriment slipped from his eyes and the
grin transformed into a grimace. The kind people make when they're delivering bad news. A
chill raced up Stafford's arm and he set his cup
back down.

"That *is* the reason I'm here, Stafford. There's
a woman claiming to be Mick's bride, or soon
to be, at the hotel." Walt shook his head as if he
didn't quite believe what he was saying, either.
"And she's got a passel of kids. Six I think, but
I could be wrong. I'd have brought them out,"
Walt went on, after taking a sip of his coffee.
"But I ain't got a rig that big."

The eerie sensation was back, suggesting the
man was serious, yet Stafford, as usual, stuck
to his guns. "The joke's on you, Walt," he said.
"Mick's not here. He and a few cowhands left
last month. I don't expect them back until the
snow flies, or next spring if he buys cows."

"Oh," the man said, as if that was news. Bad news. Shaking his head, he added, "I ain't trying to fool you, Stafford. There's really a woman, and she's really claiming to be Mick's bride."

Stafford bolted out of his chair and was halfway across the room before he knew he'd moved.

"What are you gonna do?" Walt asked.

"What am I going to do?"

Rubbing his stubble-covered chin, Walt appeared to be contemplating the ins and outs of the world. "Well," he said slowly. "I suspect you could hire one of Skip Wyle's freight wagons."

Growling and rubbing at his temples, Stafford silently called both Mick and Walt a few choice names. His question had been hypothetical. He didn't need a freight wagon. Mick hadn't been any more serious when he'd talked of marriage this time than he had been dozens of times before.

Don't be surprised if I come home with a wife, Mick had shouted as he'd kneed his horse out of the yard. But he said those same words practically every time he left for town. As usual, Stafford had replied that Mick had better add on to his cabin first. His partner's reply had been the same suggestion as always. That Stafford could do that as a wedding gift, since he was the one who liked to build things.

The sensation that came over Stafford was that of breaking through ice on a frozen lake. That had actually happened to him once, and Mick had been there to pull him out and haul him home.

Right now he wasn't remembering how sick he'd been afterward, how he still hated walking on frozen water. Instead, he was recalling how his parting conversation with Mick hadn't ended as usual. This time Mick had told Stafford that he'd better hurry up, have the cabin done by the time he returned.

"Damn," Stafford muttered before he spun to stare at Walt who was refilling his coffee cup from the pot on the stove. Another shiver rippled down his spine. "Six kids?"

Walt nodded.

Marie Hall sat on a patch of green grass in the field next to the hotel, watching Terrance and Samuel play with the dog they'd discovered begging for food last week. A stray, possibly left by someone traveling through, that's what Mrs. Murphy, the aging woman who cooked for the restaurant and who'd saved scraps for the animal, had said.

Marie smiled to herself, for the dog—white with brown patches—had been just the diversion the boys needed. Marie shifted her gaze to make sure Beatrice and Charlotte were still picking daisies, and then she glanced toward Charles and Weston. Never far apart, the youngest of her wards were chasing grasshoppers and mimicking them, which had Marie chuckling at their somewhat awkward leaps. The twins were only four so their coordination wasn't the best.

They were adorable, though. All six of the Meeker children. Strangers on the train, and here in town, had commented they all looked identical, not just Charles and Weston, and would ask how she could tell them apart. It was easy. Perhaps because she knew them so well.

Like right now. "Charles," she said warningly. "Do not put that in your mouth."

Little blue eyes surrounded by thick lashes looked up at her mournfully. Marie forced her gaze to remain stern as she shook her head. He dropped the pebble and returned to jumping, following his brother.

A heavy sigh settled deep in Marie's lungs. It had taken four months to break him of sucking his thumb, and ever since the fire, rather than his thumb, Charlie was forever putting things in his mouth. Anything he could find. It was comforting for him, she understood that, but also extremely dangerous. Some days she wondered if she should allow him to suck his thumb, just until things were settled. The poor dear had been through so much.

They all had been through a lot, and it wasn't over.

"Marie Hall?"

Startled, for she hadn't heard anyone approach, Marie snapped her head around so fast her neck popped, making her flinch.

The bright sun only allowed her to make out the silhouette of a tall man with a wide-brimmed hat. Gathering her skirt, she rose to her feet. "Yes," she answered, standing and shading her eyes with one hand.

Besides the hat, he had on a gun belt and a black leather vest. Dark brown hair hung past his shoulders and his chin was covered with a similarly colored beard. Marie couldn't stop the involuntary shudder that raced over her skin. She'd come to understand most men out here wore guns, but she'd sincerely hoped Mick Wagner would be more civilized.

A lump formed in her throat. "Yes," she repeated. Her nerves wouldn't allow her to offer a hand in greeting, so she rested hers atop the heads of the twins who now stood one on each side of her. "I'm Marie Hall."

"Are you the cowboy that's gonna be our new da?"

That was Weston. He was the most verbal of

the twins, and Marie stopped herself short of correcting him to say *father* instead of *da*. She had more important things to worry about. Such as how rough around the edges Mick Wagner appeared to be.

The others had gathered close, and Terrance pushed Weston's shoulder. "We don't need a new father."

Being the oldest, Terrance was greatly opposed to Marie's plan. She could understand a boy of ten wouldn't want a new father, and she'd tried to explain they didn't have another option. By proxy, Mick Wagner was now responsible for all six Meeker children. Making the man understand they came along with her was a concern. She hoped, with all she had, he would see their inclusion as a benefit.

There had been rumors, after a man named Walt Darter had ridden out to Mr. Wagner's ranch last week, that Mick hadn't ordered a bride. No one mentioned it to her, especially not Mr. Darter. He'd simply said Mick wasn't home but that a message had been sent to him. She'd thanked Mr. Darter for his efforts and never let it be known she'd heard the whispers or seen the finger-pointing. Partially because it wasn't a rumor. Mick Wagner hadn't ordered a bride. And partially because she had no idea what she and the children would do if he didn't claim them—soon.

"I—" She had to clear the squeak from her voice. "I'm assuming you're Mr. Wagner."

"Nope," the man said.

Marie was still processing a wave of relief when Weston asked, "You're not our new da?"

"Nope," the man repeated.

"Are you a cowboy?" the child asked.

"Yep." He winked at Weston. "Just the wrong cowboy."

Marie couldn't let Weston's questions continue, yet hers floundered as she said, "Is Mr. Wagner…"

"I'm his partner," the man said. "Stafford Burleson."

Terrance snorted and bumped his shoulder into Samuel's. "Stafford," he whispered, as if finding great humor in the name. Samuel, seven and always eager to follow his older brother, snickered, as well.

Marie chose to ignore them. She'd learned, while being trained as a nursemaid, which battles were worth fighting when it came to children of every age. This wasn't one. Besides, she couldn't quite fathom a cowboy having such an unusual name, either. Not to mention she was more than a bit relieved to know this wasn't the man she'd told everyone from here to Chicago had ordered her as a bride. "Is Mr. Wagner in town?" she asked. Several people had told her Mick Wagner's ranch was a distance from Huron—too far for her and the children to travel alone.

Tipping the edge of his hat back, and giving her a very penetrating stare from eyes that looked to be as gray as a storm cloud, the man acted as if he wasn't going to answer her questions.

Marie's nerves started jumping faster than the grasshoppers the twins had been chasing. She'd been charging things in Mr. Wagner's name since leaving Chicago. Soon the bills would be more than she'd be able to repay. That wasn't her major concern—the children were—but with each day that passed, their financial situation had started to trouble her more and more.

Finally, when the air in her lungs had built up a tremendous pressure from his stare, Mr. Burleson said, "I'm here to take you to Mick's place."

It wasn't the answer she'd expected, but her sigh was so long she wondered if her toes had been holding air. When it was all out, she nodded. "Well, thank you. We've been expecting he'd send someone." In truth she'd been praying he'd come, or send someone, but she'd never allow the children to know she'd been worrying about the outcome of their adventure.

The man nodded. "We can head out in an hour."

"An hour?" Still shaky with relief, it took Marie a moment to process his statement. Her thoughts shifted to everything that needed to be done before they left, and she shook her head. "That's not possible. We'll leave tomorrow morning."

Mr. Burleson's stormy eyes glared again. "We'll leave in an hour."

"No, we won't." She spun about, gestured to the children. "Gather your playthings. It's time to return to our rooms."

They minded without question, for once, and she turned back to the man. "We'll be ready to leave tomorrow morning, after breakfast."

"It's barely noon," he said. "We can get a good number of miles under our belt yet today."

"Tonight is bath night, Mr. Burleson," she said, holding her ground. When it came to the children and their needs she'd argue until the sun set—dealing with the solicitor back in Chicago had taught her to not back down. No matter how frightening it was. "I will not have the children's schedule upset."

"You will not—"

"That's correct," she interrupted. "I will not." No good nursemaid would, and she was the best nursemaid that had ever come out of Miss Wentworth's training course. The owner herself had said as much. Marie had a document that proclaimed it in writing. She'd used it as a testimonial when interviewing for positions. Not that she'd need it anymore. Abandoning the Meekers was something she'd never do. That's what she'd told Mr. Phillips, the solicitor, back in Chicago, as well as several other people who'd suggested such a thing. She'd been hired as their nursemaid, and she would fulfill her duties.

The children had gathered around again, holding their toys and looking at her expectantly. So was Mr. Burleson. With so much to do, Marie couldn't waste any time. "You can see to the hotel bill and the train fares, Mr. Burleson, and then bring the wagon around. A large number of our possessions can be loaded this afternoon."

"Hotel bill? Train fares?"

"Yes. For the children." She didn't explain she'd paid her own way, by selling her necklace and ear bobs. It wasn't necessary. The letter she'd written Mr. Wagner prior to leaving Chicago explained it all. How his cousin, Emma Lou Meeker, and her husband, John, had perished in the fire that burned down the entire block surrounding the gas-fitting firm Mr. Meeker had owned. And how, a mere week after the funeral, Mr. Phillips had appeared at the Meekers' big brownstone home, explaining that the

bank owned everything. He'd stated the children
were to be put in an orphanage until Mr. Wagner
could be notified. Upon his approval, the children could then be put up for adoption. Mr. Phillips had gone on to explain a few neighboring
families were interested in adopting one or two.

Marie held off her shiver of horror. That would
not happen. Either option. The only chance the
children had of staying together was Mr. Wagner. Emma Lou had listed her cousin as the
benefactor on a small life insurance policy. The
paperwork for the policy was safely tucked away,
and Marie would present it to Mr. Wagner upon
their meeting. The policy would be more than
enough to reimburse him for the travel and lodg-
ing expenses the children had incurred, though
not enough to raise all six children to adulthood.
That was something Mr. Wagner would have to
see to. She'd help, of course, as much as possible.
She owed Emma Lou and John for paying off
her debts, and this was how she could repay their
kindness. If not for them she wouldn't have the
small amount of money she did have. Above all,
though, the children needed her, and she would
not let them down.

Clapping her hands, she said, "Children."

Stafford stared as the woman, nose in the
air, marched away, followed by the flock of

red-headed kids like a mother duck leading her brood to water. Or like Custer leading the 7th Cavalry Regiment into battle. That conflict might have had a different outcome if Marie Hall had been leading the troops. She fired demands like bullets.

He'd met her kind before. Saw the way she shuddered and the disdain in her eyes as she took in his appearance. So he needed a haircut and a shave. That was none of her business. He'd considered visiting the barbershop before meeting her, making himself presentable, but curiosity had won out. The chance to get a glimpse of the woman who was claiming Mick had ordered her had been too strong when Walt said the bride-to-be was behind the hotel in Huron.

Stafford hadn't planned on heading home until tomorrow, either, but her haughty attitude had changed his mind the moment she'd stood, lip curled, as her eyes roamed over him from nose to tail like he was a mangy cow on the auction block.

His partner didn't have any more time to visit the barber than he did—the cattle company kept them both busy. Then again, it was highly unlikely Mick and Marie Hall had ever met. They might have corresponded though. Most likely last spring, while he'd been gone, down in Texas rounding up cattle. Mick had been home, then, and she could have sent him a picture. His partner was a sitting duck when it came to a pretty woman. He went half crazy over them. Women, foolish as they were, fell for Mick's boyish charm, too.

Stafford took another long look as the woman turned the corner, kids trailing behind.

He'd never seen so many freckles. Not all at once. And not one of those freckle-faced little kids looked anything like her. They were all fair skinned with copper-colored hair, whereas she had dark hair and eyes in shades of brown that teetered on black. That had him wondering what happened to her husband. The father of all those kids, or *da* as one had called him. That little guy had quite a lisp, and as much as Stafford hadn't wanted it to, a grin had won out when the kid spoke.

They disappeared around the corner of the hotel, every last one of them. Stafford took a step to follow, but paused. Miss Marie Hall. That's what Walt had called her. Miss. It made sense, too, considering she didn't look old enough to have one kid, let alone six.

Whose kids did she have?

Stafford scratched his chin, which itched due to the inch-long whiskers. Mick may have ordered a bride, but there was no way he'd have ordered six kids. That much Stafford would bet his life on.

Huron was a busy place, the railroad made it so, and someone knew something. She'd been here over a week, and with a town this size, people would know her story. He'd start at the depot. Find out about those fares she was referring to, as well as a few other things.

An hour later, Stafford concluded Mick was going to owe him more than money when he finally returned. Those weren't her kids—as he'd suspected. They were a stack of orphans she'd rustled up after their parents died in a fire. The ticket master had told him that, and how she'd promised Mick would pay their fares upon his arrival. She'd paid her own fare, though, which didn't make a lot of sense and left more questions in place of the few Stafford had found answers for.

After leaving the depot, he'd rented one of Skip Wyle's freight wagons—had to after learning about the amount of luggage she had. From what he'd heard, it took up one entire hotel room. *"The children's things,"* she'd called them— that's what he'd been told.

This woman was pulling one over on Mick. That was clear. A part of Stafford didn't mind that. It was time Mick learned a lesson, a hard one about women. All the warnings Stafford had supplied over the years sure hadn't done anything.

The wagon had been sent to the hotel, along with a couple of men to load it, and though Stafford considered leaving his hair and beard as they were, since it clearly disgusted Miss Marie Hall, he couldn't take it. His razor had snapped in two last month and he'd been itching—literally—to get a new one ever since, not to mention how his hair had grown so long it continuously whipped into his eyes.

Besides, men waiting for a haircut gossiped more than women sewing quilts, and that alone was enough to make Stafford head straight for the barber shop. By the time Mick arrived home—which would hopefully be soon because Stafford had sent a telegram to Austin, knowing his partner would make a stopover there—Stafford would know everything there was to know about Miss Marie Hall. He'd fill in the blanks for Mick—those that he instinctively knew she'd leave out—long before wedding bells rang.

Stafford just didn't want to see Mick bamboozled. They might both get married some day, raise kids across the creek from each other, but neither of them would be conned into it. He wouldn't because he was smart, had long ago learned what to watch out for, and Mick wouldn't because they were best friends, and friends looked out for each other.

Stafford's confidence was still riding high the next morning as he headed toward the hotel. He hadn't learned a whole lot more about Miss Marie Hall, but what he had fit perfectly with what he already knew. He still doubted—as he had from the beginning—that Mick had ordered her. It was possible she'd somehow heard about a cowboy—well on his way to becoming a wealthy rancher—who spouted off about wanting a bride. The fact that Mick wasn't around played into Stafford's thoughts, as well. Without his partner to interfere, he'd be able to show her just what living on the plains meant. Men had to be tough, but women, they had to be hard, and that was the one thing Miss Marie Hall wasn't. He could tell that by her hands. They were lily white.

There was a definite spring in his step as he made his way down the hotel corridor to knock on her door. Upon hearing movement, he shouted, "Burning daylight."

All Marie saw was the back of a stranger turning the corner, heading for the hotel stairway, when she opened the door. She'd been awake for some time, assembling the essentials the children would need this morning and making sure they each had specific items in their satchels.

The men who'd packed the wagon yesterday said they'd have to spend one night on the road, most likely in the wagon, before they arrived at Mick Wagner's ranch, and she wanted to make sure the children wouldn't be put out much by the travel. The train trip had taught her to pack books and toys, things to hold their attention. It was for her sake as much as theirs. She'd been frazzled by the time the train had arrived in Huron, and didn't want to be that way upon meeting Mr. Wagner.

"Is it time to leave?" Beatrice asked.

"It's time to get up," Marie answered, glancing toward the child sitting in the middle of the bed. Peeking back into the hall, though she knew it was empty, Marie frowned. The voice had made her skin shiver, and she'd thought it was Mr. Burleson, yet it must not have been. At least, the man turning the corner hadn't been him—far too well groomed. Which was just as well, she'd see enough of Mr. Burleson for the next day or two, and not telling him he needed a shave and haircut was going to be difficult.

He'd occupied her thoughts since meeting him yesterday. For the first time since embracing her plan, an unnerving dread had settled in her stomach and remained there. She'd imagined Mick Wagner would be like his cousin. Refined, with a kind and gentle nature. Someone who

would see the children's welfare as the priority.
That's how Emma Lou and her husband, John,
had been. If Mr. Wagner was anything like his
partner, he wouldn't have any of those qualities.
Mr. Burleson surely didn't. The only time he'd
looked remotely pleasant was when he'd winked
at Weston. Thank goodness there would be others traveling with them today. Being alone with
Mr. Burleson…

She gulped and slammed two doors shut,
the one to the room and the one allowing crazy
thoughts into her mind.

Beatrice and Charlotte chatted excitedly about
the adventure of riding in a covered wagon, and
Marie feigned enthusiasm, to keep them from
worrying. That was part of her job. Children
should never worry about being safe, or going
hungry, or any of the frightening things she'd
encountered growing up.

In no time, the girls and all four boys, who'd
been staying in the adjoining room, were dressed
and ready for breakfast. After checking under
the beds one final time to ensure nothing would
be left behind, Marie led her charges out the
door.

In the dining room she settled everyone upon
the chairs at their customary table and caught her
breath before taking her own seat. That's when
she noticed the man watching her. Her cheeks

grew warm from his stare, and she quickly averted her eyes. A good nursemaid never noticed men, no matter how handsome, and she was the best.

His ongoing stare gave her the jitters, and Marie did her best to ignore the stare and her fluttering stomach. Meals were ordered for the children, along with toast and tea for herself, which she would once again pay for separately. She'd never be indebted to anyone ever again, including Mr. Wagner. Her meager savings were dwindling quickly, but hopefully Mr. Wagner would see her worth and hire her. She'd be able to replenish her monies then. Right now, the children's future was her priority and worth every cent she spent. They were also what gave her the courage to stand up to the men at the bank, the railroad, even the hotel and everyone else they'd encountered during this journey.

With appetites that were never ending, the children cleaned their plates, even Charlotte, who was a finicky eater. Marie was savoring her last sip of tea when a shadow fell upon the table. It was the man. She knew that without looking up, and fought the urge to do so, hoping he'd move away. He was a stranger, not one of the locals they'd come to know the past week.

"You should have eaten more than that," he said. "It'll be a long time until we eat again."

The voice sent a tremor down her spine, and Marie couldn't stop her head from snapping up. It couldn't possibly be Mr. Burleson, yet the vest, the hat, the gun belt…

One brow was raised when her eyes finally found their way all the way up to his face, which was clean shaven. His features were crisp now, defined, including an indent in the center of his chin, and his eyes seemed no longer gray but faded blue and almost twinkling. That's when Marie saw his smile. It slanted across his face in a cocky, self-assured way that was extremely vexing. Not exactly sure she could, or should, speak at this moment—for something deep in her stomach said he wouldn't be as easy to deal with as the other men she'd encountered—she pinched her lips together.

"You said it was bath night," Stafford Burleson stated, as he practically pulled the chair out from beneath her.

Chapter Two

The tension inside her was not a good sign, especially when Marie knew it had very little to do with the children or the wagon or even the bumpy ride. It was him. Stafford Burleson was the reason. Not just his good looks. Her efforts to ignore him weren't working. Who would ever have known that under all that hair...

She shook her head, tried again not to think about his looks. If only her friend Sarah were here now, she'd have some thoughts on what to do about that. And other things.

Sarah was the Hawkins family's nursemaid. They'd lived down the road from the Meekers and the two of them often took the children to the park together. Sarah had said the Hawkinses had made inquires about eventually adopting the twins—Charles and Weston—having only girls themselves. Knowing how Marie felt, Sarah had helped formulate this mission—taking the children to meet the guardian named in their mother's will.

Sarah had known a woman who'd gone west as a mail-order bride, said the man who'd ordered her promised the railroad he'd pay for her fare at the other end, and insisted Marie could do the same thing. Uncomfortable expecting Mick Wagner to pay for her fare, Marie had sold the jewelry the Meekers had given her for Christmas—it wasn't like she'd ever have the occasion to wear such things, anyway. The children's fares were a different issue. Therefore, she'd used the mail-order bride ruse, and was thankful it had worked as well as it had.

Sarah said Mick Wagner would probably be glad to hire her as the children's nursemaid, which is exactly what Marie hoped. She couldn't imagine being separated from the children. However, she wished she'd asked Sarah a few more questions. Her friend had a much broader understanding of men, and often spoke of the day she'd be married with her own children to raise. She'd declared that marrying Mick Wagner would be a good choice, if he was so inclined, because Marie would never have to worry about finding another job. She didn't want another job, but every time she glanced at the man beside her, the idea of marriage made her insides tremble.

She closed her eyes and fought against another

tremor. If Mick Wagner was anything like the brute sitting beside her, he could very well demand things. Things she couldn't even fathom. Holding her breath, Marie pressed a hand to her stomach. Surely a man with six children to raise wouldn't insist on embarking upon behavior that might produce another one? Miss Wentworth's lesson on copulation had been extremely embarrassing to sit through, and the lesson on childbirth downright dreadful.

"Marie."

The whisper in her ear had her turning around, purposely not glancing toward Stafford Burleson beside her on the front seat of the wagon. The bouncy ride made the train journey they'd experienced seem comfortable in comparison, and the hot sun blazing down on them was relentless.

"Yes, Weston," she replied to the child standing behind the seat, protected from the sun by a billowing canvas. "What do you need, dear?"

The child whispered in her ear.

"Very well." Still without glancing his way, she said, "Mr. Burleson, we need to stop."

"Stop?"

"Yes."

"What for?"

Marie played with the bow at her chin that kept her bonnet from fluttering off with the wind, willing herself to maintain the nursemaid calm she'd perfected. The man's tone was laced with impatience—as it had been all morning—which grated on her nerves. Patience was the number one trait a person working with children needed to maintain, and he was souring hers. "Weston needs to take care of something," she stated.

"What?" Stafford Burleson asked, as he flapped the reins over the horses' backs, keeping them at a steady pace.

"I'm sure I don't need to explain what he needs to take care of," Marie said, nose forward. "At least, I shouldn't have to."

A low growl rumbled before he said, "Didn't you tell them to do that before we left town?"

Biting her tongue would not help, even if she had a mind not to speak. "Of course I did," she declared, "but small children have small bladders."

"Not that small," he exclaimed. "I can still see Huron behind us."

She couldn't help but glance around and gaze through the front and back openings of the canopy covering the wagon. The dark cluster on the horizon ignited yet another bout of tremors. She and the children were now completely at the mercy of this insufferable man, with nothing more than prayers for protection. Refusing to panic, she said, "In country this flat, I'm sure a person can see for ten miles or more."

"We haven't gone ten miles," Mr. Burleson insisted. "We've barely gone two."

"That, Mr. Burleson," she said, "makes no difference. Weston needs to relieve himself and you will stop this wagon immediately."

The snarl that formed on his face was frightening, but it also snapped her last nerve in two. He was the most insufferable man she'd ever encountered. If it had been just her, she might have cowered at his bullying, but she was the only protection the children had. She would not see them harmed, and that gave her the courage, or perhaps the determination, to return his stare with one just as formidable.

Marie was sure he cursed under his breath, but since he also pulled the horses to a stop and set the brake, she ignored it—this once—and turned around.

Climbing out of the high wagon was like climbing down a tree. Instead of branches there were steps and wagon spokes to navigate—an extremely difficult task with her skirt flapping in the wind. The alternative, having Mr. Burleson assist her as he'd tried to in town, was out of the question, so Marie managed just fine, apart from a stumble or two.

She kept her chin up, suspecting the foul

man was now chuckling under his breath, and marched toward the back of the wagon where she lifted Weston to the ground.

"Go behind that bush," she instructed, gesturing toward a scattering of shrubs a short distance away.

Weston scurried away and Marie glanced toward the wagon, prepared to ask if any of the other children needed to relieve themselves.

"If anyone else has to go, do it now," a male voice demanded harshly.

Spinning about, she eyed him. "I was about to suggest that, Mr. Burleson."

He folded his arms across his chest. "Were you?"

"Yes, I was." Arguing in front of the children should be avoided at all measures, so she took a deep breath and turned, poking her head over the end gate. "Does anyone else need to join Weston?"

Five little heads, those she'd protect with her life, gestured negatively. The quivering of Charlie's bottom lip had Marie's ire flaming. Whirling round, she grabbed one solid arm and dragged Mr. Burleson a few feet away from the wagon. "I will not have you intimidating these children."

"You will not—"

"That's right," she interrupted. "I will not permit you to speak to them so. There is no need for you to use that tone of voice around them. They are small children and—"

"Where the hell did you come from lady?" Stafford interrupted. One minute she was shaking like a rabbit and the next she was snapping like a cornered she-wolf—demanding things. Their luggage took up one entire freight wagon, leaving him no choice but to buy a second one this morning that included *some kind of covering to keep the children out of the sun*. It was now well past noon, and at the rate they were traveling it would take three days to get home. If he was lucky.

"There's no reason to curse. You know perfectly well the children and I are from Chicago," she said, pert little nose stuck skyward again.

Stafford shook his head. Didn't anyone know a rhetorical question when they heard one?

"Get that kid in the wagon," he barked, walking toward the team. Mick was going to owe him so much he might as well sign over his half of the ranch the moment he rode in. Dealing with Miss Marie Hall and her brood was costing more than money. Stafford's sanity was at stake.

August was the hottest month of the year, and here he was traipsing across the countryside with a wagonload of kids and the haughtiest woman he'd ever met.

If he'd been thinking, he'd have hired another man to drive this rig and ridden Stamper, his horse, back to the ranch.

The wagon seat listed as Marie climbed up the side of the rig with about as much grace as a chicken trying to fly. So be it. He'd offered his assistance once—back in town—and wouldn't do that again. He'd never been a slow learner.

Eventually, she got herself hoisted up and Stafford had to clench his hands into fists to keep from setting the team moving before she got herself situated on the seat. He'd have gotten a chuckle out of watching her flail about, but he wasn't in a chuckling mood.

"We may proceed now, Mr. Burleson."

"You don't say," he drawled, simply because he had to say something. Her uppity attitude had him wanting to show her just who was in charge. Him.

Stafford snapped the reins and let the horses set a steady pace forward. The trail was relatively smooth and driving the rig didn't take much concentration or effort. Anyone could do it.

"You know how to drive a team?" he asked.

She didn't glance his way, just kept her snooty little face forward. "Of course not. I am a nursemaid, not a teamster."

It had probably been a bad idea anyway.

He just wanted to be anywhere but here right now. She was like every other woman he'd ever known, with a way of making a man feel obligated to be at her beck and call. He'd given up on that years ago and didn't want to go back.

"A nursemaid?" he asked, when his mind shifted. "I thought you were a mail-order bride."

Her sigh held weight. "A person can be two things at once."

"That they can," he agreed. Snooty and persnickety.

A cold glare from those brown eyes settled on him, telling him she knew he was thinking unkind thoughts about her, and he couldn't help but grin. Let her know she was right. He even added a little wink for good measure.

Huffing, she snapped her gaze forward again.

Darn close to laughing, Stafford asked, "So how'd you and Mick meet?" The ranch was still a long way off and he might as well use the time to gather a bit more information. If she and Mick had corresponded, and if she had sent Mick a picture of herself, Mick would have waved it like a flag. Therefore, Stafford was convinced there had been no picture sharing. He also knew he'd need all the ammunition he could get once Mick saw her. Even as testy as a cornered cat, Marie Hall was a looker. Her profile reminded him of a charcoal silhouette, drawn, framed and hung on a wall to entice onlookers to imagine who the mysterious woman might be.

Not that he was enticed. He knew enough not to be drawn in by the graceful arch of her chin or how her lashes looked an inch long as she stared straight ahead.

After another weighty sigh, she said, "Mr. Wagner and I have not officially met, yet."

"Lucky man," Stafford mumbled, trying to override the direction his thoughts wanted to go.

An owl couldn't snap its neck as fast as she could, and he was saved from whatever she'd been going to say when one of the kids—he couldn't tell them apart for other than a few inches in height they all looked alike—poked their head through the canvas opening and whispered something in her ear.

Stafford's nerves ground together like millstones at the way her voice softened. When she spoke to those children honey practically poured out of her mouth. When it came to him, her tone was as sharp as needles. He couldn't help but imagine it would be the same for Mick. The poor fool. What had he been thinking?

An hour later, Stafford had flipped that question around on himself. What had *he* been thinking? Though he wasn't an overly religious man, he found himself staring skyward and pleading. *Save me. For the love of God, save me.*

Traveling with six kids was maddening. They flapped around more than chickens in a crate and argued nonstop, not to mention he'd had to halt the wagon again, twice, for people to relieve their "small bladders." No wonder. She passed the canteen between those kids on a steady basis. Insisting they drink in this heat.

He'd had enough. That was all there was to it. Enough. Even before discovering the dog—which looked more like a rat—the kids had been hiding in the back of the wagon. It had been clear Marie hadn't known the older boys had smuggled it aboard, not until it, too, had to relieve itself. A dog that size wasn't good for anything except getting stepped on, and from the looks of its round belly and swollen teats, there'd soon be a few more of them running around. Marie had been surprised about that, too. When he'd pointed it out, her cheeks had turned crimson.

Before she began loading the children and the dog back into the wagon, Stafford leaned through the front opening of the canvas, gathered up both canteens and stashed them beneath the seat.

They'd be putting on some miles before anyone got another drink. He wasn't being mean, wouldn't let anyone die of thirst, he was just putting his foot down.

It was a good ten minutes before everyone

was settled in the back of the wagon and she'd once again stationed her bottom on the seat beside him. Stafford didn't bother waiting for her signal, just gave out a low whoop that sent the horses forward.

A short time later, when the little guy with the lisp said he was hungry, Stafford merely shook his head.

She on the other hand, said consolingly, "I'm sure we'll stop for lunch soon, Weston." Flipping her tone sour as fast as a cook turns flapjacks on a grill, she added, "Won't we, Mr. Burleson?"

"Nope," Stafford answered.

"Yes, we will," she insisted. "Children have small stomachs, and—"

"And Jackson is probably a good five miles ahead of us." Pointing out the obvious, in case she'd forgotten, he added, "He has all the food with him. You were the one who said it wouldn't fit in this wagon."

Marie had to press a hand to her lips to contain her gasp. The wagon bed was so small, barely enough room for each child to sit comfortably, she'd had to insist all other items be placed in the larger freight wagon. Surly even someone as vile as Mr. Burleson could understand that. Though the freight wagon, once a dot on the horizon, was gone.

"Why did you let him get so far ahead of us?" she asked.

"I didn't," Mr. Burleson answered with a clipped tone. "You did." He gave an indifferent nod over one shoulder. "Small bladders."

Pinching her lips together didn't help much. Neither did searching her brain full of nurse-maid training. None of it had prepared her for this. Her education focused on what to do inside the home of her charges. Improvise. She had to find something to take the child's mind off his hunger, and then she'd be able to work out what to do about it. Turning she reached for one of the canteens. "Have some water for now, dear."

Neither container was where she'd left it. "Who has the canteens?" she asked, looking mainly at Terrance. Though she tried not to single him out, he was usually the culprit.

The boy shook his head. "I don't have them."

"I do."

A nerve ticked in her jaw as she turned to look at Mr. Burleson. "Why?"

"Because I'll say who can have a drink, and when."

"The children—"

"Won't starve or die of thirst before we catch up with Jackson."

That would not do. "Mr. Burleson—"

Despite the heat of the sun, his cold stare had her vocal chords freezing up.

"No one is getting a drink of water, Miss Hall," he growled. "And we aren't stopping until I say." He twisted his neck a bit more, glancing into the wagon bed. "You kids pull out some of those books she made you pack and start reading."

Six sets of startled eyes—for the children had never been spoken to with such harshness—instantly turned to their bags. In a matter of seconds, they were all reading. Or, at least, holding books in their hands with their heads hung over the pages.

She shouldn't feel this thankful to see them all sitting quietly, but in truth they hadn't sat still for more than five minutes since leaving town. If someone hadn't been complaining they didn't have enough room, someone else was hot, or thirsty, or had to go. Yet she was their nursemaid, not Stafford Burleson, and he had no right to speak to them so.

Under her breath, so the children wouldn't hear, Marie started, "Mr. Burleson, I cannot have—"

His glare came from the corner of one eye as he once again interrupted, "Don't you have a book you can read, too?"

Floored, she huffed before finding her voice. "I—"

"I," he broke in, "need some peace and quiet."

She hadn't been spoken to that way, either, not in a very long time. Besides the shivers racing up her arms, her throat locked tight. *Peace and quiet.* Blinking back the tears threatening to fall in a way they hadn't done for years, Marie turned her gaze to the horses and focused on the harnesses going up and down, trying to forget. Or just not let the memories come forward. She'd been sent back to the orphanage because of those words. That had been years ago, she told herself, and could not happen now. Could never happen again.

It took effort, lots of it, and by the time everything was suppressed, Marie was breathing hard and deep, as if she'd just run several miles. She'd been here before, this emotionally exhausted, but not in a very long time.

"Here."

Marie blinked at the canteen before her chin.

"Take a drink," he said.

Her hands shook, but the tepid water flowing down her burning throat was such relief Marie took several swallows before worrying about the few droplets that dribbled down her neck. Her breathing was returning to normal, and by the time she'd replaced the cap and wiped away the droplets, she had much more control.

"Better?"

"Yes," she managed, handing back the canteen. She couldn't bring herself to glance his way, not even as his gaze blistered the side of her face. "Thank you."

"They'll be fine," he said.

His voice was hushed, soft and even kind-hearted, which threatened the control she'd mustered. "I'm sure you're right," she answered as firmly as possible. He *was* right. It took more than a few hours before a person's stomach ached. A day or more until the pain became so strong that cramps set in. Those memories weren't easily repressed, but they did remind her she was glad to have been sent back to the orphanage all those years ago.

"Look at that," he said, one hand stretched out, gesturing toward the land covered with brown grass that went on for miles.

She'd been shocked at first, by the landscape so different from that of the city. Barely a green blade could be found, but she'd grown accustomed to it since arriving in Huron. That's how life was, a series of changes one eventually got used to.

Marie also understood he was trying to redirect her thoughts, and she let him. No good ever came from dwelling on the past.

"It's a deer," he continued, "and two fawns."

It wasn't until the animal turned and leaped that Marie noticed two smaller ones bounding through the waist-high grass. "How did you see them?" she asked. "The grass is so tall."

"Practice, I guess."

"They're so graceful," she commented, watching until the deer disappeared. "Do they always run like that? Almost as if they're flying?"

"Yes, deer are pretty swift animals. Haven't you seen any before?"

"Just pictures."

He seemed different, quiet, thoughtful, and the moments ticking by threatened to set her back to thinking, so she added, "There aren't any deer in the city."

"The city being Chicago?"

"Yes."

"You lived there your entire life?"

"Yes," she answered.

"Never left?"

"Not until boarding the train for Huron." Marie bit her tongue then, hoping she hadn't just provided him with an opening to start asking questions again. Partner or not, she wouldn't explain everything to anyone but Mr. Wagner.

"What are their names?"

She had to glance his way, and was a bit taken aback by the grin on his lips. It was really only a fraction of a grin, but friendly nonetheless. How could he do that? Go from formidable to pleasant like someone flipping a coin? Thankful her spinning mind could form a question, she asked, "The children?"

"Yes. What are their names? How old are they?"

All on its own, a smile formed. The simple thought of her wards did that all the time. "Terrance is the oldest. He's ten. Next is Charlotte, she's nine, and Samuel is seven. Beatrice is six and the twins, Charles and Weston, are four."

"And why do you have them?"

Her initial response was to state that it was none of his business, but, in fact, he had come to collect them and was delivering them to Mr. Wagner's ranch. A small portion of an explanation wasn't completely out of the question.

After a glance backward that showed the children were indeed reading—well, the older ones were, Weston and Charles had stretched out between the others and were dozing—Marie leaned toward him slightly, so she could speak as softly as possible. "Their parents perished in a fire."

"I'd heard that," he answered just as quietly. "Where?"

"From the ticket taker at the train depot."

"Oh." That wasn't alarming. She had made mention of it, just so the man would understand her delay in payment more clearly.

"That doesn't explain why you have them," he whispered, leaning closer yet.

Marie had to swallow and sat back a bit. "I was hired as their nursemaid last year, after the one they'd had for several years got married."

"Is this your first job? The first time you've been a nursemaid?"

Ruffled slightly, wondering if he was suggesting she wasn't capable, she squared her shoulders. "It was my first permanent position, but I graduated at the top of my class five years ago."

"Whoa," he said. "I can tell you're well trained and confident in what you do."

"Thank you," Marie said, although a lingering doubt had her wondering if that had been a compliment or not. Men were difficult creatures to understand. This one more so than any other she'd encountered.

"How old are you?" he asked.

That was an inappropriate question, but being in the wild as they were, he was their only hope of survival, so she should attempt to be civil to him. Besides, he probably didn't know the difference between appropriate and inappropriate questions. "I'm twenty."

A brow was lifted as he asked, "Twenty?"

She nodded.

"So, if you graduated five years ago, and just got this job last year, what did you do in between?"

"I worked for several families," Marie answered. "Just for short terms, helping out as families looked for permanent nursemaids or while others were ill and such." She attempted to keep the frustration from her voice. Moving from family to family, staying only a few weeks or days at times, was extremely difficult. She'd barely get to know the children in her charge before being assigned elsewhere. It had been expected, though, because of her age. "A large number of families like their nursemaids to be on the older side. Even the Meekers, but they were willing to hire me permanently considering their last nursemaid, though she'd been a woman well into her thirties, had chosen to get married and end her employment."

"Had she become a mail-order bride, too?"

Marie chomped down on her lip, preventing a startled *no*. How had she talked herself into this corner? Not seeing a direct escape route, she took the only one she could fathom. "My letter to Mr. Wagner explained everything."

He was frowning deeply and holding those gray eyes on her. "Mr. Wagner isn't here right now."

"I know that," she snapped, unable to stop herself.

He lifted an eyebrow as his gaze roamed up and down her for a moment, and then he turned and stared at the road ahead of them.

The pressure was enormous, but Marie held in her sigh. They'd talked enough. Silence would be a good thing for a few miles. No longer thinking about her past, the future and its dilemmas were clamoring for her attention.

"He's not at the ranch, either," Mr. Burleson said then.

"Mr. Wagner?" she asked, even though she knew that was exactly who Stafford Burleson meant.

"Yes."

"Where is he?"

He shrugged. "Texas. Mexico."

Marie couldn't deny a quick flash of relief washed over her. Maybe she wouldn't have to face the marriage issue right away. She and the children could get settled in and… "For how long?" she asked.

His gaze never left the road. "Can't rightly say. Could be next spring before he gets back."

"Next spring?" Panic overtook any sense of relief. Her funds were almost gone. The children would starve to death by then, unless… She shivered at the thought, but unfortunately, Stafford was her only hope.

Something in his eyes, the way they shimmered, had her mouth going dry, her nerves tingling as though a storm was approaching.

Maybe there was another option. "Who lives at Mr. Wagner's ranch in his absence?"

"Me."

She swallowed. "You?"

Nodding, he said, "Yep. I told you I was his partner."

An icy chill raced up her spine. "So the children and I will be living with…"

"Me."

Good heavens, what had she done? Not thought her plan out clearly, that's for sure. Living with this man had to be worse than marrying Mick Wagner.

Chapter Three

Stafford told himself a hundred times over that he shouldn't get pleasure out of someone else's fear, but he just couldn't help it. When he'd said she'd be living with him, it had scared her into next week, but he was enjoying how it had knocked some of the haughtiness out of her.

She was still uppity, and continued to use that insufferable tone with him—when she had to speak to him—but she was wary. That's the part he liked. She needed to be wary. Very. A nursemaid hauling someone else's kids across the country as a mail-order bride? What kind of tale was that? There was more to it. The way she wouldn't look him in the eye when she talked said that. If he didn't know better, he'd wonder if she'd kidnapped those kids. She'd left too clear a trail, though. Anyone could have followed her, if that was the case.

He had a lot to learn, and with all that was

going on, Stafford was discovering one thing about himself. Flipping the cards, so to speak, on a woman, was rather exciting. That opportunity had never come up in his life before now. Being raised in a family of seven children with only one brother had given him plenty of experience with women. He'd been born in the middle of five sisters. His brother, Sterling, was the oldest, and had already been working alongside their father by the time Stafford had come along. That meant he'd been told what to do and when to do it by women since the day he was born. Not to mention Francine Weatherford. She, too, had thought a man was little more than a dog that needed to be trained. He'd grown and changed a lot since leaving Mississippi ten years ago, on his eighteenth birthday, shortly after Francine broke their engagement and announced she was marrying Sterling.

Out of duty, and at his mother's insistence, he'd stuck around for the wedding, and he'd even been back a half dozen times over the years to check in on everyone, but there wasn't a day that went by when he wasn't thankful he'd made his escape when he had. Sterling had a load of kids now, too, almost as many as their parents' house had held. And Francine, well, last time he'd seen her, she hadn't been nearly as pretty as she'd looked to him all those years ago.

A ferocious round of barking had Stafford lifting his head from where he was harnessing the team. The little dog, dubbed Polly by one of the kids, was kicking up a dirt storm near a thick patch of bushes several yards away. Stafford made a quick head count. All six kids were piling things in the back of the wagon as Marie had instructed. It was she, he noted, who was missing from the campsite. He'd quit thinking of her as Miss Hall sometime yesterday. Using her given name seemed to irritate her, and he liked that, too.

"Jackson," he shouted toward the teamster readying the freight wagon. "You know where Marie is?"

The man, a big blond Swede with a voice that came from his ankles, shook his head. "Nope."

They'd caught up with the freight wagon before sunset the night before, where Jackson had chosen a good spot to call it a day and had a pot of rabbit stew ready to be devoured by six hungry children. Never unprepared, Stafford had had a bag of jerky and apples they'd all consumed as they'd traveled, but still, once they'd hit camp, those kids had all but licked their plates clean. Actually, the two little ones *had* licked their plates. Marie had scolded them while he and Jackson shared a grin. They weren't so bad—those kids—once they'd figured out that they couldn't run roughshod over him the way they did over Marie.

Polly was still going wild, and Stafford settled a harness over one horse's neck. "Finish this up, will you?" he asked Jackson, already moving toward the dog. If the crazy thing had a skunk cornered they'd all pay for it.

Stafford was almost to the edge of the thick bush when a noise caught his attention above the barking. It was faint, and subtle, but the kind of sound that a man never forgets once he hears it. Drawing his gun, Stafford scanned the ground cautiously, meticulously. Rattlers were shady and had the ability to blend in to their surroundings like no other creature.

"Get out of here, Polly," he hissed, kicking dirt to scare the dog aside. It didn't help. She started barking faster, louder. A movement near the roots of the bush proved it was a snake, shaking the buttons on its tail. The head was hidden and Stafford eased his way around the bush. He saw it then, arched up and drawn back, ready to strike.

Stafford fired.

The bullet hit its mark. The snake flew backward into the bush. At the same time, a scream sounded and Stafford saw little more than a flash of white out of the corner of his eye. He took a step, rounded the bush fully and stopped.

Hands over her ears, flat on her stomach with her skirts up around her waist and her bloomers around her ankles, lay Marie. It had to be her. She was the only woman for miles around, and that was about the cutest bare bottom he'd ever seen. So lily white, round and somewhat plump, he had a heck of a time pulling his eyes off it.

Screeching and thuds said the children were approaching so he holstered his gun and bent down, taking her arms to haul her to her feet. "Come on."

Wrestling against his hold, she demanded, "Why were you shooting at me?"

He grasped her more firmly and twisted her about. "I wasn't shooting at you. Now pull up your bloomers before the kids see you."

Her eyes grew as round as dish plates and her face turned redder than last night's sunset. "Ooh!" She threw into a fit. Mouth sputtering and arms flaying so out of control she couldn't stand.

He hoisted her to her feet. "Pull up your bloomers," he repeated and then spun around, blocking her from view of the children racing around the bush.

"What did you shoot?" asked Terrance, the oldest and first to arrive.

"A rattler," Stafford answered, pointing toward

the bush. "Stand back, I gotta make sure it's dead. Keep your brothers and sisters back, too."

Terrance held out his arms, stopping the others from coming any closer as they arrived, and Stafford spun back around to check on Marie. The expression on her face was pure mortification. Could be the gunshot or the snake, but he was putting his money on the fact he'd caught her with her bloomers down, and it took all he had not to chuckle. "You all right?" he asked, tongue in cheek.

She nodded.

He picked up a stick and used it to poke at the snake before hooking it. Dead, it hung limply over the stick, and a tiny quiver inched up his spine as he pulled it clear of the foliage. It was a good-size rattler. Pushing four feet or more.

"I thought you said you shot a rabbit," Terrance said. "That's not a rabbit, it's a snake."

"It's a rattlesnake," Stafford explained. "They're called rattlers because of the sound they make."

The children oohed and aahed but it was the shuddering *"Oh,"* coming from behind him that had him twisting around. Marie's face had about as much color as a cloud, and she appeared to be drooping before his eyes.

Stafford dropped the snake and caught her

elbow. She slouched, but didn't go all the way down. "Here," he said, "sit down."

She half nodded and half shook her head at the same time. "No, I'm all right. I don't need to sit down." The hold she had on his arm tightened. "Just give me a second to catch my breath."

An odd sensation ticked inside him. She had guts, he had to give her that. Plenty of women, men, too, might have fainted dead away to see the size of the snake that had almost sunk its fangs into her backside.

"She didn't get bit, did she?" Jackson asked, squeezing between the bush and the children to pick up the stick holding the snake.

Stafford waited for her to answer. Rattlers usually only bit once, because as soon as they sank their fangs in they held on and started pumping venom.

"No," she said weakly. "I wasn't bitten."

"Good thing," Jackson answered. "A rattler's bite can be deadly."

Her hold increased and Stafford experienced a bout of frustration at the Swede for being so insensitive. Not that he'd been overly sensitive to her during the trip, but that was different. At least, in his mind it was.

"Gotta lance open the wound," the Swede went on. "Bleed out the poison as soon as possible and the person still might not make it."

For a split second Stafford's mind saw her backside again, and he cringed inwardly at how much damage that snake could have done.

"Whatcha gonna do with that?" Terrance asked, nodding toward the snake.

"Well, we could have snake stew for supper," Jackson answered.

Marie made a quiet wheezing sound as she drew in air. She also straightened her stance and didn't lean so hard against him. Stafford watched her closely as she shook her head. It was almost as if he could see her gumption returning.

"We will not be eating that," she said sternly. "Not in a stew or any other way you might consider preparing it."

Jackson nodded. "Most folks don't take to eating them very well. I'll get rid of it." The man laid the snake on the ground and pulled a knife from his boot. "Just gonna cut off the rattles."

"Why?" Terrance asked.

"'Cause that's what you do," Jackson said. "Look here." He waved for the children to step closer. "Each one of these buttons, that's what they're called on his tail, was formed when it shed its skin. By counting the buttons, you can guess how old the snake might be."

The children had gathered close, even the girls, and Stafford took a couple of steps backward, taking Marie with him. "You doing all right now?"

Her gumption may have returned, but there was something else about her that caught him off guard. She looked all soft and feminine, especially her big doe eyes.

"Yes, thank you," she said softly.

"Thank your little dog, there," he said roughly, not too willing to accept her gratitude. "If she hadn't started barking, you may have gotten bit."

Her cheeks turned bright pink. "I threw a pebble at her, trying to hush her up."

"That couldn't have been what riled up the snake," he said, setting her arm loose and stepping away. "They usually skedaddle when it comes to things bigger than them."

Another shudder of sorts was creeping its way up his spine. He wasn't entirely sure, but he sensed it had something to do with standing this close to Marie, touching her, whispering. Those were not things he did.

"Well, thank you, and Polly, for coming to my rescue," she said.

"There was no rescuing involved," he clarified.

She was wringing her hands and cringing slightly, her face still flushed. He knew why a moment later.

"Mr. Burleson, about...about the position—"

Now *that* he could laugh at. "No one will ever know I saw your bare bottom, Marie."

The exact look of mortification he'd seen on her face earlier reappeared. Too bad he hadn't bet on the cause of it—he'd have won. At that moment, he chose to take it one step further. "That is, if you call me Stafford. I'd say the formality of Mr. Burleson would just be a waste now. Considering what I saw and all."

Her hiss, along with the snap in those brown eyes told him she was back one hundred percent, and that was a good thing. So much so, he laughed, tipped his hat, and with a wink, turned around. "We're wasting daylight," he shouted, once again feeling a genuine skip in his step.

She caught up with him before he made it to the team. "Mr. Burleson—"

One look had her pinching her lips together. "Stafford."

He nodded. It really didn't mean that much, other than that he'd won, and he liked being a winner.

Some of the steam left her as she bowed her head slightly. "I appreciate your discretion," she huffed and then turned. "Children!"

He laughed, not caring that she heard and cast a very unfavorable look his way.

It didn't take long before they were loaded up and heading west again. Marie was on the seat beside him again today, and that played a bit of havoc with Stafford's insides. It hadn't yesterday and there was no reason for it to this morning, but it did, and try as he might, ignoring it was impossible. Just as it was impossible to ignore how, every so often, his mind flashed back to the image of the lily-white flesh she was now sitting on. That was bound to affect a man. Any man.

"Mr. Burleson?"

"Yes, Samuel?" he answered, thankful he now knew the children's names. The younger two, Charles and Weston, looked exactly alike and it wasn't until they spoke that he knew who was who. Weston had the lisp, Charlie didn't. Weston talked more than Charlie did, too. Probably because Charlie was always chewing on the collar of his shirt. It was pretty amazing how much he'd discovered about these kids in such a short time.

"You're really a cowboy aren't you?" Samuel asked.

"Well, I expect I am," Stafford answered. He hadn't thought of it much, but had to admit he liked who he was, now. A cowboy was as fitting a word as any, and it beat the heck out of being a cotton farmer. Not that he'd ever have been one of those. Sterling had inherited his father's farm. That's how it was with the oldest. The second son had to forge out on his own, make his own way in life. Which fit him just fine.

"Can I call you Stafford?" Samuel asked. "It sounds a lot more like a cowboy than Mr. Burleson, don't you think?"

Marie opened her mouth, but he shook his head and grinned. Giving the boy a nod, he agreed. "Sure, you can call me Stafford."

"Are there a lot of rattlers in these parts, Stafford?" the child then asked.

Aw, the real question. "Enough," he answered, noting how Marie was staring at him. Making light of the truth might ease her anxiety, but it wouldn't do any of them any good. "Rattlesnakes don't like humans and tend to shy away, but if you startle one, or corner him, he'll strike. There's no doubt about that."

"If you shoot another one, can I have the buttons off it?" Samuel asked.

Jackson had given the rattle he'd cut off to Terrance, who'd spent the last half hour making sure everyone in the wagon didn't jostle about and break his new treasure.

"Yes," Stafford answered, figuring that was fair. Then, just to encourage Terrance to share his bounty, he said, "Let me see that rattle."

The oldest boy shouldered into the opening beside his brother. "Jackson says it's fragile. That means it'll break easy."

"That's what it means, all right," Stafford said as he held the reins toward Marie. "Hold these."

* * *

Still humiliated, Marie shook her head. Never,
ever, had she been so embarrassed in her life. It
would help if Stafford—as she was now forced to
call him—didn't find such humor in it all. He'd
been grinning ever since he'd shot that snake.
Every time she glanced his way, she could tell
he was remembering what he'd seen, almost as
if he'd pressed the image in a book the way one
would a flower, to take it out and look at it every
so often.

"If you're going to live out here, Marie," he
said, thrusting the reins toward her, "you'll need
to learn to drive a wagon. Now take the reins.
I'm right here, nothing's going to happen."

It would help, too, if he wasn't so, well, right,
and so bull-headed about everything. And if he
hadn't come to her rescue as he had. Swallow-
ing a growl, she took the reins.

"That's it," he said. "Just hold them loosely.
You don't have to do anything. The horses know
to follow the road."

If she hadn't just been found with her bottom
as bare as an infant's, she might have been nervous to drive a wagon of this size—of any size—
but right now she wasn't going to give Stafford
anything else to laugh about. Consequently, she
did as instructed, telling herself she could drive

a wagon twice this size, and snuck a peek as he took the snake's tail from Terrance.

"There's twelve buttons," Terrance said.

"I see that," Stafford answered.

"Does that mean that snake was twelve years old?" Samuel asked.

"No," Stafford answered.

Marie couldn't help but relax a bit and appreciate how comfortable the children had become around Stafford. Yesterday, she'd feared the opposite, that he might have terrorized them. It appeared the children simply understood he wouldn't tolerate misbehaving, and therefore they'd conducted themselves remarkably well ever since. In some ways she'd grown more comfortable around him, too, before the snake.

Actually, he'd probably saved her life this morning. Something she did need to be grateful for. Men had always made her nervous. Before this trip west, she'd never had to deal with them, and still wasn't exactly sure how to go about it. Stafford was different, though. He was certainly stubborn and demanding, but, especially when it came to the children, she saw a softer side to him. One she couldn't help but wonder about. Even admire—just the tiniest bit.

"These rattles are about as breakable as our fingernails," he was telling the children, "and you know how easy it is to break one of them."

He shifted and held the snake's tail in front of the boys. "See this bottom button? It's called the nub. One that's never been broken is smooth and round, but this one, see how it's kind of pointed and split?"

When the boys nodded, he continued, "That means this rattle's been broken."

"So it was older than twelve?" Terrance asked, clearly enthralled.

Marie could no longer hold back her smile. Teaching was an integral part of being a nurse-maid, and whether Stafford knew it or not, he was providing the boys a lesson in animal science.

"No. There's no real way of guessing how old that snake was. Depending on the climate, how much it's eaten and how much it's grown, a snake sheds its skin several times a year. The only thing that's for sure is the more buttons, the bigger the snake."

Stafford glanced her way. He was smiling and lifted a brow as he asked, "Do you know what that means?"

Marie refrained from asking what, knowing the boys would, and they did.

"The bigger the snake, the farther away you want to stay," Stafford answered his own question.

The humor in his eyes tickled her insides,

making her want to giggle, but she held it in. Terrance and Samuel, though, laughed aloud. Stafford reached below the seat then, and pulled out a box. He lifted the lid and, after searching a bit, closed it and pushed the box back under the seat. Handing a piece of cloth to Terrance, he said, "Here. This is just a rag for greasing the wagon hubs, but it'll work. When you're done admiring your rattle, tie it up in this and then tie the rag to a brace bar holding up the canvas. That way you won't have to worry about your brothers and sisters breaking it."

"Thanks, Stafford, I will." Terrance said, taking both the rattle and the rag.

The boys sat down, still guessing the age of the snake and Marie, a bit tongue-tied at the moment over how thoughtful and caring Stafford was being, had forgotten all about the reins in her hands until he spoke.

"You're doing a good job."

"Oh, here," she said, handing over the reins. She wasn't usually addlepated and it was a bit disconcerting that he made her feel as if she was. The way she was thinking about his looks was a bit distressing, too. How when he smiled the lines around his eyes deepened, enhancing his handsomeness. Thoughts like that should not be crossing her mind. She was a nursemaid, first and foremost. The children and their safety should control her thoughts at all times.

Not taking the reins, Stafford shook his head. "No, you're doing a good job." Leaning toward her, he then added, "Actually, let me show you how to lace the reins through your fingers, so you'll have more control."

One at a time, he wove the reins through her fingers. The leather was smooth and warm; however, quite unexpectedly, it was the touch of his skin on hers that caused her hands to burn and tremble.

"You'll want to wear gloves when driving, if at all possible," he said. "The leather can chafe the skin, like a rope burn."

She nodded, not exactly sure why. Other than that she was feeling too out of breath to speak. Yesterday, sitting next to him had been no different than riding beside a stranger in a coach, or standing next to one in line somewhere, yet today, a new awareness had awakened inside her. One she'd never experienced. He was still a stranger—a somewhat overbearing one whom she really didn't like very much—and sitting next to him shouldn't be any different. But it was. Although she couldn't say exactly how or why, perhaps because she was putting too much thought into it. She was known for that. Miss Wentworth had said one of her best attributes was how she could concentrate on a problem and ultimately come up with the best choice.

"Just curve this finger a bit," Stafford said, forcing her finger to bend. "See how it tugs on that rein? And if you bend this one —" he maneuvered a finger on the other hand "—that rein moves. It doesn't take much, and is pretty easy when the road is this smooth. You'll soon learn that the rougher the road, the more control you'll need over the horses."

Marie was listening, but it was difficult to concentrate with him holding her hands as he was, and with the way he smelled. It was pleasant, spicy, and made the air snag in her chest. Telling herself not to think of such things didn't help at all.

Attempting to focus all her thoughts on the children proved to be impossible, as well. But perhaps that was her way out. She could tell Stafford that watching over six children would take all her time and, therefore, she most assuredly would not need to learn to drive a wagon. No matter where they lived she had lessons to teach—reading and spelling, geography and grammar, philosophy, civil government and a smattering of other subjects, unless of course there was a school within walking distance for the older ones to attend. It would be good for them to learn social graces by interacting with other children their age.

"You got it."

It was a moment before Marie realized he was speaking of driving the team. It had worked. Focusing on the children, what she'd need to do, had pulled her mind off him.

"You're a quick learner," he added with a nod.

A surprising jolt of happiness flashed inside her. "Thank you," she said. "I was always quick at school. Actually Miss Wentworth said I may have been her best student ever. She said I had a natural ability." Heat rose upon her cheeks. She was proud of her accomplishments, but hadn't meant to sound so boastful. A part of her just wanted him to know she wasn't a simpleton. Mainly because, even thinking of the children, the episode with the snake was still causing a good amount of mortification to fester inside her. Miss Wentworth would be appalled, too, to learn she'd let a man see her bare backside.

"I see," he said. "And who is Miss Wentworth?"

Not being from Chicago, it made sense he would never have heard of Opal Wentworth. "She owns the Chicago School of Domestic Labor. Her training classes in all positions are renowned. It's close to impossible to obtain a position without a certificate of completion within the city."

He was looking at her somewhat curiously, as if she'd said something he didn't quite believe.

"It's true," she said. "A certificate from Miss Wentworth's opens doors." A different sense overcame her, one of achievement, perhaps. It could be because she'd never driven a wagon before and was quite proud of herself for learning so quickly, or because she had graduated at the top of her class.

Then again, it could be because of something entirely different. She'd never been around a man so much before, and it was rather bewildering. All of her placements had been with married couples, but it had been the wives who'd managed the household help, including her.

Glancing forward, she attempted to keep her thoughts on their conversation. "Miss Wentworth said I was the best nursemaid she'd ever had the pleasure to train."

"You don't say," he said.

She nodded. Perhaps if she convinced him of her nursemaid abilities, he could convince Mick Wagner that hiring her would be more beneficial than marrying her. She'd always believed earning a wage would be far more pleasurable than getting married. No matter what Sarah had suggested. "Yes," Marie said proudly. "The best nursemaid ever."

Several hours later her confidence was waning. The second day on the trail was better than the first, in many ways, but in others it was worse. The sun was boiling hot today. Sweat poured down Marie's back and her temples throbbed. Stafford had taken the reins from her long before her arms had started to ache, but they did so now. Her entire body hurt from the endless bouncing, and she had to wonder if the heat and travels were getting to Stafford, too.

He kept taking off his hat and wiping at the sweat streaming down his forehead, and when someone asked for a drink of water, he never questioned it, just handed over the canteen.

The heat was taking a toll on the children, too. Their little faces were red and they drooped in the back of the wagon like a half dozen dandelions plucked from the ground. Marie's confidence in coming up with a plan to ease their plight had plummeted. There was nothing she could do or offer that would relieve the heat.

At her suggestion, they'd all walked for a while, but that had been worse. At least beneath the canopy of the wagon the children were shielded from the glare of the sun.

"There's a creek up ahead," Stafford said,

interrupting her thoughts. "We'll stop there to water the animals and ourselves."

A wave of thankfulness crashed over her. "That will be nice. This heat is deplorable."

He frowned, but nodded.

Used to explaining the definition of words, she started, "Deplorable means—"

"I know what it means."

Marie chose to ignore the bite in his tone. The heat was taxing, but she sensed it was more than the temperature getting to him. He'd turned quiet some time ago, almost brooding. It was just as well. His silence, that was. They'd conversed enough. While showing her how to drive the team, he'd talked about being little and how his father had taught him how to drive. He also shared that he was from Mississippi, where his family still lived. Then he'd started asking about her family, at which point she'd changed the subject and kept changing it every time he tried to bring it back up.

If necessary, she'd explain her history to Mick Wagner, but not to anyone else. There was no need to, and for her, it was better off left buried deep inside. She didn't like how memories could befuddle a person's mind, and the thought of telling him she'd been returned, twice, to the orphanage, made her stomach hurt. Especially after he'd told her about his family. That's all she'd ever wanted. To be part of a family. She'd gotten that when the Meekers had hired her, and she wouldn't give it up.

First one, then the other horse nickered, and Marie glanced around, but saw nothing but brown grass.

"They smell the water," Stafford said. "It's just over the hill."

The next few minutes seemed to take hours, the hill they ambled up the tallest ever, but when they crested the peak and she saw the sparkling creek trailing along the floor of the valley below, the downward trek became endless. The children had moved to the front opening of the wagon, vying for a spot to gaze at the water with as much longing as the horses showed by their increased speed.

As the horses trudged closer, the creek grew larger and a touch of anxiety rose up to quell her excitement. The road they were on entered the water on one side and appeared again on the other side. She shivered slightly.

"There's no bridge."

"No, there's not," Stafford agreed. "But the water isn't deep. We can cross safely this time of year. Springtime is a different story."

She had no choice but to trust him, which actually was becoming easier and easier.

A chorus of voices over her shoulder asked if

they could get wet, and as the wagons rolled to a stop a short distance from the water, Stafford answered, "Yes." He then turned to her as he set the brake. "We're going to unhitch the teams, let them cool off a bit. You and the children can go upstream a distance and cool off yourselves. Just not too far."

Climbing on and off the wagon had grown a bit easier, too, now that she knew exactly where to step. Marie was down in no time and lifting the twins out of the back while the older children climbed out themselves.

"Can we get wet, like Stafford said?" Samuel asked hopefully.

She should have insisted the children continue to call him Mr. Burleson. Allowing them to call him Stafford was inappropriate, but in truth, she didn't have the wherewithal to say a whole lot right now. She'd never been so hot and uncomfortable in her life.

"Yes," she said. "But take your shoes off."

They took off running and Marie didn't have the heart to call them back, make them wait for her. So, instead, she ran, too. The water was crystal clear, and she could easily see the rocky bottom. Wasting no more time than the children, she removed her shoes and stockings, and entered the creek beside them, sighing at the heavenly coolness the water offered.

She held her skirt up, letting the water splash about her ankles, and kept vigilant eyes on the children as they eagerly ventured farther in. She'd never learned to swim, so the water made her nervous, but it was shallow, only up to the twins' waists, and they were enjoying the experience wholeheartedly, as were the others.

It wasn't long before a whoop sounded and Mr. Jackson flew past her like a wild man. Arms out, he threw himself face-first into the water and sank below, only to pop up moments later, laughing from deep in his lungs.

Samuel instantly copied the man's actions, and that had everyone laughing all over again.

A hand caught hers and she twisted, ready to pull it away, for the heat was intense.

"Come on," Stafford said, tugging slightly.

"No, this is deep enough," she insisted.

"It's barely up to your knees at the deepest point." With his free hand, he pointed toward Mr. Jackson. "He's sitting on the bottom and it's not up to his shoulders."

"He's a tall man," she explained.

Stafford laughed and let go of her hand, which left a sense of loneliness swirling around her. He was gone in an instant, out in the middle with all of the children and Mr. Jackson, splashing up tidal wave after tidal wave.

The air left Marie's lungs slowly. She shouldn't

be staring, but Stafford had taken his shirt off. So had Mr. Jackson, but her eyes weren't drawn to the other man as they were to Stafford. Dark hair covered his chest, and his shoulders and arms bulged. Muscles. She'd seen pictures of the male form in her studies, but goodness, none of those drawings had looked this…real.

Marie glanced away, downstream to where the horses stood in the water, drinking their fill, but that didn't hold her attention. When she turned back, her gaze caught Stafford's.

"Come on," he said again, waving a hand as he now sat on the bottom with water swirling around his burly chest. "It feels great."

The children joined in with his invitation, waving and begging her to join them. She could say no to him, but not to them. Dropping her skirt, for she couldn't hoist it any higher, she edged toward the clapping and squeals.

And splashing. Water was flying in all directions, and it did feel wonderful. Then, all of a sudden, Marie went down. Though the water was shallow, she was completely submerged, her back thumping off the rocky creek bed.

Chapter Four

Marie came up as quickly as she'd gone down, coughing, but it wasn't until Stafford saw the laughter in her eyes that he let the air out of his chest. He tore his eyes away, a bit disgusted he'd been holding his breath. People could drown in just about any amount of water, he understood that, but there were enough of them around to prevent that. What irritated him was how every time he caught a glimpse of her air snagged in the middle of his chest and sat there until it burned.

She was a looker, he could admit that, and what he'd seen this morning kept flashing in his mind like heat lightning—a sudden flash that was nothing but an illusion.

He hadn't been drawn in by looks in ages. Frustrated in ways he hadn't been in years, either, he ducked beneath the water again and held his breath until his lungs had a reason to burn.

When he surfaced, he stood and made his way to the shore. He'd said it before and thought it again while seeing her running to the stream with the children, but had to repeat it to himself once more. Marie looked like the kids' older sister, barely more than a child herself.

It didn't help. She was a woman. An attractive one who took her job seriously. He was also willing to admit, she did it well. Not one of those kids could make a peep without her responding immediately, and right now they were gathered around her as if she was the queen bee.

Stafford stepped out of the water and bent forward to shake the water from his hair before he made his way over to where he'd left his shirt, boots, socks and hat. Right next to hers. Her little bonnet lay there, too, and he ran a hand over it, testing the thickness of the fabric. Just as he'd suspected, it was nothing more than thin cotton that didn't offer much relief from the sun. Not on a day like this.

He sat to pull on his socks and boots, and his gaze locked onto the game of water tag happening in the stream. He watched as Marie caught both twins, one in each arm, and planted kisses on their wet heads before she let them loose and chased after the two girls.

A smile tugged at his lips, and he let it form. He remembered days like this. When it was too hot to do much else, his family would head to the river and spend the day frolicking in the water. It had been fun, and something he hadn't thought of in a long time. Crazy as it was, he felt a touch homesick.

Boots on, Stafford stood and shrugged into his shirt before he made his way to the wagons where he checked hubs and axels and anything else he could think of to keep his mind from wandering deeper down memory lane. He was trying, too, to keep his thoughts off Marie. In reality, that is what he should be thinking about, figuring out what she wanted with Mick, but when he did let her into his mind, Mick didn't accompany her.

"I feel like a new man," Jackson said, leading two of the horses out of the water.

"It felt good," Stafford agreed.

"Good for those kids, too," the other man said, handing over the reins. "I know how hard it is keeping them cooped up in a wagon."

"You do?"

Jackson, already heading back to gather the other team, paused with his gaze on the group still splashing about. "Yeah. I got two boys, five and nine, we moved out here from Wisconsin last year. That was a long trip."

Stafford hadn't met the man prior to hiring him and figured it made sense, the man having kids, given the way he'd taken to Marie's bunch so readily.

"My wife's name is Marie, too." Jackson laughed then. "Maybe it's the name. Marie. I can't say, but mine is the best wife ever. She's a dream come true, and there's few prettier. Although that one comes close."

Stafford ignored the feelings nettling inside him, almost as if he didn't want other men looking at Marie and commenting on how pretty she was. He'd felt that way once, about Francine, and was never going to do that to himself again.

Jackson retrieved the other horses, and as soon as the man approached, Stafford, still trying to gain control of his mind, asked, "What are your sons' names?"

"Jack is the oldest and Henry the youngest."

"Jack Jackson?" Stafford couldn't help but ask, glad to have something his mind could snatch up. When they'd been introduced, the man had simply said to call him Jackson.

"No." The other man laughed as he started hitching his team to the freight wagon. "Jackson's just the name I go by. My real name is William Borgeson."

Buckling harnesses, Stafford asked, "How do you get Jackson out of that?"

"My folks had nine girls before I came along. My father's name was Jack, so the entire town took to calling me Jack's son. It stuck. I was about ten before I learned my real name was William."

"That's an interesting story."

The female voice, all soft and tender, caught Stafford so off guard he lost his hold on the drawbar yoke of the singletree harness, which promptly fell and smashed the big toe on his left foot. He almost cursed. The expletive didn't leave his lips because his breath had caught again, sat there in his chest as though it didn't have anything better to do than sting as sharply as his toe.

Marie was wet from top to bottom and was finger-combing her long hair over one shoulder. Her hands slid all the way to the ends, which hung near her waist, and her wet dress—once a pale blue, now much darker—and white pinafore clung to her in ways dresses shouldn't cling. Not while he was looking, anyway.

"Thank you, Miss," Jackson answered, hitching the yoke to the harness of his team. "Now that my father has passed on, the name has a bit more meaning for me, and it's pretty much the only thing I answer to." Chuckling he added, "Other than to my wife. She can call me anything she wants and I come a-running."

Toe throbbing and lungs burning, Stafford wasn't in any mood to hear how happily married the other man was, no matter how he got his name. He didn't want to think of Marie being a wife, either, not to anyone. It would be nice, though, if his partner was here right about now. Then Stafford could wash his hands of this entire mess and not have to sit beside Marie for the next several hours.

"Get the kids loaded up," he said, gruffly. "With any luck, we'll be home before dark."

Luck, it appeared, had left him so far behind he might never see it again. A couple of hours later, the freight wagon cracked a hub, and though they got it fixed, it was too late to take off again, even though he was so close to home he might be able to see it if they were atop a hill instead of in another river valley. And sitting next to Marie had been even more disagreeable than he'd imagined. This time, to keep the children occupied, with a sweet, perfect voice, she'd sung songs with them. Jaunty and silly tunes that had them all laughing and encouraging him to join in.

He hadn't, of course, and he'd bitten his lip so many times to keep from grinning there probably wasn't any skin left on his bottom one. His sister Camellia had been the singer in his family. She was married now, living down by Galveston, and he couldn't help but wonder how she was doing.

It seemed everything had him thinking about his family, his home, and the bottom line was he didn't like it. He'd rid himself of those memories at the same time he'd erased the ones of Francine and how she'd chosen Sterling over him. For ten years he'd gotten along fine without those reminiscences and didn't need them back. The few times he'd seen his family since leaving home, he'd made new memories. They were enough.

Furthermore, it seemed to him that while he and Jackson had been working on the hub, Marie could have been gathering wood, lighting a fire and rustling up something for supper—the wagon was full of food. But she hadn't. Instead, she'd led the kids into the shade and sat there reading to them and watching as they wrote on their slates. Schooling was fine, but when there was work to be done, that's what should come first.

"Terrance," Stafford yelled as he replaced the tools in the box beneath the wagon seat. "You and Samuel gather some wood for a fire."

The boys instantly jumped to follow his orders, but Marie stood, too, and took Terrance by the arm. Stafford was too far away to hear what she said, however, the way both Terrance and Samuel bowed their heads he caught the gist of it.

Sitting next to her for hours on end—including those while her hair and clothes dried, filling the hot air that had circled around him with a flowery scent—his mind bringing up memories as if it was turning the pages of an old book, not to mention the broken hub and the heat, had taken their toll. Usually a tolerant man—well somewhat tolerant—he couldn't put up with anything else. Shoving the box back in place he marched toward the trees.

She met him at the fringe of the shade. "I will not allow—"

His growl caused her to pause, but not for long.

After taking a breath she continued. "Have you forgotten what happened this morning?" she asked, red faced and snippy. "The snake?"

He'd be dead in his grave and still remembering everything about the snake incident. Taking out his gun, he stepped around the children and fired all six bullets into the underbrush. He spun around as the echoes were still bouncing. The two girls were peeking out from behind Marie with their hands over their ears, while the boys were clapping and grinning.

Stafford nodded to them before he lifted his gaze to her. "If there were any snakes, they're hightailing it for safer ground now." He holstered his gun. "Terrance, you and Samuel gather some wood."

The boys looked up at Marie. Stafford noticed

that out of the corner of his eyes. The rest of his gaze was locked on hers in a rather steely battle. Her glare didn't waver, therefore, he narrowed his eyes and gave her a good hard stare.

It took a moment or two, but eventually, with a slow lowering of those long lashes, she glanced toward the two waiting boys. "Stay together and watch for snakes."

"Yes'um," they agreed, flying around him.

While Stafford took a moment to breathe—yes, he'd been holding his breath again—Marie sent the other children off toward the wagons with a few gentle words before her glare returned to him.

"That was not necessary," she seethed between clenched teeth.

"You're right," he agreed. "If you'd have thought to gather firewood, I wouldn't have found it necessary to ask."

A frown flashed upon her brows. "Thought to gather firewood? Why would I have thought of that?"

"To build a fire?" he asked mockingly.

"For what? It's still a hundred degrees out. No one's cold."

She couldn't possibly be this dense. "To cook on?" he asked, half wondering if it really was a question.

Pausing, as if gathering her thoughts, she said, "Oh."

"You do know what that is?" he asked. "Cooking?"

"Yes," she snapped.

"Then why didn't you?" he asked as she started walking toward the wagons. Stafford hadn't completely expected her to cook, yet it seemed to him that most women would have. Catching up to her, he asked, "Why didn't you prepare supper while we fixed the wagon?"

She stopped and hands on her hips, glared at him again. "Because I am a nursemaid, Mr. Burleson, not a cook."

He didn't miss the emphasis she put on his name. "So?"

"So, nursemaids don't cook."

Realization clicked inside his head. Maybe luck was on his side. "Don't or can't?"

She continued to glare.

"I thought you graduated at the top of your class."

"I did. Nursemaid classes."

"And feeding children isn't part of taking care of them?" He shook his head then, even as another question formed. "Who do you think will be cooking for the children once we arrive at my—M-Mick's house?"

"The cook, of course."

Stafford took great pleasure in stating, "Mick doesn't have a cook."

Her expression was a cross between shock and horror. "He doesn't?"

"Nope." Having hot meals waiting for him at home was just one of the many things Mick proclaimed a wife would do, and knowing that wasn't about to happen had Stafford's mood growing more cheerful by the second.

"Who cooks for him?"

"He cooks for himself." Seeing her frown deepening had Stafford adding, "Once in a while he eats over at my place."

"Your place?"

He nodded.

"I thought you said—" She stopped to square her shoulders. "Don't you live with Mick—Mr. Wagner?"

Shoot, he'd forgotten about that. Then he'd been too happy to see her look of shock to explain everything fully. "We live on the same ranch, in different houses."

Frowning, she said, "Oh," and then asked, "Who cooks for you?"

The older boys had brought an armload of wood to Jackson, who was busy digging a fire hole, and Stafford started walking that way. "Me."

Marie was certain her stomach had landed

on the ground near her heels. Her entire being sagged near there, too. No cook? That possibility had never occurred to her. Everyone had a cook. Everyone she'd ever worked for, anyway. Miss Wentworth had assured her it would be that way. Nursemaids weren't expected to cook.

She spun, staring at the men and boys near the fire now flaming in a small hole. No cook? Not even learning she wouldn't be living under the same roof as Stafford could ease the shock of it. Before they'd left Huron, she'd wondered about meals along the trip, and had asked Mr. Jackson. He'd told her not to worry, that he had everything they needed for the journey and that he'd see to the meals.

She'd been grateful to hear that, knowing the duties of taking care of the children would keep her busy. That would continue, once they arrived at the ranch. How could she cook, as well? Well, she could—make the time that is, for feeding them was a top priority—if she knew how. Nothing in her past had included cooking instructions. She'd gone straight from the orphanage to Miss Wentworth's school and then to various positions as a nanny.

Despite the still warm and muggy air, a chill rippled across her skin. Mick Wagner would probably expect her to cook—at least for the

children—even if she didn't have to follow
through on the mail-order bride scheme.

Her chill intensified, and it didn't take much
to discover why. Stafford was staring at her and
a very distinct grin sat on his face. He thought
it was funny. Or, more to the point, he thought
she was incompetent and enjoyed it.

Marie may not have been born with much—
not a family or name—but she had been born
with determination, and it kicked in right now.
She'd show him. Graduating at the top of her
class meant she hadn't let anything stop her from
proving she could become someone—the best
nursemaid ever—and she'd prove it again. To
Stafford Burleson. She'd learn to cook. Become
the best one he'd ever have a chance to know.

It couldn't be that hard. The children would
need to eat once they arrived at the ranch, and
she would not—could not—be beholden to Stafford for anything more than this trip. Actually,
she couldn't wait to get to the ranch and bid him
farewell, watch him ride off to his place—wher-
ever that might be. Hopefully miles from Mick
Wagner's place. Ranches could be that large,
couldn't they?

Marie was determined, but she wasn't stupid,
therefore, that night she watched, making mental
notes, and did so again the following morning
while Jackson—the man had insisted she drop

the Mr. from his name—did most of the cooking. A blessing for sure, because he didn't mind her whispered questions. The meals were simple affairs. Canned beans for supper, and bacon tucked inside biscuits he pulled from a bag for breakfast. Jackson—bless his heart—even expounded upon the answers he provided. Explained how thick to cut the bacon and how to keep turning it so it wouldn't burn. He even explained how to make the coffee both he and Stafford seemed to enjoy so much.

She preferred tea. Always had, and she knew how to brew a pot, but Mick Wagner would probably rather have coffee, too, and she'd learn how to make it. If she could cook and take care of the children, there would be no reason for Mick to marry her at all. No reason to worry about some of the things Stafford had her thinking about. Things only husbands and wives did in private. Frustrating thoughts that she couldn't fathom.

The sun had barely made its way into the sky when Stafford's clipped and hard tone suggested it was time to head out.

Marie bit her tongue to keep from telling him there was no reason to shout, only because she felt a bit smug at how irritated he was with her. His brows had been furrowed all morning as he'd watched her conversing with Jackson.

If she'd slept last night, she might have had

the energy to explain how a person who graduates at the top of her class has the wherewithal to learn whatever they need to, but considering she and all six of the children slept, or tried to sleep, in the wagon, she was simply too tired.

The night before she'd allowed the boys to sleep on the ground, as Stafford and Jackson had, but after the snake incident she wasn't about to let that happen again. Therefore, with the children practically lying on top of one another, she'd squeezed into the corner of the wagon and attempted to sleep sitting up. No one, neither her nor the children, had slept much.

Once the children were safely tucked into the back of the wagon, she climbed onto the bench seat, barely acknowledging the glare coming from Stafford.

"Ready?"

Tucking her skirt beneath her knees, she nodded. "Ready."

He let out a disgusted-sounding sigh and slapped the reins over the backs of the horses.

"We won't be stopping for anything this morning," he said after they'd traveled several miles. "I want to be home by noon."

Her lack of response—a simple nod—seemed to irritate him all over again.

"Another day like yesterday," he continued,

"traveling through that heat, would be more than the horses can take."

"I'm sure it would be," she said, while smothering a yawn. A glance into the back of the wagon proved the gentle sway had lulled the children to sleep. It was playing on her already-tired body, as well, and making her eyes heavy.

Stafford's mind was fighting a plethora of things, including how Marie's head bobbed and then snapped back up. No wonder, they must have all sweltered beneath the canvas of the wagon last night. Even lying on the ground had been hot. She couldn't have gotten a wink of sleep, sitting up with her head resting on the tailgate. He'd battled with himself half the night, forcing himself not to go to her and promise there wasn't a snake within a hundred miles. She wouldn't have believed him, and that, too, bothered him.

With each moment that passed, he was having a harder time not liking her, and for the life of him he couldn't figure out why. Although, he had to admit she did have a couple of endearing qualities. Right now, the way her chin bobbed against her chest tickled his insides and made her look about as adorable as any woman had a right to.

The wagon rolled over a bump—had he been

looking he'd have steered around it—and her head jerked, but she didn't wake.

Unable to hide his grin and accepting he couldn't let her fall out of the wagon, Stafford reached over and wrapped an arm around her shoulders, tugging her to his side.

She mumbled slightly, but didn't wake as her cheek nuzzled his shoulder before she let out a sigh and slumped fully against him.

Despite the way his blood warmed—or maybe because of it—Stafford questioned his sanity all over again. The flowery, unique scent he'd come to know surrounded him, making him breathe deeper. He also repositioned himself, just so she'd be more comfortable as the miles brought them closer and closer to home.

Stafford had mixed feelings about that, too. Home. Mick would be there soon. The telegram he'd sent from Huron told his partner to return as quickly as possible. He still didn't want Mick marrying her, but another man would. Practically anyone in the territory—six kids or not.

Terrance and Samuel had answered a few questions last night while he built a fire. He'd still been wondering about her lack of cooking when the boys had piped up, said she'd grown up in an orphanage and that's why she wouldn't let the same thing happen to them. All in all, that had created more questions in his head, but he'd stopped before grilling the boys.

She on the other hand, hadn't ceased her questions—the ones she'd asked Jackson about cooking. It appeared she may not know how to cook now, but wasn't afraid to learn. He had to give her credit for that, even though he didn't want to, at least that's what he kept telling himself.

A good hour later, when they were less than a couple of miles from the ranch, she stirred. One lid opened and Stafford's insides jolted at her sleepy smile before her eye shut and she snuggled against him a bit closer.

Stafford knew the instant Marie realized she was sleeping on his shoulder. Her entire being went stiff and she bolted upright like a branch snapped in two. He laughed. "Have a good nap?"

She glared.

Just to keep the blush on her cheeks, he rubbed the shoulder she'd used as a pillow. When she frowned, he said, "Just wiping off the drool."

Eyes wide, she insisted, "I did not—"

"No, you didn't drool on my shoulder," he assured her, though he wouldn't have minded if she had. That notion set his smile aside. What was he thinking? She was his partner's soon-to-be wife.

Stafford let that thought take root and turned his attention to the horses in front of them. "You might want to wake up the kids. We'll be at the ranch in another mile or so."

She agreed and turned toward the back, but Stafford didn't acknowledge either her answer or her movement. He was too busy telling himself he was not attracted to her. Not at all. He barely knew her, and what he knew he didn't like. Teasing her wasn't fun, either.

They'd been on the trail too long. That's the problem. He'd met hundreds of women over the years, and not one of them had affected him the way she had, because he hadn't spent more than an hour or so in their company. Getting back home, becoming engrossed in his work was exactly what he needed.

By the time his house rose up on the horizon, Stafford was convinced he was back to his old self.

"Is that your ranch?" Terrance asked, leaning over the seat back.

"That's the Dakota Cattle Company," he answered. "Mick and I each own fifty percent of it." Stafford wasn't exactly sure why he wanted Marie to know that, but he did.

"You do?" she asked.

He'd purposely not made mention of the exact terms of his partnership with Mick while traveling. There were a few other things he'd kept to himself, too, and he was telling himself he would enjoy telling her about them. "Yes," he answered. "I do."

Lips pinched, she eased her gaze off him to look toward the buildings they approached, several barns and other sheds, his house as well as Mick's place. An offshoot of the river, a little creek most of the time, ran between their two places. Mick had claimed the acreage on the north side of the creek, Stafford had taken the south and they'd built the ranch itself right in the center, sealing their partnership.

"You both don't live in the same house?" she asked.

"No. We each have our own place," he answered, noting her gaze was on his house. It was rather large. Besides being a good carpenter, he'd wanted a place that would put his brother's to shame. That had been his goal when he'd started building it. Mick thought he was crazy, especially since it took him two years to complete it. Three stories, plus a cellar, nine bedrooms, three parlors, an office, a kitchen and several other rooms he hadn't necessarily named, but most were furnished—everything shipped in from the east.

"That's our house?"

Charlotte asked that, she was the older of the two girls, and for a moment the pleasure of showing Marie the house they'd live in dimmed.

Mick's place only had one bed, and there wasn't enough space to add a second one, let alone a third or fourth.

Stafford let the wagon roll past his place, toward the bridge that arched over the creek. "Nope," he said.

Marie couldn't help but stretch her neck to examine the large, rather unusual house as they moved past it. Painted white, with a porch that appeared to be never ending, it looked a lot like one of the plantation mansions she'd read about and seen pictures of in books about the South before the war. Her heart had started pounding when the house had first come into view. There would be more than enough room in there for all of the children. That had been something she'd worried about. "It's not?" she asked, when the billowing canvas blocked her view.

Stafford didn't answer until after they'd rolled over a short bridge to where another cluster of barns and buildings sat. There, he stopped the horses in front of a small, square shed of sorts. "This," he said, pointing toward the squat building, "is your house."

All of the children were vying for space behind the seat to get a look at their new home, and it was Samuel who said, "That's not a house."

"It's a cabin," Stafford answered. His gaze,

steady and rather cold, landed on her. "Mick's cabin."

The large house was in view again, over her shoulder, and after a glance that way Marie drew a deep breath. An overly large lump formed in her throat, and the tingling of her spine said she already knew, yet she asked, "Whose house is that?"

"Mine."

Chapter Five

Marie refused to jump to conclusions. The little cabin could be larger on the inside than it looked on the outside. Plenty of buildings were like that. Stafford was instructing a few men who'd walked across the bridge to help Jackson unload the freight wagon and the children were running about, stretching their legs after the long ride and investigating their new surroundings.

Attempting to summon up a positive attitude, Marie pushed the dead air out of her lungs, drew in a fresh breath and made her way to the cabin. It didn't even have a porch, just a path of well-worn dirt that led to the windowless door. It, too, reminded her of pictures she'd seen in books, those of the homes the first settlers of the West had created. That had been years before, though, and the country was well settled now. At least, that's what she'd told the children before they'd embarked on their journey.

Without further ado, she pushed open the door and stepped inside. The space was dark, but she saw enough to make her close her eyes and hope the image would change before she opened them again.

It didn't, and dread once again welled up inside her.

Four walls stood before her, containing a small cast iron stove, a table with two chairs and a bed. That was it. Besides being small, the space smelled of dust and dirt. The mud caked on the floorboards was the cause of that. Footprints could be made out. Large ones.

Still not willing to give in to panic, Marie entered the cabin fully. There were two windows on opposite walls, one over the bed and the other behind the stove. Both were covered with what appeared to be old saddle blankets. She went to the one over the bed first. The ends of the woven material were frayed and tacked to the wall with small nails. One tug and it let loose, the movement sending dust into the air. She sneezed, twice, and then had to rub her palm over the window to see if there was glass behind the thick coat of filth.

A glint of sunlight peeked through the area

she'd wiped, which revealed a heavy layer of dust covering everything else in the cabin.

Unlike cooking, she was well versed in cleaning. Not from her nursemaid classes but from the orphanage. A bucket and mop were the first things young girls were introduced to. She wasn't afraid of that kind of work and made her way to the other window, uncovering cobwebs along with the dirt. She turned back to the room then, imagining it clean and orderly.

The cabin would look better then, once she'd finished, but it wouldn't be any larger. Her optimism was waning, and her anger growing. Stafford could have mentioned this. From about any point in the small cabin, she could see out the door, and the view was the same. The little bridge and the big white house. What kind of man expected children to live in this when he had all that room?

A quiver twisted around her spine. Was he married? Did children and perhaps a wife live in that big house? If so, why hadn't they come out to meet him? Heat warmed her cheeks. She'd dreamed on the way here that she was sleeping next to him, and when she'd awakened and seen him smiling down at her, for a brief moment she'd believed it was real and had never known such joy. It had shattered, though, the moment she'd realized she was snuggled against him.

With a shake of her head, Marie stopped several other questions from forming and marched out the door.

Jackson was climbing onto the freight wagon, now empty. The other wagon, canvas collapsed, was parked next to a large barn, which is where Stafford stood.

"Mr. Burleson," she said loud enough for him to hear. "May I speak with you for a moment, please?"

He said something to Jackson and gestured toward the other side of the creek before walking to her. Marie used the few moments it took him to cover the distance to scan the area, counting the heads of all six children. Seeing them frolicking, with Polly barking beside them as they went from building to building, increased her determination.

When Stafford arrived, looking smug, something snapped inside her, even before he lifted a brow.

"So what do you think of your new house?"

Ignoring his question, she asked sternly, "Who lives in your house with you?"

"No one."

A touch of excitement fluttered in her stomach, which she promptly ignored. "You and Mick Wagner are equal partners in this ranch, aren't you?"

"The ranch, yes, not the homes."

She pulled her eyes off his big house to ask, "How can that be?"

"We each own separate parcels of land, and the buildings on them, but are equal partners in the cattle operation." Gesturing toward each place, he added, "That side of the creek is mine, this side is Mick's."

"I don't understand why Mr. Wagner wouldn't have built a larger house," she said, trying to keep her frustration under control.

"Guess he figured the cabin was all he needed."

"And you needed a house that large?"

"I wanted a big house," he said. "Like the one I grew up in down in Mississippi."

"Why? Do you plan on having a large family?" Her question caused her heart to flutter, a very unusual happening.

"Nope. Don't plan on having a family at all." He turned then. "I've got things to do, and I'm sure you'll want to get settled."

Marie couldn't say exactly what she'd imagined their new home would be like, but this wasn't it. She grabbed his arm, stopping him from walking away. A tingle entered every finger and shot up her arm, but she didn't let loose. The children depended on her for everything, to keep them safe, healthy and happy.

"Surely you realize the children and I can't live in this cabin."

His eyes went from her hold to her face. "Why not?"

"There's only one bed. Where will they all sleep? Furthermore, the bed practically touches the table, which almost touches the stove. There's barely enough room in there for one person, let alone seven." A wave of longing she'd lived with her entire life sprang forth. "Children need space of their own, to put their belongings and feel as if they, too, belong there."

He stared at her for an extended length of time, and she could only hope he was taking what she'd said into consideration. She didn't want to beg, plead with him to let the children and her live in his house, but she'd never lived outside the city before, and the vast countryside, along with the fact the ranch harbored nothing but men, had fear overtaking her senses. Stafford was a man, too, but at least he was one she knew, and he'd provided for them, kept them safe the entire trip here.

"Well," he finally said.

Hope leaped inside her.

"I guess Mick should have thought of that before he ordered a bride."

Stunned, it was a moment or more before Marie realized he'd walked away. She hurried forward, catching him before he stepped on the bridge. The cabin was close to the water, little more than several yards away, whereas his house was up the hill on the other side and grass surrounded it. Green grass the children could play in. Surely he had to see his home was a much more suitable place for children. And her. There might even still be Indian raids in this part of the country.

Holding his arm again, she said, "Mr. Burleson, I cannot allow the children to live in this cabin."

"Why not?"

Having already explained her reasons, she pointed out a suitable compromise. "It simply would make more sense for you to live in the cabin and us to live in the house."

He laughed. "That will not happen, Miss Hall."

She'd taken to calling him Mr. Burleson, but was a touch annoyed to hear him call her Miss Hall again. Actually she was more than a touch annoyed by everything. This wasn't the Stafford she knew, the one she'd come to like—strangely enough.

He patted the back of one of her hands. "Maybe when Mick gets home he'll build you a bigger house."

His complacency grated on her nerves. "We

cannot live in that cabin all winter, now, I insist—"

"Insist all you want," he interrupted, "but that's your house." His grin increased. "A person who graduated at the top of her class must be smart, Miss Hall. I'm sure you'll figure it out."

Too put out for a comeback, Marie let him walk away. He was right, though, she was smart and she would figure it out, and in doing so, she'd wipe that smug grin off his face.

She'd been in unknown situations before, every time she'd taken a new position, and had managed. This was no different. She'd just have to pretend they weren't alone, that the cabin was a fine home. No matter what, she couldn't let the children see her fears. However, she wouldn't pretend Stafford Burleson was anything less than the insufferable brute he was.

A tug on her skirt had her glancing down.

"I'm hungry," Weston said.

The fury inside her doubled.

Stafford didn't turn around until he was almost to his house, even though he wanted to. Marie and those kids would be wedged in Mick's cabin tighter than they'd been packed in the wagon. He was trying his darnedest for it not to trouble him, but it did.

He took off his hat and scratched at his head.

When she'd looked up at him with those plead-ing eyes, he'd all but told them to come across the creek with him. That was the last thing he wanted. She'd gotten to him, though, with her statement about everyone needing a place to put their belongings. His family's home had been large, but not as big as the one he'd built. Grow-ing up, he'd shared a room with Sterling, and being the younger brother, he'd been given a very small space to call his own. Furthermore, most everything he'd owned had been Sterling's first.

The one thing that had been his first had been Francine, but in the end, he'd had to share that with Sterling, too.

Stafford slapped his hat on his head and tore his eyes off Marie and how she'd gathered the children and now walked toward Mick's cabin. Spinning around, he marched in the direction of his house. The monstrous one he'd built so he'd have room for all the things that were his. Things he'd never have to share.

When he entered the house, he expected the warmth of homecoming, the satisfaction of knowing this was all his alone—for that had been his goal, and he'd relished his accomplish-ments the past few years. Instead, the echo of the door closing left him disgusted and lonely. As empty as the house.

Stafford left as quickly as he'd entered and

made his way to the bunkhouse where Shorty Jepson was sure to be. The old man had performed chow duty on every drive he and Mick had led, but when Mick was preparing to leave, Shorty had asked to stay behind. The other ranch hands were happy about that. It meant they weren't on their own when it came to mealtime.

It was all part of Stafford's plan, too. The herd was large enough now that they needed year-round help, and having a cook for the cowboys was as necessary as the men themselves.

"So, that's Mick's bride?" Shorty asked from his seat on the porch of the bunkhouse.

"Yep," Stafford answered, stepping up beside the man whose name matched his height. Shorty was whiskered, too, and gruff and opinionated, and Stafford knew he had to cut the man off at the pass. He was in no mood to answer the dozen questions in the man's narrowed eyes.

"Go over there and see if Mick left any provisions," Stafford said.

"You know he didn't," Shorty replied. "Mick never stocks up on anything."

"Well, go see anyway," Stafford said. "Take whatever you think they'll need, and show her where the springhouse is."

Other than rubbing his mustache, Shorty showed no sign of moving. "Seems odd, don't you think? Mick ordering a bride."

The lump in Stafford's stomach grew hard and heavy. "He's been talking about it for years."

"That was just talk," Shorty said. "You know that. Mick likes riding shotgun in life. Wouldn't have a pot to pee in if he hadn't partnered up with you."

Stafford made no comment. Mick liked to let people believe he was just along for the ride, but in truth he was driven, ambitious, and the bottom line was Stafford wouldn't have a pot to pee in if he hadn't partnered up with Mick.

He'd left home after Sterling's wedding with nothing but a horse, a saddle and less than a hundred bucks to his name. It seemed like enough, but by the time he hit the Rocky Mountains, he was counting pennies. His plan had been to hit a creek filled with gold and pluck out enough nuggets to go farther north and start a ranch. That's how folks made it sound, that you just had to walk along and pick up gold. It wasn't true.

Mick, originally from Texas and making his way north, too, with a similar dream, was as broke as Stafford when they met up along the trail. Having already been in Colorado for a year, Mick knew there weren't any nuggets just lying around. He'd said one man couldn't do it by himself, but if they were to partner up, they might have a chance of finding enough flakes to make both their dreams come true. Over the next year, their dreams became one, and when they left the mountains, they both had money in their pockets.

Though they shared the same dream, Stafford was the one insisting they kept things separate. Back then, his desire to never share anything ever again had been even stronger than it was now. Therefore, their partnership was more of a trio. The Dakota Cattle Company had a third of their findings, he had a third, and Mick had a third. So far it had worked out well. Kept squabbles off the table and allowed them to remain friends as well as partners.

Stafford found his eyes were glued to Mick's property, the buildings there, anyway. Cattle company funds had built the barns used for different aspects of ranching on each side of the creek, but they'd both used personal finances to build their homes. Mick had thrown his cabin up the first year they'd been there, said he'd build a bigger one when the time came, whereas Stafford had lived out of the bunkhouse for years, building on his place every chance he had. He'd known the house he wanted right from the start, and wasn't going to live in anything less. When the day came for his family, namely his brother and Francine, to see what he'd built, he wanted a showplace.

Mick had chastised him often enough. Had

gone so far as to say he was building the house for a woman who'd never live in it and he needed to get over it—Mick did know all about Stafford's past, just as Stafford knew about Mick's—but Stafford had insisted his partner was wrong. He hadn't built the house for Francine, but to prove she was wrong. A man didn't have to inherit wealth in order to provide for a family.

He'd stayed home many times when Mick had asked him to put his hammer down and come to town, spend an evening at the card games and a night in bed with a willing woman. There had been a few times he'd gone along, enjoyed the games and the women, but most of the time he'd declined.

During the hours he'd spent building, he'd thought a lot about Francine and Sterling, and how they'd both insisted they hadn't meant to fall in love. How it had just happened. Things like that didn't "just happen."

Marie flashed into his mind then. Maybe because she and the children were carrying the table and chairs out of Mick's house, setting them up on the hard-packed dirt in front of the doorway. He had to wonder how she would react to Mick's penchant for gambling and visiting houses of ill repute. The thought didn't take hold. Though he enjoyed a game now and again, Mick wasn't a gambler, and he was an honest, dedicated man. When he married, he'd be faithful and a good provider.

"You ain't heard a word I've said, have you?"

Shorty's declaration was loud enough to clear Stafford's mind, and he turned to the man. "I guess I haven't. What did you say?"

"It don't matter none at all," the old man insisted as he hitched up his britches. "I'll go see what they need."

Surprisingly, Marie's optimism had grown. Jackson had bid farewell, but before he left, he announced she could keep most of the ready-made food he'd brought along. He assured her he still had plenty for himself, and what he left was more than enough to tide her and the children over for a few days. Then a man named Shorty Jepson—who insisted she call him Shorty—came over with supplies, including milk for the children.

Shorty also gave her a tour of Mick's property that included a building he called the bunkhouse. He said the cowboys all stayed at the one similar to it over at Stafford's place. This one was only used when they had extra boys staying for a few days after cattle drives and such.

Without a stove for heat or cooking, or a lock on the door, she couldn't imagine living in the building, but she could see it as a playhouse of sorts. There was plenty of space that, once divided up, would offer each child their own private area to store their personal possessions, and the feather ticks could be carried to the cabin. With the table and chairs outside, a sleeping pallet could be created for everyone. It would take more rearranging, but she could picture it in her mind. Winter might prove challenging, being cooped up so, but she'd worry about that when the time came. The important thing was proving to Stafford that she could cope.

With newfound enthusiasm, she fed the children on the table in the yard, utilizing a few more chairs they'd found in the bunkhouse, and afterward she told them of the adventure they would have transforming the bunkhouse.

Caught up in her eagerness, they all pitched in, and by nightfall, after another meal shared at the outdoor table, the children, as exhausted as she, climbed into their new beds. Charlotte and Beatrice, as well as the twins, slept in the cabin's original bed—two at each end—and Terrance and Samuel occupied the two narrow mattresses now laid out where the table had been. She'd hoped for room for at least one more, for the twins, which would have provided her space with the girls, but no matter how'd they moved things, it just wouldn't fit.

There was room, though, between the foot of

the bed and the wall, and that's where she'd laid out a blanket and pillow. She'd had worse accommodations in her life. The children's comfort and safety came first. The bolt lock on the door was reassuring, as well, and though she tried not to include him in her thoughts, knowing Stafford was just across the creek helped, too. She had no doubt he'd come to their rescue if needed. Although he'd tried to stay hidden, she'd seen him watching them all day, and that increased her determination to make Mick's cabin livable.

In the days that followed, when not providing lessons, she scrubbed and cleaned the cabin and the bunkhouse. She and the children also created partition walls in the bunkhouse out of the canvas once used to cover the wagon, as well as other canvas pieces they found in one of the barns.

The children were adapting well to their new home, probably better than she was. However, the canvas walls did help her ignore how the bunkhouse reminded her of the orphanage. In their Chicago home, the six children had shared three rooms, so having a small space all their own was new to them, and that, too, made her look at things differently.

"Marie, can I go see if Stafford wants to come see our rooms?" Samuel asked. He'd arranged his entire set of toy soldiers upon the floor in his area and was admiring his handiwork with great pride.

"He's not home," Terrance replied from his space on the other side of the canvas.

"How do you know that?" Charlotte asked. Her area included two crates upon which several porcelain dolls sat.

"I saw him ride out a while ago," Terrance replied. "Most likely to check the herd. He does that daily, you know."

Marie was biting her tongue, as she had to do quite often. The children had made a habit of crossing the bridge several times a day to visit Stafford. She'd questioned the appropriateness of that, but, missing him herself, she'd allowed it to continue. Not that she truly missed him. He was just different from any other man she'd ever encountered, that's what she suspected, anyway. She saw him often, from afar. He still watched them closely, and somehow she knew he was the main reason she wasn't scared witless. In some ways she found the isolation of the ranch comforting. The chances of anyone finding them, attempting to take away the children, was very remote. Out here, she could almost believe she had the family she always wanted.

The children discussed things Stafford had told them over the past few days, about cattle and such, while she set a brace board in the trunk that held Charlie's toys so the lid wouldn't accidently fall on him, and she waited until there was a break in their conversation. "Perhaps after lunch he'll have time to come see your rooms," she said brightly. "And speaking of lunch, it's time I go prepare something to eat."

Despite the nervousness fluttering in her stomach, she walked out of the bunkhouse. The last of the food Jackson had left had been used for breakfast, but that wasn't her real concern. Shorty had brought over a basket of eggs, and he'd explained how she could scramble them for the children. It sounded easy enough. However, this would be her first attempt at using the stove. Something she had to learn to use, not just for cooking. Tonight was bath night. They would need hot water.

The thought hadn't frightened her until this morning, when Shorty brought over the eggs. He'd warned her that Mick's stove was finicky. In his gruff way, he'd said she'd need to leave the door open or it wouldn't catch enough air for the fire to take off. He'd said to be careful. One spark could set the cabin aflame.

Never, not once, had she been in charge of starting a fire, and she felt a little overwhelmed at the prospect.

To be on the safe side, she stacked the extra mattresses on top of the bed, and considering

Shorty had said the fire needed air, she made sure both windows were open as well as the door.

Marie started with a few small pieces of wood and a handful of straw. It took several matches and a second handful of straw before the flames caught. At that point she added a larger piece of wood, and then, because she had no idea how much wood she would need, she filled the entire space with two more logs.

The only cupboards in the cabin were a set of shelves nailed to the wall that held plates and such, so she carried a bowl and the basket of eggs to the table outside.

Milk. She'd forgotten that needed to be mixed with the eggs, so she hurried toward the creek and the little structure Shorty had called the springhouse. He'd explained that the constant flow of water kept the milk and butter, as well as several other things, cold, and she was amazed at how well it worked.

Emerging from the dark little building, Marie's heart leaped into her throat at the smoke billowing out the cabin door. It was the Meeker's house in Chicago all over again. She dropped the milk can and ran.

The thundering of hooves sounded behind her, as well as a shout, but she ignored everything in her quest to get to the cabin. She was almost at the door when brute force shoved her aside.

"Get back!"

Marie stumbled, but recognizing both his voice and his bulk as he entered the cabin, she found her footing and moved forward again.

The room was clouded with smoke, but she saw Stafford kick the stove door closed with one foot while doing something with the handle on the pipe that stretched up to the roof at the same time.

"What were you trying to do?" he shouted. "Burn the place down?"

"Of course not," she yelled in return. The smoke filling her nose and mouth made her cough before she could finish. "I was cooking lunch for the children."

"You don't know how to cook," he yelled, grabbing her arm and pulling her toward the door.

"I'm learning," she shouted back.

"Well, learn how to build a fire first."

They were outside now, in fresh air, which got her lungs working again. "Shorty told me to leave the door open so the fire would take off."

Stafford had a hold of both her upper arms. "You also have to open the damper so the smoke goes up the chimney," he shouted inches from her face.

Over the noise of his voice she heard the trampling of footsteps on the wooden bridge and turned, a multitude of thoughts vying for space in her mind. Number one being that, even though he was shouting at her, she was rather delighted by the sight of him. It was like seeing the first robin in spring, when it made a person happy, even if there was still snow on the ground. Then again, maybe she was happy because she'd been right. He had come to the rescue.

"Everything all right, boss?"

It was one of the ranch hands asking the question. She hadn't been introduced to anyone besides Shorty, but the children had, and by the descriptions they'd provided, she assumed this man was the one named Red. The children had asked how that could be when *Red* had black hair and a rather comical-looking black mustache.

"Yes," Stafford said. "She just forgot to open the damper."

"All right, then." The other man tipped the brim of his hat and gave a little nod. "Ma'am."

She gave a slight nod in return. Her mind was still racing, and still in one direction. Stafford. It had only been a few days, but she'd forgotten how handsome he was, and how tall. Right now, if she stared straight ahead, her eyes landed on the buttons of his shirt. She had to tip her head to see his face, which she was afraid to do again. A moment ago, while gazing up at him, her heart had started beating so frantically it hurt to breathe.

The hold he had on her arms softened and his hands rubbed the area instead. The action caused a multitude of feelings inside her, and she could no longer keep from glancing up.

His expression was no longer hard and fierce, and she couldn't find a way to describe how he was looking at her. The tenderness in his gaze, though, made her gulp. It seemed as if time stopped, as they stood simply looking at each other.

He was still rubbing her upper arms and the commotion inside her was growing stronger. She had an undeniable urge to step closer and stretch her neck so—

The realization was startling, and Marie stepped back. Stafford moved at the same instant, separating them further. While she pressed a hand over her racing heart, he took off his hat and glanced around before replacing it.

She'd never, ever thought of kissing a man before.

"Make sure you open that damper," he said gruffly.

Her meek reply of, "I will," caused her cheeks to grow even hotter. What was it about him that left her completely out of sorts? She didn't have a lot of experience around men, but one hadn't intimidated her for a very long time. That thought triggered a response.

"I wasn't trying to burn the cabin down," she shouted at his back, needing to show him he hadn't frightened her and never would.

He spun around, frowning. A moment later, he nodded. "Good, see that you don't."

"I won't," she insisted, marching toward the table and the eggs that still needed to be cooked.

Marie did cook the eggs, and did so several more times, until a week later, when she burned down the cabin.

Chapter Six

After the last bucket of water was thrown and the smoke had cleared, there was nothing left of Mick Wagner's cabin but ashes and a still-smoking black stove missing one side. Standing beside the charred ruins, Marie wanted to run over and start pounding on that stove. It had become her worst enemy. The inanimate object had taken on an evil personality, fighting her every time she had to build a fire in its belly. If it wasn't filling the cabin with black smoke—open damper or not—it was smothering flames as fast as she could strike matches.

This morning, after fighting it for more than an hour, she'd filled it with straw, determined to win. There was no explanation for what happened. An explosion of sorts inside the stove had knocked the door wide open and spewed flaming bits of straw into the air.

She'd grabbed the water bucket and thrown

it at the stove, and that's when one entire side of the stove had flown across the room. Screaming, she'd run for help, but it was too late. By the time the men rushed over the bridge, the entire cabin was in flames.

The desire to throttle the stove left her, or maybe she was just completely depleted. When her knees wanted to give out, she let them, sinking slowly to the ground. She'd failed. Her dream of having a family, a home that was hers, had gone up in smoke. She'd be sent back, just as before, but this time was worse. The children would be returned, too.

She heard Shorty shout for Stafford, and her stomach filled with knots.

"The kids are just fine," Shorty said, patting her shoulder. "I took them to Stafford's house and told them to stay there."

"I know." She'd watched as the old man ushered them all over the bridge to the big white house while the other men fetched buckets of water. "Thank you."

"It was bound to happen," Shorty continued. "That stove's been a pain ever since Mick hauled it home."

In his own gruff way, he was attempting to make her feel better, but instead, tears started to drip from her eyes. A rarity. It had been so long since she'd cried, Marie had forgotten what it felt like. Her throat started to burn and her temples pounded. She'd sworn this would never happen again. The pain of being rejected, of being returned to the orphanage, not once but twice, rushed forward. She closed her eyes, swallowed a sob and tried to fight the memories.

Quietly, Stafford arrived at her side, and Shorty wandered back toward the smoldering ruins.

"Come on," Stafford said softly.

Shaking her head, she refused to budge. "You can't send them back."

"Send who back?" he asked.

"The children. You can't—"

"The children," he said, taking her arms gently but firmly, "will want to know you're all right."

With his strength pulling her up, Marie had no choice but to stand, but her feet didn't want to move and she stumbled.

Stafford grasped both of her hands, examining them thoroughly. "Did you get burned?"

"No." More tears were threatening to start falling. He'd come to her rescue again, been the first to arrive, and that filled her with raw frustration. She'd tried so hard. Wanted him to see how capable she was, how needed—more so than ever before—and now... Oh, that stupid, stupid stove. Everything else she'd managed to make work, but he wasn't going to see that. No one would. Not with Mick Wagner's cabin in cinders.

Stafford's hands gently cupped her cheeks. She tried not to look up, but when his thumbs wiped away her tears, she had to, and had to blink at what she saw. He should be furious with her, shouting and saying *I told you so,* but he wasn't. Instead, he was looking at her as if she was fragile and might break at any moment. He had no idea how close she was to that. Breaking.

"Please don't send us back to Chicago," she whispered.

He frowned slightly, and then wrapped an arm around her shoulders and held her against his side as he started walking. "No one's going anywhere," he said, "other than you going to my house to check on the children."

The sensation that washed over her was new, one she couldn't explain, yet inside she believed him. That he wouldn't send her back. "I don't know what happened," she said.

"The stove got too hot," he said. "When cold water hits hot cast it can make it crack, and it's not unusual for a seam to give way."

She'd seen men be kind before. John Meeker had always been cordial, and some along the trip had been helpful, but no man had ever been this understanding, not to her, and that had odd things happening inside her. Just as when he'd saved her from the snake. Though she'd been mortified, she'd also been in awe. He was so strong, so masculine, and deep down, she really wanted him to like her. She'd never, ever, wanted that before. A man to like her.

She sniffled and he squeezed her shoulder.

"Doing better?" he asked.

"You're being awfully nice about this." She hadn't meant to say that aloud.

Stafford knew his behavior was surprising her. It was a bit astonishing to him, too. Mick's cabin being burned to the ground didn't bother him as much as it should, and knowing she and the children now had to live with him wasn't a worry, either. All of them living in that cabin, with only one bed had been.

For the past several days he'd tried to come up with a reason to make them move into his house, but Marie, in her own stubborn way, had made the best of the situation and there wasn't anything he could use as an excuse. Not one she'd have accepted.

Watching from the other side of the river had been worse than sitting next to her on the wagon seat, but moments ago, when she asked him not to send her back to Chicago, his heart had flipped in a way it never had.

They crossed the bridge, and while walking up the steeper slope that led to his house and barns she said, "I think it would be better if you yelled at me."

The urge to kiss her had hit new heights a short time ago and the way those big, luminous brown eyes were looking at him right now was making it all but impossible. "Why?"

She shrugged. "Then I'd know how you feel."

He felt, all right. Things he shouldn't be feeling for her. As though if he didn't kiss her soon, he might explode, about like that stove had.

Maybe that was exactly what he needed to do. Just get it over with. Release all this pent-up tension inside him.

He led her up the hill and around to the back side of his house. There he stopped, twisted her so she faced him, and cupped both of her cheeks. One kiss was all it would take. That would get her out of his system, let him think about other things and prove he truly had no feelings for her.

"Are you going to yell at me now?" she asked.

"No."

"Why not? You told me not to burn down the cabin."

"It was an accident," he said. "Accidents happen." He tilted her head back slightly. "As long as everyone's all right, nothing else really matters."

"You aren't going to send us away?"

"No."

She was watching him closely, and he waited, biding his time until she sensed what was about to happen. Her eyes widened, and she swallowed, but she didn't try to pull away as he half expected. He'd kissed one woman before who hadn't wanted him to—Francine, after she'd told him about Sterling—and he'd sworn he'd never do that again.

"I'm going to kiss you, instead," he declared quietly.

Eyes wider, she asked, "You are?"

He nodded, grinned.

"Why?" she asked, biting her lips.

"Because I want to."

"You do?"

This type of buildup wasn't something he'd done before, but he found the excitement growing inside him refreshing. He answered her with a slow nod.

"When?" Her whisper was almost breathless and quite intoxicating.

"As soon as you stop talking."

"Oh."

The sparkle in her eyes was so amazing he had a hard time blinking. He dipped his head, watching her slightest movement, which was little more than her lashes lowering. When his lips brushed hers, she let out a little gasp. He held her face and pressed his mouth completely against hers, absorbing the warm moisture of her lips for a moment before pulling back and then kissing her again, longer and with more intent.

That kiss led to another and another.

Stafford attempted to pause, just let their lips rest upon each other. It usually didn't take long for his desire to evaporate, but that wasn't happening this time. If anything, new cravings were coming to life and kept his lips moving over hers. Hard and fast, and soft and slow.

The kissing continued, winding him tighter than a spring. Stafford knew he had to stop, but doing so was another story.

For the life of her, Marie couldn't make her lips stop. They just kept following Stafford's. Kissing him. Her heart was racing, too, and her hands were pressed against his hard chest. It was all more wonderful than she ever could have imagined.

She'd never kissed a man before, but recently she'd thought about it. A lot. Even dreamed about it, and would wake up sweating and gasping for air. It had been Stafford she'd been kissing in her dream, just like now.

Lately, she'd found herself thinking more and more about Emma Lou and John Meeker, too. How they'd smiled at each other, as if talking to each other secretly, and how they'd kissed before he left each morning. John had usually kissed Emma Lou's cheek, but one day Marie had seen them kissing on the lips. The way she and Stafford were doing. She'd been embarrassed that morning and had rushed the children back into the dining room, but she wasn't embarrassed right now. Not at all. She wanted to go on kissing Stafford for hours on end.

At first, when his mouth had touched hers, she'd been startled, had no idea what to do, but her lips had. Still did. They kept moving beneath his in ways that had her insides dancing with ecstasy.

No wonder Miss Wentworth had been so strict in her instructions about staying away from men. Kissing Stafford was amazing. Wonderful. Spectacular.

Her stomach, full of enchanting flutters, dropped. What was she doing? Kissing a man was the fastest way to get fired. No, she didn't work for him, but she did depend on him for everything, at least until Mick Wagner returned.

Marie pushed against Stafford's chest, stumbling backward, and before he could speak, she spun around and raced up the back porch steps. Gasping for air, she wrenched open the door and slammed it shut behind her.

Stafford cursed. One kiss was all it had taken in the past to remind him he didn't want a woman, didn't want to care about anyone the way he had about Francine, and he wasn't happy that he didn't feel that way this time.

He should send Marie back to Chicago, but unfortunately, that wasn't an option. However, the way he'd just attacked her, she might leave all on her own. Spinning around, he made his way back toward the destroyed cabin. There, along with Red Scott and Mike Jones, two ranch hands, he used a shovel to make sure no embers lay hidden, waiting to burst into flames. He also tried not to think of kissing Marie. Actually, he was trying to justify kissing her. Which wasn't happening. He was no better than Sterling.

"Looks like Mick's bride is gonna have to live in your house," Red said. "Then again, she ain't Mick's bride, yet, is she?" the man added with a laugh.

Stafford let his glare speak for itself. Red caught it fast enough and shoveled his way to the far end of the charred ground without another word.

No one had to tell him Marie wasn't Mick's bride yet. That fact was circling his head like a flock of buzzards over a dead cow. Mick was his best friend, had been for years, and coveting his bride was more than wrong. It was disloyal and disgusting, and something Stafford never imagined doing. It also was something he would not do.

Anger flared inside him and Stafford kicked a beam, made it fall among the ashes. Mick should be here, or at least have sent word he was on his way. Stafford had wired him almost two weeks ago.

"Looks pretty good to me, boss," Shorty said, kicking his way along the edge of the burned area. "I'd say it's all out." The old man pulled a hanky from his pocket and blew his nose loudly. "Darn stove. I told you Marie and those kids shouldn't be living here. She and those babies didn't have enough room to turn around in that cabin."

"Good thing all their stuff was in the bunkhouse." Mike, a young cowboy Stafford had hired in Texas last spring stopped next to Shorty. "They've only been sleeping in the cabin."

Stafford wasn't surprised everyone knew Marie and the children's comings and goings, the ranch wasn't that large, but it irritated him to know others had kept such a close eye on them. It shouldn't. Mick would expect everyone to keep an eye on his bride. Maybe that was more where his irritation festered.

"Haul their belongings up to my place," he told Mike while walking over to hand his shovel to Shorty.

"Where you going?" Shorty asked.

"Same place I was going before the fire happened," he said. "To Merryville." There was a woman he'd visited at a saloon a time or two. Maybe that's what he needed. It sure couldn't hurt.

Marie had no idea how long she'd been standing just inside the door, trying to gather her wits. Stafford was sure to send her away now. If by some odd chance he didn't, Mick Wagner would. She'd have to beg Miss Wentworth for another position, which would cost her another seven years of servitude. Her small savings wouldn't give her any other choice. She'd just put herself back in the place she'd worked so hard to get out of.

She pressed a hand to her lips. How could something so wonderful be so terrible at the same time?

Voices, those of the children, had her pushing off the door. Here she was, thinking about herself again instead of her charges. Kissing men. Burning down cabins. She deserved to be sent back to Chicago.

The long hallway boasting rooms off both sides ended in an open area where the front doors, two of them, side by side with beveled glass and flanked by windows, took up a large portion of the wall.

"Marie, there's a piano here," Charlotte exclaimed through an arched doorway on the right. "I've missed the one we had so much."

The piano was in the far corner of the room. Potted plants sat on pretty stands near the curtain-covered windows and a fireplace made of stone took up one entire wall—the back one where a staircase in the corner led upward. While filling in for other nursemaids, she'd been in some large and lavish homes, but this one was different. It was big and fully furnished, yet the knotty pine walls, or maybe the way it was built, with archways instead of doors, made it feel open, friendly and, well, comfortable. Or maybe she was just noting everything because she didn't want to leave.

"Shorty told us to stay right here," Samuel said.

"We didn't touch anything," Beatrice added.

"Did they get the fire out?" Terrance asked.

Marie swallowed her worries and moved farther into the room. "Yes, the fire is out." Nodding toward Charlotte, she answered, "I see the piano." Turning to Samuel and Beatrice she added, "Thank you for minding so well."

"How bad was the fire? Did it hurt the cabin?"

Terrance asked, climbing off the long sofa he sat upon with the twins and Samuel.

She couldn't make light of it, they'd soon see the entire cabin was gone. "Yes, it hurt the cabin," she said, stopping to lay a hand on his shoulder. "It's gone."

"Gone?"

Nodding, she repeated what Stafford had said, "But no one was hurt. That's the important thing."

"Where are we going to live now?" Charlotte asked.

Marie held her breath, hoping an answer would form. It didn't. Not a definitive one. "Well, all of our belongings are in the bunkhouse." She tried to sound excited. "We could make that our home."

"But there aren't any beds or a stove," Samuel said.

"I know, but—"

"Stafford will let us live here," Terrance interrupted. "I know he will."

The children all jumped to their feet, talking at once, asking if they could live here, with Stafford.

"I can give you a tour," Terrance said. "Samuel, too. Stafford showed us everything in the house."

"Uh-huh," Samuel agreed. "There's even a water closet."

"There is," Terrance assured. "Just like what Mama wanted Papa to build in our house in Chicago."

The room grew quiet then, and Marie's insides jolted. The fire had to have the children thinking of their parents. Their sadness was not something she could stand, so she forced excitement to ripple her voice. "A water closet? Oh, yes, you must show us that."

It worked, grins replaced frowns.

"This way." Terrance waved an arm. "It's down the hall, next to the vestibule. That's a room that leads to another room. Stafford says when he's full of mud from working cows, he comes in the vestibule first and takes off all his muddy clothes so the rest of the house doesn't get dirty."

Marie's mind flashed to the cabin and the muddy footprints it had taken her two days and five buckets of water to get rid of, but her eyes stayed focused on the hopeful faces gazing up at her. "That's what a vestibule is, and it's a very good idea," she told Terrance, encouraging the others to follow him out of the room.

After the water closet, which was even finer than the one she'd seen in a home where she'd worked for two days, Terrance and Samuel led

the way as they roamed from room to room. All
the way to the top floor, which consisted of one
large room with windows that looked out in all
directions.

From there she saw Stafford walking across
the bridge with Shorty. Her insides skipped and
she turned away, telling herself she didn't want
the children to notice the patch of black ground
where the cabin had been.

"There's no furniture up here yet because
Stafford doesn't know what kind to put in this
room," Terrance explained.

The twins were running from one end to the
other, and as Marie rounded them up, heading
them toward the doorway, she could imagine the
children playing up here on long winter days.
Though there was only one staircase leading to
this floor, there were two leading to the ground
floor from the second floor. The one that ended
in the front parlor and a second one that ended
in the kitchen, which was the set they used.

Her eyes went to the stove. It was four times
the size of the one in the cabin, and she could
only imagine how difficult building a fire in
one that big would be. She would never find out.
Using it would never happen.

The sound of voices and a door opening had
her and the children entering the hall and hurry-
ing toward the front door. Two ranch hands, the

ones that had helped put out the fire, were carrying things through the open doorway.

"Hey, that's our stuff," Samuel said.

"It sure enough is," the younger of the two men said.

Marie believed his name was Mike, from what the children had told her.

Shorty entered the house next, and he must have noticed the confusion on her face because he said, "Stafford said you and the kids will have to live in his house now." He waved a hand toward the children shouting with joy. "He says there's a bedroom up there that has two beds and suggested the twins take that one."

"No," Weston said. "We want the one with all the windows."

"That's not a bedroom," Marie said. Although she was more than a little apprehensive, she followed the children up the stairs off the parlor, and ultimately agreed on each of the rooms they picked out.

"I believe this is yours, ma'am," the cowhand named Red said as he held up her carpetbag. "Which room do you want it in?"

She looked at her belongings in one of his hands, and reality shook her. If the cabin, the one she'd just burnt to the ground, had been bigger all of their possessions would have been lost. She should be grateful, instead she grew sick. Everything that had been destroyed had belonged to Mick Wagner.

"Take this room, Marie," Charlotte said. "It's right next to mine."

Marie removed the hand covering her mouth to offer the girl a false smile and then nodded at the ranch hand. It truly didn't matter what room he put her things in, she'd just destroyed someone's home. A man she'd never met. One she'd hauled six kids across the country toward, expecting him to raise them. If it'd been possible, she'd have stayed in Chicago, raised the children as her own. She'd thought about getting a job to raise enough money, but there would have been no one to watch the children while she worked.

The squeals coming from across the hall forced her into action. Weston and Charlie were jumping on two beds separated by a table holding a lamp that she caught moments before it tumbled to the floor. "Stop," she said loudly and sternly enough that it captured both boys' attention. "There will be no jumping on the beds."

Once they were both standing on the floor, with their bottom lips quivering, Marie went into the hall and requested that the rest of the children join her. In the twins' room, she sat them all down on the beds.

Taking a deep breath, she forced her mind to recall her training.

Ground rules—all nursemaids knew they were a must, yet she wasn't sure where to start. She'd just broken the most important rule by kissing Stafford.

All six children were waiting expectantly, and for the first time since leaving Miss Wentworth's, Marie was scared. They were her responsibility—every freckled face and each set of the blue eyes gazing up at her. She couldn't let them be placed in an orphanage or separated from one another, yet she had to wonder if she'd done the right thing. Not just because she burned down Mick Wagner's cabin—and kissed Stafford—but because the children needed more than she could give them.

Not just rules. Not just guidance. They needed a family. All children did.

Marie closed her eyes for a moment, trying to shake the fear building inside her. What entered her mind surprised her. It was a statement Stafford had made.

A person who graduated at the top of her class must be smart, Miss Hall. I'm sure you'll figure it out.

Though he'd said it mockingly at the time, it had resonated with her, and did so again now.

She had graduated at the top of her class, and that meant she wasn't a quitter.

Lifting her chin, she drew in air until her

lungs couldn't hold any more. "It's very kind of Sta—Mr. Burleson to allow us to stay here," she started.

"You mean Stafford. He likes being called that better than Mr. Burleson," Samuel said. "He says Mr. Burleson was his father and he's not that old yet."

Marie bit her bottom lip as the child made his explanation. Other things about Stafford were flashing in her mind. Not just his kiss. Without his kindness, she and the children wouldn't have a single bed to share between them. They wouldn't have food, either, or the other necessities they were going to need while she figured this all out. Everyone was allowed one broken rule, as long as they learned from it. Didn't let it happen again.

"It's very kind of Stafford," she said, eyeing each child individually, "to allow us to stay here."

Once they'd all nodded, she continued, "And you each must remember that. We are his guests, and you know what it means to be a guest, don't you?"

They nodded, but she felt a refresher course was in order.

"It means," she said slowly, "that we must be on our best behavior. No running in the house. No shouting in the house. No touching things that don't belong to us. Everyone must pick up after themselves, including making their beds each morning, and there will be no arguing." She took note of that last comment for herself—to not irritate Stafford, even when he angered her. It might be difficult, but it was necessary.

"What happens if we do?" Samuel wanted to know. "Argue?"

"You'll be sleeping in the bunkhouse back over at Mick's place," Terrance said.

Marie pressed a hand to her churning stomach. That was something else she had to figure out. How to replace Mick Wagner's home. The sinking feeling overcoming her said she didn't need to think harder. She needed a miracle.

"What if we don't know how to make our bed?" Charlie asked with worry.

"I'll teach you," Marie assured him.

The child smiled, and though Marie smiled back, her lips wobbled. Who was going to teach her all the things she needed to know?

Chapter Seven

It didn't help. Visiting the girl at the saloon. Stafford couldn't even muster up a smile for her, let alone anything else. Not with the taste of Marie's lips still lingering on his and her image floating before his eyes. Therefore, he spent his time in town seeing to a variety of errands, including a stop at the telegraph office.

Rex McPherson had seen him ride into town and waved him over. A telegram from Mick had arrived just that morning. It didn't say much, other than that he couldn't come home right away. He'd just arrived in Austin and was going to Mexico before coming home.

Stafford wrote out a reply, with the hope Mick hadn't left yet. A simple one.

Your bride is here STOP

He had it sent right away, and told Rex he'd be in town for the next few hours in case Mick sent one in return.

That had been before the saloon. He'd planned on killing a few hours there. When that didn't work out, Stafford went to the feed store and placed an order. Then he went to the general store, where he placed an even larger order. It hadn't started out that way, but after listening to two women discussing the dresses they planned on sewing, he tried to remember if he'd seen Marie wear anything other than her light blue dress. He hadn't; therefore, recalling many shopping trips with his sisters, he added several lengths of material, thread and buttons to his order.

There was a hat that caught his eye, too. It would provide her head much more protection than her thin bonnet, and as long as he was buying one for her, he picked out six small ones, too. Straw hats, like the one he'd picked out for Marie, for the girls, and ones that looked a lot like his for the boys. Terrance was going to like that, so would Samuel. The twins might not get much use out of theirs. They were always running so fast, hats might not stay on.

"Anything else, Stafford?" Henry Smith asked, piling the hats on the counter.

"A dozen of those peppermint sticks." Stafford pointed to the candy jars lining a shelf on the back wall. "Those I'll take with me."

Henry's green eyes had been full of curiosity

since Stafford had walked into the store, and it appeared the man couldn't contain it any longer. "You got newcomers out at your place?" he asked, handing over the candy sticks he'd wrapped in paper.

Word traveled fast, and there was no doubt the merchant already knew. "Yeah," Stafford answered, pocketing the candy.

Henry counted the hats again. "So, she really has six kids?"

"They aren't hers." For the life of him, Stafford couldn't guess why he chose to explain that.

Bald, with two chins and no neck, Henry leaned over the counter as if to say something he didn't want anyone to hear. Stafford wasn't too sure he wanted to hear what that might be. It was hard to know what kind of rumors were already floating about. Nonetheless, disappointment hit his stomach hard when Verna, Henry's wife, chose that moment to walk through the curtained doorway behind the counter.

"So, who do I charge this to?" Henry asked, standing straight again. "You, the ranch, or Mick?"

Verna Smith was a good foot taller than her husband, and her eyes, two narrow beads deeply set above a nose that was as pointed as her chin, leveled on Stafford. He'd been about to tell Henry to charge him, but Verna might use that bit of information, just as she would if he said to bill Mick.

He'd never been the subject of her gossip, at least not that he knew of, and didn't want to start now, so Stafford said, "The ranch." Transferring funds was easy enough, and even if it wasn't, it would be well worth not having Verna know his business. "Shorty needs his regular order, too," he added, just to distract her attention. "He's wondering if that new coffee grinder he ordered has arrived yet."

"Yes," she answered, eyeing him up and down. "Just this week."

"Good," Stafford said, and then repeated what Shorty had told him this morning when he'd mentioned riding into town. "The handle broke on the old one, and this time he can't repair it."

"Do you want to take it with you now, or…" She paused, eyeing the pile of merchandise on the counter. "Have it delivered?"

Henry already knew, but Stafford repeated it anyway. "Alfred's bringing a load of seed out later this week. He can bring it out then."

Verna elbowed Henry aside to stand directly across the counter. "I suppose you want your mail? Most of it is Mr. Wagner's so I've held it here, knowing he went to Texas."

More than one person claimed Verna Smith opened and read letters before delivering them, and since neither he nor Mick ever received anything too important, it had never bothered him before. Today, however, the idea had the muscles in his neck tightening.

"I'll take it now."

She pushed her husband aside as she made her way to a desk surrounded by shelves in the corner at the end of the counter. The apologetic gaze in Henry's eyes wasn't lost on Stafford, and he found himself wondering if the merchant regretted marrying the woman. Most men, at one time or another, probably questioned their choice, but Henry had it worse. Verna had been married twice before, and more than one whisper referred to her as a black widow. Her first husband had died from some kind of infection, her second, from a form of poison. If he were Henry, Stafford would be sleeping with one eye open.

"Here you are." She returned with several envelopes.

Stafford took them and flipped each one over. He normally didn't do such things, but today, he made a point of examining the wax seals. None appeared to be broken, but the bitter scowl on Verna's face had him wondering if she'd discovered a way to reseal them.

He tapped the edges of the letters on the counter. "Thanks, Henry." Then with a nod, he said, "Mrs. Smith." Turning, he left the store, and it wasn't until he was outside that he discovered why his hand felt as if it was on fire.

One letter, addressed to Mr. Mick Wagner, Dakota Territory, had a Chicago return address and the name above that was none other than Miss Marie Hall.

An eerie sensation had Stafford twisting his neck, looking back over one shoulder.

Verna Smith stood on the other side of the window, peering out at him with her lips pulled into an almost wicked smile. He considered staring her down, but in the end he turned away.

After stopping at the telegraph office, where there was no message from Mick, Stafford made his way down to the bank and found Ralph Peterson pulling the key out of the door lock.

"Stafford," the man greeted him. "Good to see you. I was just locking up for the day, but can reopen if there's something you need."

Glancing toward the setting sun, Stafford shook his head. "No, I was just making a social call as long as I was in town."

Ralph, a tall, gangly man originally from Boston, had arrived shortly after Merryville was established in order to create The Bank of the West, which was proving profitable. His enthusiasm alone had been enough for Stafford to buy in.

"Well, in that case," the man said, "come to

the house with me. Becca will be happy to see you. You can join us for supper."

The banker's wife was the complete opposite of Verna Smith. Plump, without a single gray strand in her coal-black hair, there wasn't a woman more personable than Becca Peterson in all of Merryville. "I wouldn't want to intrude," Stafford said, even while recalling the apple pie she sent to the ranch every time Ralph rode out to visit.

"Nonsense. Becca always makes more than enough, and she'll scold me blue if she hears I didn't make you join us." Hooking the back of his arm, Ralph started walking. "You can count on there being pie, though it might not be apple." After a low chuckle, he said, "We can talk business as we walk."

As a major investor in the bank, Stafford latched on to that comment. "Is something wrong?" Mind made up, he untied his horse from the rail.

"No, oh, heavens no," the banker assured him as they started down the dirt road. "We've just had the best quarter ever. I actually want to ask your opinion on hiring an assistant. I'm hardly able to keep up."

"I'd say if you need an assistant, hire one."

"It would be more of a teller position. Someone to assist the daily customers," Ralph said.

"I've run the numbers and our operating budget can afford it."

As shareholders, he and Mick, as well as a few other community members, had voting rights on all operational changes. "Anyone opposing it?"

"No. Joe Jepson and Nick Harmon already cast yes votes. Your vote and Mick's would make it a majority."

Stafford had authority to vote for Mick, as Mick had in his absence, so he asked, "Reed Simons still in Kansas?"

"Yes, and Axel Turner is up at the railhead."

"I can't believe either of them would oppose," Stafford said.

"I can't, either." Ralph paused, shook his head. "With the mail clerk we have in town, I try to minimize the information I send through the postal service, so I haven't tried to contact them about it yet."

"I wouldn't, either," Stafford agreed. Verna Smith would find a way to get the entire town riled up over the simple hire. "You've got my vote and Mick's, so go ahead. I'll sign a ballot if need be."

Ralph lifted the leather bag he carried in one hand. "Have one right here. We'll dig it out after supper."

Business done, and since they'd stopped at the

edge of the yard of the banker's house so he could tie up his horse, Stafford asked, "Pie, huh?"

Laughing, Ralph slapped him on the back. "If there isn't any when you arrive, there will be before you leave. I guarantee it."

There was indeed pie, peach not apple. But the entire time Stafford was at the Petersons' he wondered about things. Lots of things. Ralph and Becca had two children. A boy and a girl, probably close to Terrance and Charlotte's ages. It would be good, he thought, for the kids to meet. Marie meeting Becca would be a good thing, too, especially considering how hard she was trying to learn how to cook. The pie had literally melted in his mouth, and he declined the second piece Becca offered only because he didn't want to seem greedy. The ham had been tasty, too, as well as the sweet potatoes and cabbage.

He almost made a suggestion, that the banker and his family should visit the ranch soon, but didn't. Neither he nor Shorty—though the cowboys never complained—could put on a meal fit for company.

After bidding farewell to the man's family, Stafford walked out the front door with Ralph, and remembered one other thing he'd wanted to ask. "How's that new lumber mill coming along?" He'd planned on riding the three miles north of town to where the mill was being built, but it was too late now.

"I haven't been out there this week," Ralph answered. "But it was close to completion last weekend. There was a community picnic out there after church. Everyone's excited we won't have to have lumber hauled in—except Verna Smith. Lumber orders all went through her before. Why do you ask? Wondering about the loan we made Otis, or planning to build something?"

"We had a little fire," he said, tightening the saddle he'd loosened before entering the home earlier.

"Anyone hurt?"

"No." He let out a sigh. "Thankfully." Flipping the stirrup down, he said, "But I'll need lumber as soon as I can get it."

"I'll check for you."

"Thanks, I appreciate it." Stafford swung into the saddle and steered his horse around. "Thank Becca again for supper." Bringing up a question asked of him earlier, he said, "And tell her I don't know if apple's still my favorite or if it's peach now."

Ralph laughed. "I will. Take care."

"You, too," Stafford said, pushing Stamper into a trot.

The buildings were soon all behind him, and dusk had given way to night. The quiet darkness gave him little to think about, so his mind found other things. Plenty of them. As a rancher, a well-to-do one, he should consider hosting visitors. Not just the Petersons, but other folks. Merchants from town, other ranchers, even the railroad men and business owners that traveled through. His father used to do that. Host parties and gatherings for people from as far away as New Orleans. As a kid, he'd looked forward to them, knowing there would be others to play with besides his sisters.

The idea grew on him. Mick would like it, too.

Shifting then, he wondered about what kind of house to build for Mick. A cabin would no longer do, yet his partner swore he'd never want anything as large as Stafford's. It wouldn't have to be that big, but it would have to have several bedrooms.

That thought churned his stomach, and since he didn't want to ruin the meal he'd enjoyed so much, he quit thinking about Mick and his house. Marie, however, was still on his mind. Kissing her was, anyway. Had been all day.

He was in the midst of reliving those moments when Stamper nickered. The answering whinny told Stafford what he already knew; he was home, and that left him with mixed emotions.

A light flickered, over on Mick's property. It

looked as though someone carrying a lantern had just entered the bunkhouse. Stamper wasn't impressed when Stafford forced the horse to walk past the barn and over the little bridge. If Marie had refused to move into his house, he'd set her straight. There was no way she and those kids could live in the bunkhouse. Well, they could. Practically had the past week, but not anymore.

Stafford swung out of the saddle and slapped the horse on the rump, letting it make its way back to the barn. The clip of hooves trotting over the bridge echoed in the air as Stafford strode toward the bunkhouse.

Marie set the lantern on the table, noting how naked the bunkhouse looked without the canvas dividers and no mattresses on some of the wooden bunks. She was wiping the tears off her face when the sounds of a horse crossing the bridge echoed for a second time.

Good. She didn't want anyone to know what else she'd done.

"What are you doing?"

The question sounded at the same time as footfalls and she squeezed her eyes shut, trying to hold back a fresh bout of tears. She'd known Stafford would be home, sometime, but she certainly hadn't wanted him to find her.

Not like this.

"Marie?"

She swallowed the burning in her throat and wiped her nose on the back of her hand, still fighting the tears pressing hard at her lids.

"Marie?" he repeated.

His hands settled on her upper arms, from behind, and she couldn't quell the gasp that ripped out of her mouth. He was so strong and powerful, and she wished she could share all her burdens with him.

"What's happened?" he asked, forcing her to turn around.

Biting her lips together, she shook her head, but as he forced her chin up, the tears escaped.

"What's happened? Is it one of the kids?"

The concern in his voice left her no choice but to answer. "It's Polly." She swiped the tears off both cheeks at the same time. "She's missing."

"Polly?"

"I've l-looked everywhere," Marie stuttered. "But I can't find her. She must have b-been—" she had to swallow a sob "—been in the cabin."

She wanted to lay her head on his solid chest and cry her eyes out, and when he let out a little shushing sound and wrapped his arms around her shoulders, she slumped against him.

"Hush, now," he whispered. "Polly wasn't in the cabin."

Her fingers curled into the material of his

shirt as she pressed her forehead harder against his chest. "She must have been. I've looked everywhere."

His hands slid down her back to her waist, and then he pulled her entire body against his. He started swaying then, just slightly back and forth. It was uniquely comforting, and the pressure in her lungs released as the air slowly escaped.

"Where did you look?" he asked softly.

She twisted her neck so her cheek rested on his chest. "Everywhere."

"In the daylight?"

"No, but the children looked, and they didn't find her, either."

"Are they out looking for her now?"

"No, they're sleeping. I waited until they were before I started to look for her." The tears had completely stopped and she lifted her head enough to wipe her cheeks again. "I told them she probably figured she couldn't sleep in your house and was off pouting somewhere."

"Pouting?"

"I didn't know what else to tell them." The large clump of self-pity in her stomach rolled over. "I not only burned down their home, I killed their dog."

He let out a chuckle and she lifted her head to look at him. The twinkle in his gray-blue eyes made her frown. His behavior, up until now, certainly hadn't been insensitive.

"It's not funny." She pushed at his chest, trying to break the hold he still had around her waist.

"Polly's not dead," he said.

Hope flared. "She's not? Did you see her when you rode in? Where?" Craning to see the doorway around his broad shoulders, she asked, "Where is she?"

"I don't know where she is—"

Her optimism plummeted. "Then how do you know—"

"Because," he interrupted. "The door to the cabin was wide open. She wouldn't have stayed in a burning building."

"What if—"

This time it was his hold that interrupted her words. His arms had tightened, forcing her hips firmly against his thighs. "My guess is she's hiding somewhere because she's having her pups."

"Why would she do that?" Marie had to shake her head to clear her thoughts—they were shooting off in another direction. One that hadn't been far away all day. Kissing him. "Hide?"

"Animals do that," he said. "She wouldn't have come when the kids called for her."

Hope was rising again. "Really?"

"Yes, really."

Marie tried to read his face, make sure he wasn't trying to fool her, but all she could think about was his mouth touching hers again. Pretending that was the furthest thing from her mind, she said, "I hope you're right."

His eyes were on her lips, making them quiver. "I know I'm right."

There wasn't a single part of her that wasn't aware of what was happening. Every breath she took was filled with the spicy scent she'd become so accustomed to on the wagon ride here. Her body, even where it wasn't touching his, had grown overly warm and tingling. She was trying to tell her hands to push against him and her feet to take a step back, but her fingers wouldn't let loose of his shirt and her toes had curled inside her shoes at the heat racing down her legs.

She could feel his breath on her lips and that made things worse. The warmth pooling in her stomach floated throughout her system, making her eyes want to roll back in her head at the delicious sensations. It was crazy. Ridiculous. Wonderful.

And then, his lips touched hers. Softly, barely connected, it was both heavenly and torturous. Torturous because she suddenly knew she'd want his kisses for the rest of her life. Anything this sweet, this delirious, would be too hard to forget.

"I've never tasted anything as sweet as you,

Marie," he whispered, kissing the corners of her mouth one at a time.

Unable to respond with all that was going on, she closed her eyes and wasn't sure if that made Stafford's kisses more intense, or if the pressure really had increased. Either way, she tightened her hold on his shirt to keep from toppling as he kissed her square on the mouth again.

The throbbing inside her grew harder, more forceful and concentrated, and she wasn't sure what that meant, but certainly didn't want him to stop.

Eventually, he did. His lips left hers to kiss her cheek, then her forehead, before he rested his chin on top of her head and started to rock her back and forth again as he had before.

Marie kept her eyes closed and his hold encouraged her to relax, just rest upon him. Slowly her entire system grew calm and tranquil, and a long slow sigh emptied her lungs.

He leaned back then and she lifted her head, felt a flash of heat in her cheeks at the smile on his lips. "Come on," he said, releasing his hold. One arm stayed around her, though, while the other reached over to pick the lantern up off the table by its handle. "You've had a long day. It's time for bed."

A little amazed she was able to walk after all that, she waited, unable to speak until they were outside, heading toward the bridge. "Do you think Polly will let us find her tomorrow?"

The arm around her shoulder tightened slightly as his hand rubbed her upper arm. "I promise we'll find her tomorrow."

No one had ever promised her anything, not ever, and she couldn't help but glance up. There was nothing but sincerity looking down at her. He was so unique. Right from the start there had been something about him that had eased her usual nervousness around men. She'd thought it was because he irritated her, but that didn't make sense.

He walked her to the front double doors, and then handed her the lantern so he could turn the knob. "Go to bed now, it's late."

She entered the house, but when he didn't attempt to follow her, she turned around. "Aren't you coming in?"

"I have to go unsaddle my horse."

"Oh." Not wanting him to leave, she held out the lantern. "Do you want the light?"

"No. You go to bed. I'll see you tomorrow."

He reached for the door, and unable to come up with anything else to say, she whispered, "Good night."

"Good night, Marie."

He pulled the door closed and she stood there until long after his footsteps no longer sounded on the porch or the steps. It was a shiver that raced over her body that finally had her trudging toward the staircase. She'd kissed him again! Something a good nursemaid would never do.

Perhaps that was the problem. Maybe she wasn't a good nursemaid. She had taken the children away from all they'd ever known, hauled them to a stranger's home, burned that one down, lost their dog and kissed a man. Twice. On the same day, no less.

She might as well rip up that recommendation from Miss Wentworth along with her training certificate. Ultimately, neither one of them meant squat.

As frustrated as she was with herself, she made the rounds of the children's rooms, sneaking in to make sure each child was covered. It was comforting to see them sleeping in real beds again, but she'd had very little to do with that.

In her room, she removed her dress—uniform, actually. Upon obtaining the position at the Meeker home Miss Wentworth had presented her with two work dresses. Simple gowns of pale blue.

Her carpetbag, holding her other dress, still sat at the foot of the bed. Actually, the bag wasn't hers. It had been Emma Lou Meeker's, but since the woman would no longer need it, and Marie didn't have one for the trip, she'd used it for her belongings. It had been the only thing she'd taken, and looking at it made guilt rise up inside her. Sarah had said it wasn't stealing, and eventually Marie had given in, agreeing to use the bag, but it was stealing. Another thing a good nursemaid would never do.

"Oh, good heavens," she growled in self-admonishment. "Whether you're a good nursemaid or a terrible one has very little bearing on what needs to be done. Now stop feeling sorry for yourself and go to bed."

Marie changed into her night dress and climbed between the covers. She was just closing her eyes when she heard the front door close. Pulling the covers over her head, she whispered, "And stop thinking about him, too."

Chapter Eight

Stafford was up early, and Polly, whom he'd found behind the woodshed at Mick's place along with her four pups, was now in the vestibule in a blanket-lined box. He grinned when he heard movement upstairs while pouring himself a cup of coffee. He carried the coffee to the table where he sat down to glance at the paper he'd picked up in town yesterday.

He'd slept remarkably well, all considered, yet nothing in the paper enticed him to read more than a line or two. His ears were too busy listening. He hadn't been this excited for a long time. Seven people were going to be very surprised when he told them to look in the vestibule. The commotion upstairs increased, and Stafford tried once again to focus his attention on the newspaper. The typeset letters swirled into one another. He'd imagined Marie would come down first, even anticipated showing her Polly—and her reaction—and how the two of them would then surprise the children. As if it was Christmas morning or something.

He snapped the paper open, scanning the words with more determination. He hadn't celebrated Christmas, not by exchanging gifts and such, since he'd left home. And he liked it that way. That was the way things were going to remain, too.

The footfalls on the stairway leading into the kitchen off the far wall sounded like a tribe of Indians on the warpath, and as hard as Stafford fought it, a smile won out. He folded the paper in half as Terrance bounded off the bottom step.

"Hey, Stafford," the boy greeted him, showing two front teeth his face still had to grow into.

"Morning," Stafford responded.

If his ears weren't still peeled, he might not have heard the gasp that sounded somewhere up the staircase, or the somewhat harsh whisper, "Children!"

The rest of the tribe, all five of them, raced down the steps and collided with Terrance's back. The boy's spine had gone stiff. One by one, the other five children, right down to Charlie, who plopped his thumb in his mouth, but then quickly pulled it out, straightened their stances, and moved to form a straight line next to their brother with their lips clamped tight.

Stafford frowned. Faces shining, they all stood board stiff as Marie entered the kitchen behind them. Moving nothing but their eyes, all six kids looked at her as she skirted around them.

For no apparent reason, Stafford's heart slapped the inside of his chest. She was dressed in her normal blue dress, and her hair was once again braided and twisted into a coil at the back of her head. He'd watched her tame the long brown locks after they'd gone swimming that day, and how she'd deftly looped it around and pinned it in place. One pin was all she'd used. He'd been amazed it held. Still was.

"Children," she said tartly. "Say good morning."

"Good morning, Stafford," they said in chorus.

Somewhat hesitantly, for they sounded like a well-trained classroom—completely out of the ordinary for them—he replied, "Good morning."

She nodded then. "Take your seats."

Seats? It was a kitchen.

With slow even steps, they crossed the room and sat down at the table. Their grins, when they looked his way, were familiar, but disappeared quickly and they averted their eyes.

Marie's steps were no more relaxed than the children's had been as she walked across the room. She stopped facing the stove, her back to him, and he noted the deep breath she took by the rise of her shoulders.

After casting a wary gaze around the table, noting the bowed heads, Stafford stood and made his way to her side. "I already built a fire," he said, taking a guess at how hesitant she'd be about having anything to do with stoves for a day or two.

Her sigh was audible before she caught herself. "Oh, thank you."

"There's flour in the pantry and eggs in—"

"I know how to scramble eggs," she said quickly.

A faint groan came from the table, but when he glanced that way, no one had moved. The boys all had their hair combed, although the cowlick on the top of Weston's head was fighting the water that must have been used to calm it. Copper-colored hairs were popping up one at a time to stand as proudly as a rooster's comb. Charlotte's hair was braided with yellow bows tied on the ends, and a large clump of Beatrice's red curls had been tied back with a blue ribbon. No one and nothing, other than Weston's wayward hairs, still popping, so much as twitched.

Stafford shifted his gaze back to Marie, who'd moved to the counter where he'd set the basket of eggs Shorty had given him this morning. The old man had said he'd brought over stew for them to eat last night, so Stafford had also taken a pan out of the cupboard in case she hadn't had time yesterday to discover where such things were located.

She picked up the frying pan and moved toward the stove, but stopped a good three feet away to reach over and gingerly slide the pan across the top of it. As if it might get bitten, she pulled her hand away and quickly returned to the counter where she started cracking eggs.

He couldn't blame her for being skittish after what had happed with the other stove and was about to cross the room, take over making breakfast, but he stopped. He didn't have time to cook every meal, and eventually she'd have to get over it.

Battling that thought with another one that said it wouldn't hurt him to make breakfast this morning, Stafford glanced back to the table and all the little people sitting there as quiet and immobile as a litter of scared-stiff rabbits.

Terrance lifted his gaze, and with a solemn nod, he said, "It sure is nice of you to let us stay in your house, Stafford."

Stafford bit the inside of his cheek, taking a guess at what was going on. She'd told the children to be on their best behavior, and they were minding. He should appreciate that. Kids should mind, he'd be the first to admit that, but this group was as grave as a houseful of inmates with armed guards standing over them. It had been years, but not so many that he didn't remember how it felt to be *on your best behavior*. He'd had to do it every Sunday, when visiting his grandmother's house. Sitting in her flower-filled parlor he'd always felt as though he'd swallowed a handful of grasshoppers. Even his toes had been jittery back then, full of energy that wanted out. It had been a cruel torture, one his mother never grasped.

Tiny clicks, in a quick clip-clop pattern sounded, and he leaned slightly to see around the table. Sure enough, Polly had heard a voice she recognized and come exploring.

He grinned and gave a tiny nod, encouraging the children to look toward the doorway.

The table practically exploded as the kids flew off their chairs, shouting the dog's name. Marie fluttered past him, kneeling down along with the children to greet the dog, whose little brown-and-white body was wiggling with delight. Stafford was enjoying the sight, but the reunion didn't last long.

Marie scooped up the dog, whispering, "Who let Polly in the house?"

They started answering at once, each child assuring they hadn't and shaking their heads.

"I told you yesterday," she started.

Stafford arrived at her side in time to interrupt and to take the dog from her arms. "I let her in the house." Nodding to the children, he added, "Follow me."

They did so without questions, which goaded him a bit. They'd started to speak, but Marie, in that obey-me-or-else voice had hushed them.

He led them to the box and gestured with one hand for them to view its contents. Polly wriggled in his arms, letting out little whines as they gathered close. Stafford slowly knelt, so the dog could be reassured he wouldn't let anyone injure her pups.

Marie was the first to coo, and she didn't scold anyone when they leaned closer, copying her behavior. After everyone had a good look at the white-and-brown pups—that in Stafford's mind were quite homely—he set Polly in the box.

"You can't play with them yet," he cautioned, "but in a few weeks, they'll be running along behind you." There had been plenty of dogs and puppies in his childhood. Up until now he hadn't missed them.

Of their own accord, his eyes found Marie. She'd backed away from the box. He stood, catching her subtle nod, and moved to stand alongside her. About to comment on finding Polly, Stafford frowned when she gestured toward the hallway.

His heart did a double take. She had to be excited he'd found the dog. As he followed her, his mind conjured up kissing her. Just accepting her tiny thank-you kiss.

That was before she opened her mouth.

"Mr. Burleson, dogs do not belong in the house," she hissed.

Disappointment hit hard and fast. Especially as she licked her lips. But it was how she called him Mr. Burleson that aggravated him. Less than twelve hours ago they'd been kissing, now he was Mr. Burleson?

"It's my house," he said, before pointedly adding, "Marie."

"I realize that," she all but spat. After a deep breath, she started again. "The children—"

It was impossible not to stop her. "Are children," he said. "And this is now their home."

"I appreciate that, but I cannot—"

"You don't have a say in what can and can't happen. It's my house. I'll say if a dog can live in it or not, and I say Polly and her pups stay right where they are." It was foolish to argue over such a thing, but watching her pinch those lips together was driving him crazy. "And I say kids don't have to sit with their heads bowed and their hands in their laps."

"What?" Her eyes snapped more sparks than the fire that burned down Mick's house. "They have to learn—"

"Learn?" He grabbed the frame of the kitchen doorway over her head with one hand, mainly to keep it—and the other one—from shaking her. "I'll tell you who needs to learn." He leaned close, almost nose to nose, and had a bird's eye view of her licking those lips again. The way she kept doing that drove him crazy. "You."

"Me?"

"Yes, you." There were a dozen thoughts racing through his mind, and not one of them would be an appropriate thing to say. Therefore, he used the only piece of ammunition he could. "Those kids are sick of scrambled eggs."

Her expression grew rather traumatized, and that didn't feel nearly as good as he wanted it to. All he'd wanted was a little bit of gratitude for searching the ranch for a foolish dog this morning. Which, in its own right, was crazy. He hadn't expected appreciation from anyone in years. Pushing off the wall he said, "I'd have thought someone who graduated at the top of their class could have figured that out."

Without waiting for a response, Stafford twisted and grabbed his hat off the table by the front door on his way out of the house.

Marie attempted to catch her breath. The way Stafford had held on to the overhead doorframe had impressed on her just how tall he was, and the way he'd leaned close reminded her how sweet his lips had tasted last night, but the way he'd so arrogantly pointed out her inabilities prompted her to recall just how bigheaded he was, too.

Of course she knew the kids were tired of scrambled eggs. She was too, but there wasn't a whole lot she could do about it. Knowing how to cook didn't just happen. It's not as if people were born with that skill.

She spun around, still gasping for air, and stared at the monstrous stove. Gleaming black, it looked as new as everything else in the home. Cleaning she'd learned as a child. Taking care of children she'd learned as a scholar. She was trying, but without someone to teach her, cooking...

Hurt, that stomach-sickening sensation she remembered so well, rolled dangerously inside her, threatening to boil up and consume her. That would not happen. She'd figure this out all right, and she'd show Mr. Stafford Burleson just how smart she was. Starting with never, ever, kissing him again.

Tightening her jaw, she fought the bile trying to work its way up her throat and clenched her shaking hands into fists. Her eyes settled on the stove with purpose. She could do this. And would.

It turned out the stove wasn't as intimidating as it looked, and whether they were tired of scrambled eggs or not, the children ate them. Then they started in on the chores she assigned them. Keeping a house this size in order would take cooperation. She'd do the heavy cleaning, but dusting and seeing to the needs of Polly—the dog didn't seem to be tired of scrambled eggs—and her pups were things the children could handle.

Marie had finished the dishes, when Beatrice, after wiping the table, asked, "Where should I put this?"

"I'll take it," Marie answered, noting the newspaper needed to be refolded. While doing just that, opening it to once again fold it on the creases, an advertisement caught her attention.

Cook Wanted. Twenty-five cents a day plus room and board. Striker Hotel.

Excitement had a smile tugging at her lips. If the hotel could hire a cook, why couldn't she? She still had nearly ten dollars from her savings and selling her jewelry. Spending it on a cook wasn't in her plan, but ten dollars wasn't enough for one return ticket to Chicago, let alone seven. If she could hire a cook, perhaps they could teach her....

Nibbling on her bottom lip, she tossed the

thought about. It would take a good portion of her money, but it wouldn't have to be for long. She was a fast learner. Two weeks would be more than enough time.

The idea grew more enticing with each thought. Cookies. The children would be so happy if she learned to make the cinnamon cookies Mrs. Garth had made back in Chicago. Hiring someone like Mrs. Garth wouldn't work though. She hadn't allowed anyone in her kitchen.

Still, there had to be someone in Merryville willing to take the job. Someone who wouldn't mind sharing their skills. If she learned how to cook, maybe, just maybe, Stafford would hire her to cook for him. Not for money, but for room and board. Then he wouldn't send her back, or the children, before Mick Wagner arrived. And once Mr. Wagner did arrive, perhaps he'd hire her and... A thrill overtook her. Convinced this would work, Marie tucked the newspaper under her arm. "Children!"

They came running. After a moment inspecting faces and hands, she announced, "We are going to town."

"Town?" Samuel asked.

"She means Merryville," Terrance supplied, then frowning, he asked, "How we gonna get there?"

"How *are we going to* get there," she corrected him.

He nodded. "How?"

"We'll walk."

"That's a long walk. Stafford says—"

"We shall walk," Marie interrupted, gesturing toward the hall. "Wait on the front steps. I'll be right back." So excited she almost missed the first step, Marie dashed up the staircase.

The children were lined up on the porch when she exited the house, and Shorty was standing near the bottom step.

"Kids say you're going to town," he said, rubbing his chin.

"Yes, we are."

The man shuffled from foot to foot. "You plan on coming back?"

Six pair of nervous eyes glanced up at her. "Of course," she replied. That consideration had never entered her mind. Where else would they go? Tossing those nagging thoughts aside, she said, "There are just a few things we need."

He nodded, and wiped a hand over his mouth. "I'll get the wagon."

"That's not necessary, Mr.—Shorty." Calling all these men by their first names was very difficult. It went against all of her formal training. "We can walk."

"It's a long ways, Marie," he answered. "You

wouldn't get home until late. And how would you carry what you purchase?"

She planned on their purchase walking alongside them, but that sounded a little presumptuous.

Her silence had Shorty repeating, "I'll get the wagon."

Stepping around the children, she hurried down the steps and caught up with him on the grass. The small amount of time she'd held the reins while traveling from Huron couldn't be considered training, and certainly hadn't taught her enough to feel comfortable doing so again.

"I don't know how to drive a wagon," she whispered. Her insides flinched, but Shorty—unlike Stafford—seemed to understand her lack of knowledge in some areas. She'd considered asking Shorty to teach her how to cook a few things besides scrambled eggs, but she'd tasted his stew. Beggars can't be choosers, but she wanted to know how to cook things that were a bit more edible.

He glanced toward the bunkhouse before nodding. "The boys are out checking the cattle. I've got time to take you to town."

"But what will Mr.—Stafford think of that?"

Shorty shrugged. "He ain't here. Rode out a while ago."

Offering her newly hired employee a ride

home would be more presentable than asking her to walk, so Marie nodded. "Thank you, Shorty. We appreciate that very much, and will enjoy your company."

Ha-ha you keep her STOP I'll get another one STOP

Stafford stared at the telegram one more time, trying to come up with a response. He'd read Mick's reply a dozen times since it had been delivered to the ranch, shortly after he'd stormed out of his house. His house. The one that now had six kids, five dogs and one very uppity nursemaid living in it. Trouble was, none of that bothered him as much as it should.

"You want to send a telegram, Stafford?" Rex asked, pulling a stubby pencil out from behind his ear. "Or just keep reading that one?"

The air in his chest pushed its way out. Stafford waited until it was all gone, took in a supply of fresh air and then nodded. "Yeah, I want to send a reply. Same address."

Rex set the pencil to paper and glanced up expectantly.

When the man started tapping the tip against the paper, Stafford said, "I'm thinking what I want to say."

"That one came in late last night," Rex said.

"I just happened to catch Newly Cross, heard he was heading out your way this morning."

Still contemplating, Stafford nodded. "Thanks, I appreciate how quickly you delivered it."

"This one gonna be just as urgent?"

"Yes."

"But you don't know what you want to say?"

Stafford set a solid glare on the man, then cringed. It wasn't Rex's fault. It was Mick's. Keep her? What kind of answer was that? Nobody in their right mind would want to keep a woman around who burns down houses, can't cook, is— He stopped the thought short. It wasn't Marie's fault, either.

After cursing Mick under his breath, calling the man several names, Stafford said, "Just put, *You ordered her. Now come claim her.*"

Rex lifted a brow, but didn't say a word. The man was not a gossip and would go to his grave with a large number of messages no one else would ever hear about. If Stafford didn't believe that one hundred and fifty percent, he wouldn't be standing where he was right now.

"You want the reply sent to the ranch?"

"No, I'll be in town awhile. I'm riding out to the new lumber mill. I'll stop back."

"Good enough." Rex carried the slip of paper to his desk and his fingers started tapping away on the telegraph key even before he lowered himself onto his short swivel stool.

Stafford left, wondering if he should have said more. Telling Mick how pretty Marie was would have helped. His partner would catch the first train heading north then. He paused on the boardwalk, contemplating reentering the telegraph office.

"I didn't expect to see you again so soon."

Stafford pulled up a grin for the approaching banker and tucked Mick's message in his pocket. "I decided to ride in and check out the lumber mill myself."

"I just hung a note on the door of the bank so I could ride out there," Ralph explained.

Glad his mind was working again, Stafford said, "Proof you need an assistant."

Ralph laughed. "Guess so. I was going to wait until this evening, but Becca's making fried chicken for supper and I don't want to miss that."

"You're a lucky man." Stafford's insides did a double take. Those were not words he ever expected to leave his mouth, yet he knew they were true. The banker not only had a sweet wife— one who could cook up a storm—Ralph seemed content, satisfied with his life. Stafford doubted he'd ever felt that way.

"No one has to tell me that," Ralph says. "I give thanks for my blessings every night."

Stafford questioned that, too. He'd spent many Sundays in church growing up, but, couldn't recall the last time he'd actually given thanks. Or if he ever had.

"So, how much lumber will you need?" Ralph asked.

"Not really sure," Stafford answered. "Haven't given it much thought, I guess."

"I suspect not, if the fire just happened."

"It just happened, all right," Stafford answered, thinking of several things.

Ralph let out a good-natured laugh. "Well, last I talked to Otis, he was considering putting together packages. Lumber precut to frame in a house along with preassembled doors and windows. He asked if the bank might consider backing him on the idea. I'm sure he'd appreciate your thoughts. As would I."

Intrigued, Stafford tossed the notion about for a moment. "That's not a bad idea. With the way this town is growing, it might make good business for both Otis's lumberyard and the bank."

"And once the railroad depot is built, it'll only grow more." Ralph patted him on the shoulder. "It's amazing, isn't it? Seeing a town rise up from the ground, being a part of shaping it. That's the reason Becca and I came west, to become a real part of this great nation."

Stafford took a moment to ponder that. It

wasn't something he'd considered—being an integral part of the town—yet it sparked something inside him. He and Mick had built the ranch, and that had been exciting, still was, but in all honesty, the ranch was more of a self-centered goal, for themselves. The town was a community, a unit of people coming together for a common good. That appealed to him, though he wasn't exactly sure why.

They stopped outside Ralph's barn, and Stafford, waiting while the other man entered, took a moment to examine the banker's house. New, as all the houses were, it wasn't extravagant or presumptuous. Solid, though, and well built. A good home to raise a family in, to really set down roots and build a life. His house, as big and full of every modern convenience as it was, didn't have that. Roots.

Ralph led his horse out of the barn, a big red roan, and Stafford hoisted himself into the saddle on Stamper's back. He and the black paint had traveled a lot of miles together. He'd bought Stamper from a neighbor down in Mississippi shortly before leaving.

As they rode out of town, Ralph started talking about Otis's house idea, and interested, Stafford answered, but in the back of his mind other things were going on. No matter how he tried to repress it, one niggling notion stuck. Maybe

Mick's idea of a wife wasn't such a bad one. When a man set down roots, a family was usually involved.

Chapter Nine

To say she was surprised would be an understatement. Marie wasn't exactly sure what she'd expected from the town of Merryville, but it wasn't to see people living in tents. Big ones, small ones and in-between ones. There were buildings, too, and real houses, but only a few compared to the tents. What she saw had pinpricks of chagrin jabbing her. As small as Mick Wagner's cabin had been, it was certainly more of a home than canvas walls and dirt floors. And Stafford's house, which might be considered small compared to some of the homes she'd worked in, was nothing short of a mansion next to the dwellings in Merryville.

She needed to count her blessings. Something she'd been amiss in doing lately. She and the children certainly could have fared far worse than they had. Very well still could, if her plan didn't work.

"There's Striker's place," Shorty said, pointing out the largest building in town. Unpainted, other than the word *Hotel* across the front, the wood still held its natural shine. "I'll drive round back."

"Round back?" Marie asked. The man knew their mission. He'd even read the newspaper advertisement now clenched in her hands.

"Yep." Shorty steered the wagon down a side street. "You can't very well walk in the front door and ask Chris Striker if you can hire away one of his employees."

"I suspect you're right about that." There were many things she hadn't considered when the idea had popped into her head, but Shorty had been the right person to hash it over with. He was not only in agreement, but rather giddy about the idea of hiring a cook. Feeding the cowboys would still be his responsibility, he'd said, but having someone around who could bake bread and maybe a pie or two would suit him just fine. Stafford, too, he'd insisted.

Marie hadn't wanted to quell his hopes by saying the cook's main objective would be to teach her, neither did she want to think about how Stafford might react, so she'd remained quiet, as she was right now, staring at the back of the hotel. An older woman sat on an overturned bucket, doing something with what looked like a chicken. A dead one.

"The kids and I will wait here," Shorty said.

Marie nodded, and although thankful she'd mastered climbing in and out of the wagon Shorty had explained Stafford had bought, not rented as she'd assumed, back in Huron, her nerves were jumping beneath her skin. She'd never hired anyone.

Chin up, hoping it helped, she began walking across the well-packed dirt.

The woman didn't look up from her task, yet spoke before Marie arrived. "Mr. Striker's inside the hotel. That's where you'll want to go."

Marie continued forward, even though the smell of wet feathers was rather pungent.

The woman, middle-aged by the look of her brown hair, looked up then. "If you want a job, you have to talk to Mr. Striker. I can't hire anyone." Her tired-looking eyes went from Marie's head to her toes and back again. "You might want to rethink applying. Mr. Striker isn't easy to work for."

Turning back to her task, the woman plucked feathers out of the wet carcass and threw them into a second bucket by her feet. Two other chickens, dead, of course, were floating in another bucket of steaming water.

"Do you work here?" Marie asked. As soon

as the words were out, she wished she could pull them back in. Of course the woman worked here. Why else would she be doing what she was doing?

"Unfortunately, darling, I do. Told Striker a month ago I can't do it all myself," the woman answered. "But you might want to reconsider that ad you have tucked under your arm. It's not easy work."

Marie pulled out the paper. "I'm not here to apply for the job."

The woman glanced over her shoulder, to the wagon, where Shorty gave a slight nod. "What are you doing then?"

"I'm looking to hire someone. A cook." She opened the paper. "It says here you are paid twenty-five cents a day plus room and board."

"Yeah, so?"

"Would you consider working elsewhere for that price?"

The woman set down the chicken and wiped her hands on a very bloody apron. "I might. Where you got in mind?"

"We," Marie gestured toward the children, "live on a ranch a few miles from here."

A frown so deep her eyes almost disappeared, the woman asked, "That your husband?"

"Oh, no," Marie said quickly. "I'm not married."

"Are those your children?"

"Yes. I mean, no." Marie shook her head. "I'm sorry. They are my charges. I was their nanny in Chicago, before their parents died." Now wasn't the time to explain everything. Stepping forward, she held out a hand. "I'm Marie Hall."

"Gertrude Baker," the woman replied with a quick handshake. Her eyes were on the wagon again. "So they're orphans?"

"That's not a word I'm particularly fond of," Marie replied, stiffening her shoulders at a familiar sting. "We have recently arrived, and I'm in need of someone to cook for us and teach me how to cook."

"You don't know how?"

"No, there has never been a need before."

Gertrude Baker shifted her gaze to the hotel, and then to the chickens and then back to Marie. "When would I need to start?"

As wonderful as that question made her insides feel, Marie shook her head. "I need to conduct an interview first, make sure you have all the qualifications I seek."

The woman sat back down and picked up the chicken. "Ask away, then, but I gotta keep working while you do."

Questions were what she needed. Marie tried to remember some of the ones asked of her by potential employers, but none that formed fit the situation. If Stafford was here, he'd know what to ask. She held her breath for a moment, attempting to dispel how deeply she'd come to depend on him. Questions couldn't be that difficult, considering there were things she wanted to know. "How long have you lived in Merryville?"

"No one's lived here long. The town just took off 'bout two years ago, when the railroad was being built. That's when we arrived, George, my husband and I. He worked for the railroad." The woman set the chicken down again. "We used to live in Illinois, too. Had a little place near Springfield." Her eyes grew sad. "George had big plans on moving west. To Wyoming. He'd signed on to work for the railroad that far, thought by then we'd have all the money we'd need for a new start."

The sadness surrounding the other woman had Marie's heart aching. "What happened?"

"George died." Gertrude wiped her face with the back of one hand. "Went to work one morning but didn't come home that night. An accident unloading railroad ties."

Unsure what else to say, Marie whispered, "I'm sorry."

Gertrude smiled slightly, sadly. "Thanks." Shaking her head, she said, "I cooked for the railroad for a time, but once they moved on…" She shrugged.

"Why didn't you move on, too?" Marie asked.

"Have you ever followed the rails?"

"No."

"It's not good. Worse for a woman alone." Gertrude picked up the chicken again. "I worked for the Hoffmans up until they closed their boarding house to follow the line." With a glance over her shoulder, she added, "Had to go to work for Striker a couple months ago. He's gone through more cooks than an Indian has arrows."

Indians were not a subject Marie was prepared to discuss. She'd yet to see one, but had heard enough to hope she didn't. "Do you know how to bake bread? Make pies and cookies?"

"You name it, and I can cook it," Gertrude answered. "Food that not only sticks to your belly, but tastes good while going down. If you need to learn how to cook, you wouldn't find a better teacher than me. My George would have told you that."

The interviews she'd had in the past were much longer than this, but Gertrude Baker was exactly what she'd hoped to find. "I can pay you the same amount you're earning here." Marie's lack of funds had her adding, "For a two-week trial period."

"Trial period?"

"I'll need to make sure you're the right fit." Her funds could stretch into a month, but she couldn't say that right now. Promising more than two weeks wouldn't be fair to Mrs. Baker. Asking the woman to leave her current employment wasn't really fair, either, but what the children needed came first.

Gertrude glanced behind her and then stood. "Striker's not going to like it, but I've had enough of that man." Extending a hand, she said, "It's a deal, Miss Hall."

Excitement flared. "Wonderful," Marie said. "Will you be able to leave now?"

"I'll go inside, tell Striker I quit, and then I'll have to gather my belongings. How about I meet you on the road out front in an hour?"

"Excellent," Marie said. "Thank you."

"No, thank you." Gertrude left the chickens where they were, and turned, walking toward the back door of the hotel. "I'm in need of a change, and there's nothing better than cooking for a passel of kids."

Marie spun around and scurried across the yard. Seeing Shorty's hopeful expression, she answered his silent question, "She said yes."

He let out a whoop, so did the children, and Marie all but skipped her way around the wagon.

"Mrs. Baker, that's her name," Marie said while climbing in the wagon. "Gertrude Baker. She'll be ready to leave in an hour."

"That'll give us time to pick up some things at the dry-goods store," Shorty said. "Stafford placed an order yesterday. I wanna check to make sure he got everything. I'll order up some supplies for your new cook, too."

She hadn't thought of supplies, but couldn't believe Stafford would be upset about that. "All right," Marie answered, and then turned to encourage the children to be on their best behavior again.

Minutes later, she couldn't say if the children were being extraordinarily good, or if they were scared out of their britches by the store owner. The woman stood as tall as any man and was rather frightening looking. More so with the dark mole right in the center of her chin that had three hairs sticking out of it. Her eyes, dark and narrow slits, didn't allow a person to know exactly where she was looking, but she was certainly glaring at them, Marie and the children.

Shorty seemed to know the husband well. A short man, without a single strand of hair, named Henry Smith. Mr. Smith had introduced his wife as Verna, but she'd emphasized her name was Mrs. Smith. Marie had nodded appropriately, but chose to hang close to the door along with the children. She had no money to make purchases, and even if she did, she'd have preferred not to spend it here.

The store was neat and clean, although tiny and cramped, but it was the atmosphere, controlled by the woman behind the counter, that didn't sit well.

Shorty and Mr. Smith were discussing a grinder of some kind, when Mrs. Smith walked around the end of the counter. Everything inside Marie began to jitter. Dressed in black other than a snow-white apron, Verna Smith approached with a definite purpose.

"So these," she asked with a raspy voice that sent a shiver clear to Marie's toes, "are the Meeker children?"

A chill settled deep in Marie's spine. She'd made no introductions as far as the children were concerned, and neither had Shorty. People would soon know, and there was no reason to hide it, yet Marie was very uncomfortable. "Yes."

"And you are their nursemaid?"

"Yes," Marie said again, ignoring the weight the woman used on the word nursemaid, as if it was a rather appalling thing to be. "I am."

The children were easing their way toward the open doorway, and Marie had a desire to follow them but knew there was no escaping. The determination in Mrs. Smith's glare, along with her evil-sounding whispers, said she'd give chase. Marie's thoughts dashed to Stafford again, wishing he was here.

"They're Mick Wagner's relatives, are they?"

It wasn't the snarl in the woman's words, but

the fact Marie hadn't told anyone that, other than Mr. Wagner, in the letter she'd written him, that worried Marie. Though she didn't want to answer, for it was truly none of Mrs. Smith's business, she didn't want to increase the woman's wrath.

"Yes, they are," she answered.

"He's in Texas. Won't be home until next spring."

"I'm aware of that," Marie said, keeping her chin up. She also cast a glance toward Shorty, wishing he'd hurry up or notice Mrs. Smith had practically cornered her near the door.

"I'm aware of a few other things, too," the woman said.

"I'm sure you are, Verna."

Marie spun. Relief and confusion hit at the same time when she saw Gertrude Baker in the doorway.

"And, I'd say most of it is none of your business," Gertrude continued as she took a hold of Marie's hand. "Come. Let's wait in the wagon."

More than happy to comply, Marie scooted out the door.

"Why would you need to wait in their wagon?" Verna Smith asked, clearly addressing Gertrude.

Walking beside Marie, Gertrude whispered, "Something she doesn't know. I love this job already." She then glanced over her shoulder to say aloud, "I work for them."

"You work for Stafford Burleson?" Mrs. Smith asked.

The shock in the shop owner's voice was apparent, but it was Gertrude Baker's wheezing that caused Marie's stomach to hit the ground.

"You've just hired me to work at Stafford Burleson's ranch?" Gertrude hissed.

Marie swallowed the lump in her throat before nodding. Gertrude looked as if she was going to quit before she'd ever started.

After placing his lumber order, which would be ready by the end of the month, Stafford returned to town, said goodbye to Ralph and, with a churning stomach, headed down Main Street. The house he was imagining for Mick would have plenty of room for the kids, and that wasn't setting as well as it should. There wasn't anything saying he had to start on Mick's house right away, other than his conscience.

Mick wouldn't build a house for him, but that was only because Mick wasn't a carpenter. He'd do anything else, though, that was for sure. Just as Stafford would for him. Friendships were like that. The one he and Mick had, anyway. A man was lucky to have a friend like that.

The other thing a man always knows is

when someone's talking about him, and Stafford turned in the direction the warning sensation was coming from. Verna Smith and Chris Striker were on the walkway in front of the Striker Hotel. The two of them were rather well suited, like two weasel-faced badgers.

Stafford tipped the brim of his hat with his finger and thumb as he rode past. Their glares grew more menacing. Why, he had no idea, but neither the man nor the woman were worth spending a moment of time worrying over. They were both obsessed with themselves.

Obsession, now that he might ponder. Not with himself, but a certain nursemaid. She'd been on his mind all day. All week. Actually, ever since Walt Darter's visit, Marie had been on Stafford's mind, and it was taking its toll.

She was memorable. And when her dander was up, spitting out *I will not* or *I cannot,* well, there wasn't a woman more adorable. She was cute when she was sad, too, like last night when she was out scanning the darkness, looking for Polly, and his mind still flashed the picture of her lily-white backside every so often.

Actually, more often than not. Getting Mick's house built, and her and the kids moved into it as soon as possible was the best plan.

It was then—when he was halfway home and started thinking about Mick's house again, Stafford realized he'd forgotten to stop by the telegraph office.

Going back now would be a waste. He'd already been gone most of the day. Rex would send a message out to the ranch when it arrived. More than likely it would say Mick was on his way.

It's what he wanted, so why was he dreading that message?

Stafford shifted in the saddle and urged Stamper into a faster pace. It was natural for him to think so much about Marie and the children. As Mick's friend it was his duty to take care of them until his partner returned home.

It really didn't matter how cute she was, or how stubborn, he'd keep them safe and fed, until Mick arrived. Maybe then he'd head down to Texas. Or even Mississippi, say hi to the family. Tell them about all the things he had going on around here. The life he'd built for himself. Better yet, maybe he'd invite them all up here. See everything first hand.

Stafford was still tossing future plans around when he rode into the homestead. The big house, the one in which he'd driven every nail, sawed every board, looked the same, yet the sight of it made his heart tick a bit faster than it ever had before. It wasn't pride, either, that of accomplishment or, in a sense, revenge. It was true, what Mick had said. He'd built this house, with its big white column porch pillars and windowed top floor for Francine—to prove she was wrong. He said he would amount to something, and he had.

In all the times he'd gazed upon his handiwork, it had never given him a sense of homecoming the way it was right now. The two little girls hosting a tea party on the porch had him smiling. That, and how they had Charlie and Weston sitting in the extra seats, most likely against the twins' wills. His grin increased as the older boys came running out of the barn, waving and shouting his name.

It had been years since anyone had welcomed him like that. Maybe it had never happened before.

He greeted them in return while dismounting and half listened to their chatter as his gaze went to the house, wondering if anyone else might walk out to say hello.

"And then there was this woman with a black wart on her chin, she was *scary!*" Samuel said.

"What?" Stafford asked. "Where did you see a woman like that?" Verna Smith formed in his mind, but it would have been impossible for the woman to be out here. He'd seen her in town.

"It's a mole, not a wart," Terrance corrected Samuel.

Stafford could almost hear Marie explaining the difference between a mole and a wart.

It would have been a teaching moment. She'd explained those to him on the ride from Huron. Teaching moments. He could think of a few of them himself.

"We saw her in town," Terrance said.

"When were you in town?" he asked.

"We just told you," Terrance answered. "This morning. That's where we got the cook."

"Cook?"

Freckle-covered faces with ear-to-ear grins nodded. Stafford was searching his mind, trying to piece things together when their faces fell. The sensation floating over his back said Marie had just closed the front door of the house. Even with the birds chirping nearby he'd heard the click.

"Ask Shorty to put Stamper up, will you?" Stafford asked, handing the reins to Terrance. A cook?

He turned, found Marie standing exactly as he'd pictured. She had a proud stance. Shoulders straight and chin up.

Outwardly she appeared unyielding, completely in control, but she couldn't hide, not from him anyway, how nervous she was inside. The way she wrung her hands was a dead giveaway. He saw more, though, and had the urge to comfort her again, as he had last night in the bunkhouse.

Stafford slowed his approach, giving her time. Or maybe he was giving himself time.

"Hello," she greeted him.

"Who took you to town?" The question shot out before he'd known it had formed.

"Shorty."

"I see." That, at least, was a relief. Her driving a wagon—full of rambunctious kids—would have been dangerous all the way around. He arrived at the bottom of the steps. "Why did you need to go to town?"

Her chin lifted another notch. "You told me to figure it out."

Lost for a moment, he asked, "I told you to figure out how to get to town?"

"No." Her lips pinched away the smile that had flashed for a brief moment. "You told me to figure out how to cook."

He did recall saying something along those lines this morning when his mind had been focused on her lips. How perfectly they'd fit against his last night.

"So I did," she said. "Figure it out, that is."

"How's that?"

"I hired one."

"You hired a cook?" A blind man could do a better job of picking out a newspaper.

"Yes."

She was adorable, standing there trying to appear all sober and stoic. He climbed the steps. The urge to kiss her was growing as strong as it had been this morning, and last night and yesterday. He'd tried that, though. Kissing her. It hadn't gotten her out of his system. In reality, it had backfired.

And would again.

His life was about to get messy unless he put a stop to it all right now.

Chapter Ten

Marie might as well be facing down the evil-looking Mrs. Smith with the way her insides were trying to work their way outside. There was a tick in Stafford's cheek she'd never seen before, and his usual sparkling eyes, something she'd come to take for granted, had all of a sudden turned stormy-gray again. As they'd been the first time they met.

She drew a deep breath in through her nose, hoping it would help the trembles working their way up her legs, down her arms, across her stomach.

Gertrude had held her silence on the way home, but once they'd arrived at the ranch and the children were sent outside to play, the woman had shared reservations about working at the Dakota Cattle Company. Said the ranch, and its owners, had a reputation. Folks claimed Mick Wagner and Stafford Burleson had hit it big in the gold mines of Colorado, and now, besides spending money on their ranch, they were inclined to spend their riches on gambling and loose women.

In the end, and much to Marie's relief, Gertrude said she'd stay for the promised two weeks. Only because she couldn't let Marie and the children live out here alone—with those men.

So many things had changed since this morning. Living out here with such men had her insides churning, but she had very few choices. The children were her first priority, and they, legally, belonged to Mick Wagner.

"I suggested you learn how to cook," Stafford said. "I just laid out a good sum of money to replace the cabin you burned down, and now you spend more by hiring a cook?"

The lump in her throat was too large to swallow. It just sat there, throbbing as if her heart was a part of it. Some of the things Gertrude said about Stafford had seemed impossible. Now, she wondered why she'd thought that. He was acting so superior, righteous even, the way he had back in Huron. Having seen the other side of him, the one the children had taken to so readily, the one she—well, what she thought wasn't important. The children were, though.

"I used my money," she said pointedly.

"You have money?"

The doubt in his tone struck a chord inside her. "Yes," she said. "I have money."

"Enough to hire a cook?"

Skirting around the amount of money she had, Marie answered, "I wouldn't have hired Mrs. Baker if I didn't have enough money to do so."

Stafford's glare grew darker. "If you have that much money, what are you doing here? You and the kids could just stay at the hotel until Mick gets home."

Flustered, Marie admitted, "I don't have that much money."

"How much do you have?"

Her insides were clenched together. Ten dollars wouldn't provide for her and the children until next spring. Stafford was her only hope of making it through the upcoming winter that Gertrude had said could carry blizzards that left mountains of snow, trapping them all at the ranch for months.

Frustrated, Marie huffed. "I have ten dollars. Well, had ten dollars. It'll be significantly less after I pay Mrs. Baker."

"Less than ten dollars? How long did you hire her for? A day?"

Marie spun around, noting for the first time that the children were watching with interest, and headed toward the front door. Stafford was right on her heels, but she hadn't expected anything less. Arguing in front of the children wasn't acceptable, and it was obvious there would be an argument.

Stafford shut the door behind them, but not wanting Gertrude to hear, either, Marie walked across the entranceway and down the hall, all the way to the vestibule where Polly and her babies resided in their box. There she opened the back door and stepped outside again.

With a severe frown, Stafford followed.

"I've hired Mrs. Baker for two weeks," Marie said, stopping near the porch railing. She might as well tell him her plan, perhaps knowing that she'd found an acceptable arrangement would change his attitude. "During that time she will not only prepare meals for the children, she will teach me how to cook."

"Two weeks, huh?"

She spun to face him. A grave mistake. The way he stood there, looking so serious, reminded her of yesterday when he'd led her to this very spot. What had she been thinking? This is where he'd kissed her. Her stomach flipped and Marie shook her head in an attempt to clear the vision forming.

"Yes," she answered. "Two weeks."

"You're paying her ten dollars for two weeks?"

"No, I'm paying her twenty-five cents a day plus room and board." Lifting her chin, she added, "That's the same amount Mr. Striker paid her."

"Striker?"

She nodded. "He owns the hotel."

"I know who he is." He rubbed his forehead. "You just hired his cook away from him?"

"Well, she wasn't happy there." Marie chose not to add Gertrude wasn't overly happy about being here, either.

"That explains—" Stafford stopped whatever he'd been saying and moved closer. Leaning forward until his nose was very close to hers, he said, "A good cook costs more than twenty-five cents a day."

"Plus room and board," she whispered. His nearness had her heart trembling, but she couldn't say it was fear. It was that unique excitement she'd felt before when he'd kissed her.

"Even with room and board."

Marie closed her eyes, which was a big mistake. She'd thought if she couldn't see him, she wouldn't, well, feel him. But with her eyes closed everything was more intense. She could even feel his breathing. Not just hear, but feel each breath he took as if it was a part of her as much as a part of him, and for whatever reason, she didn't want to open her eyes, lose that feeling.

It took great effort, but she lifted her lids and forced herself to think of the situation at hand.

The children. "You won't make her leave, will you?"

He stared at her for an extended length of time. There was a mysterious softness in his eyes, but it made her want to close her eyes again, and the urge to lean forward was terribly difficult to fight. Her breath was catching in her throat, too, making her lightheaded.

Stafford leaned back, and then, as if that wasn't far enough, he took a step backward. "No," he said, "I won't make her leave."

That's what he did, though.

He left.

Just walked down the steps.

Marie, however, had to grab on to the railing to stay upright. Relief, most likely that he wouldn't force Gertrude to leave, left her legs weak and wobbly.

The air gushed from her chest in a huge rush. She'd never been good at lying. Not even to herself. There wasn't an ounce of relief in her, and what she was feeling had nothing to do with cooking or the children. She still wanted Stafford to like her. Actually, that seemed to grow more each day. Sometimes, she thought he did like her, but other times, she sensed he didn't. It was so confusing, and she didn't understand why it mattered to her so much.

Stafford rounded the corner of the house,

and Marie's mind turned a corner, as well. Did he think she was like the women he visited in town—the ones Gertrude told her about? Is that why he'd kissed her before? Even a nursemaid knew what type of women Gertrude had spoken about, and that alone would make most well-educated, smart, sensible nursemaids distance themselves from any man who pursued such women. That had been part of Miss Wentworth's lessons, how to stay clear of the men who resided in the same homes as the children, employers or not. Her instructor had emphasized that the fastest way to get fired was to associate yourself with the man of the house.

Perhaps that was part of her problem. Stafford wasn't her employer. Maybe if he was, she wouldn't keep forgetting that part of her training.

Stafford couldn't say he'd ever met Gertrude Baker before, but it was apparent the woman didn't like him. It showed in the blue eyes she used to watch him like a hawk. He could barely turn a corner in the house without running into her. Fortunately he wasn't choosing to spend much time in the house at the moment. It had only been three days since her arrival, so it wasn't as though they'd encountered each other very many times, but considering that she, too, was living in his house, they did run into each other three times a day. Mealtimes.

Marie had outdone herself in that respect. Gertrude Baker could cook. Therefore, Stafford attempted to be on his best behavior around the woman. A part of him even felt sorry for Chris Striker. No wonder the man had been glaring at him when Stafford had ridden past the hotel the other day.

"Thank you, Mrs. Baker," Stafford said, laying his napkin next to his plate. They were eating in the big dining room off the hallway—the one he'd never eaten in before the cook had arrived. "That was some of the best roast beef I've ever had."

The children were nodding, agreeing with him as they continued to shovel food into their mouths. He'd made a point of glancing at each of them before allowing his gaze to settle on Marie at the far end of the big table.

"Thank you, Mr. Stafford. I'm glad you approve," Mrs. Baker said as she refilled Marie's teacup. The cook then set the teapot on the large buffet and picked up the coffeepot—both made of silver and so fancy he'd never used them before. "Would you care for more coffee? I will serve dessert in a moment. Spice cake with frosting."

His insides melted. Spice cake. He hadn't

had that since leaving home. "Yes, I would. Thank you."

While the woman filled his cup, his mind went back to Mississippi—a portion of his thoughts anyway. He was comparing this—a wonderful meal at a table full of people, being waited on by a servant—to his childhood. There were a lot of similarities, and as much as he'd told himself it wasn't what he wanted, it was gratifying. As if he'd come full circle. Become the person he'd told his family he had no desire to be.

They'd scoffed at him, and over the years he'd laid out an agenda that didn't include one thing he was looking at right now. Yet, even while convincing himself it wasn't what he wanted, he'd swayed in that direction. The house he'd built was proof of that. Even after building the house, he'd denied he wanted it full. Claimed living alone was the life he wished for.

It was rather sobering, discovering he'd been wrong all these years. More sobering than it was knowing this wasn't real. The house was real, the furnishings and the fancy dishes. Yet whilst the children and Marie and Mrs. Baker were real, they weren't his. They were all Mick's. And they were exactly what Mick had wanted. His partner had spoken of it since the day they'd met.

Mick had been raised in Texas. Not on a ranch, but in town. Austin. His father had been a doctor. When he'd died and Mick's mother re-married, Mick had left. Said their house hadn't been big enough for two men, but he always stopped to see his mother—and stepfather—when he went south. Mick had a couple of much younger stepbrothers and often said he wished he'd had brothers and sisters while growing up. He also said he wanted a house full of kids.

Stafford's gaze landed on Marie again, who was waiting for Mrs. Baker to set a plate of dessert in front of her.

Hence the mail-order bride. Mick had known what he wanted, and when he hadn't found it, he'd ordered it. Complete with kids.

Stafford had told his partner that having siblings, a big family, wasn't all it was cracked up to be, yet in that, too, perhaps he'd been wrong.

The gurgling in his stomach should have ruined his appetite, but when Mrs. Baker placed a china plate before him, holding a large slice of spice cake, he picked up his fork and all but moaned when the sugary treat hit his taste buds. It was better than he remembered. Then again, maybe his mother's cook's spice cake hadn't been this good.

He ate the entire piece, savoring each bite, and then congratulated Mrs. Baker on her abilities.

"I didn't make the cake," Gertrude Baker said,

offering the first real smile he'd seen her give. "Marie did."

The red blush covering Marie's cheeks revealed that the cook spoke the truth.

"My compliments, Marie," he said. "You really must be an apt student."

"That she is," Mrs. Baker said as Marie's cheeks turned a shade darker. "Not one mistake."

Stafford couldn't come up with a comment, not with the way his mind was twisting about. He was thinking about Ralph Peterson, and how proud the banker was of his wife's cooking abilities. Stafford could relate to that. And he now had everything at his disposal to invite Ralph and his family out to the ranch.

He pushed away from the table then, and complimented the cooks one last time before taking his leave. There were always things that needed to be done at the ranch, chores and such, yet, as he paused on the front step, not a single task came to mind. It was evening, the cowboys were settled into the bunkhouse, and visiting them wasn't the escape he needed.

As he walked down the steps his gaze settled on the burned piece of ground on the other side of the creek. He set out in that direction. There was plenty of daylight yet to stake out the footings for Mick's new house.

A short while later Terrance joined him.

"Why are you pounding those boards in the ground?" the child asked, kicking at the black clumps of dirt.

"I'm staking out where we'll build the new house," Stafford explained.

"Mick Wagner's new house?"

The boy's tone held a definite hint of disgust. "Yes, Mick's new house," Stafford answered. "Don't worry. It'll be much larger than the cabin."

"I don't see why we can't just live in your house," Terrance said, bending over to inspect a rock. "It's even bigger than the one we had back in Chicago."

Stafford laid down his hammer and stepped over the string he'd stretched from end stake to end stake. More than once he'd thought about the children and the changes that had happened to them. It had tugged at his chest before, but was stronger tonight. Maybe because of Terrance's meekness, which was unusual, or maybe because he was remembering his own childhood more fondly lately. He knelt down next to the child and feigned interest in a couple of rocks near the boy's feet. "I think you'll like this new house. It'll have plenty of bedrooms."

Terrance tossed his rock away. "Just 'cause he's our cousin shouldn't mean we have to live with him."

Stafford leaned back on his heels. "Who's your cousin? Mick?"

"Yes," Terrance said. "That's why we're here."

Both Terrance and Samuel had chattered endlessly while tagging along beside him over the past weeks, but he'd never heard this. "Mick Wagner's your cousin?" Stafford repeated, just to make sure his hearing was working.

"Well, he was our mother's cousin," Terrance answered. "And she gave us to him. That's what the lawyer said when he told us we had to leave. He said we either come live with Mick or go to the orphanage in Chicago. No one would ever want all of us, so Marie wrote a letter to Mick."

With everything else happening, Stafford had forgotten about the letter Mrs. Smith had given him. It must still be in his saddlebag. "And Mick wrote Marie back?" he asked, questioning the sense of hope rising inside him.

"No," Terrance said, tossing another rock. "We ran out of time." The boy stuffed both of his hands into his pockets. "Marie doesn't know, but I heard what the man from the bank said. Two days. We had to be out of the house in two days or they'd take us all to the orphanage." He wiped at his cheek with one hand, which left a dark smear, before asking, "You ever been to an orphanage, Stafford?"

"No, I can't say I have."

"We went there last Christmas. Marie took us to give the kids there some of our toys." He shook his head and huffed out a breath as if he was older than Shorty. "It wasn't a place I'd want to live, I'll tell you that." Then, after kicking at another dirt clump, he added, "I can't say I'll like living at Mick Wagner's place, either."

This was a conversation he should be having with Marie, not Terrance, therefore Stafford stood. Ruffling Terrance's copper-shaded hair, he said, "Well, for right now, you're living in my house, and I like it."

Something akin to hope glistened in the child's eyes. "You like us living in your house?"

"I sure enough do," Stafford answered. "Who wouldn't?"

"Because we've been on our best behavior?"

Stafford grinned. "You've been behaving, that's for sure, but, truth is, I like you."

A blush covered the boy's face. "I expect you were a bit lonely before we came along. Living in that big house all alone."

"I expect I was," Stafford answered as he walked over to pick up his hammer. Terrance had followed, so he gestured toward the string. "Carry that for me, will you?"

"Sure," Terrance replied, more than happy to comply. As they started walking toward the bridge, he asked, "Hey, Stafford, do you think you could write Mick a letter? Maybe tell him to stay in Texas a bit longer?" Then as if trying to explain his reasoning, he said, "We're comfortable at your house. There's no need for him to hurry home."

Stafford couldn't let on just how close Terrance's thoughts were to his own. First, though, he had some questions for Marie.

Terrance must have taken his silence as an answer, because he said, "I guess not, huh?"

"Well, Terrance," Stafford said, laying a hand on the boys shoulder. "Mick's a lot like you. A lot like me. He's got a mind of his own. It wouldn't make any difference if I wrote him or not. He'll come home when he's ready to come home."

Peering up, Terrance asked, "You think I'm like you?"

Not exactly sure why he'd thought the boy would like to hear that, other than he remembered how much it meant when his father said it to him, Stafford nodded. "I sure do. We both like dogs and horses. And," he said, lowering his voice, "we both have so many brothers and sisters we don't know what to do with them."

Terrance laughed. "Ain't that the truth." More serious, he asked, "You have brothers and sisters?"

"Yep. Five sisters and one brother."

After a moment of thought, Terrance exclaimed, "That's more than me."

"Yes, it is," Stafford answered.

"Where do they live?"

"Mississippi, most of them. One of my sisters lives in Texas now."

"That's a long ways away," Terrance said, frowning.

"That's what happens when you grow up, people move away." Stafford gestured toward the shed where they'd put away the tools they both carried, and in hopes of bringing a smile back to Terrance's face, he asked, "Where's the hat I bought for you?" Though it was evening, he explained, "It'll keep the sun off your head."

The child set the spool of string on the shelf before asking, "What hat?"

"It should have been in the freight wagon that arrived the other day," Stafford answered as they walked out the door.

"There's some stuff in the room by the back porch. A couple of crates full. Marie said it must be yours and that we shouldn't—"

"Yes," Stafford said. "I remember, now." Marie had told him at supper two days ago that she'd put his supplies in that room. He still didn't know what to use that room for, so he just stored things in it. His mother had had a room like that, one that ran along the back of the house. She'd called it a lady's parlor and he wasn't ever allowed in it.

"You bought me a hat?" Terrance asked. "Is it like yours?"

"Yep."

"Can we go get it?"

"Yes," Stafford answered. "There's one for each of your brothers and sisters, too."

Marie was on the porch, feeding Polly, when the door flew open. Her heart skipped several times, which had nothing to do with the speed of Terrance's steps. She simply had no control over her insides when it came to Stafford. Since Mrs. Baker had arrived, she'd barely seen him. Other than mealtimes, which she'd grown to love. Sitting around the table, her on one end, Stafford on the other, was just like a family. Just what she'd always wanted. He liked it, too; at least, it seemed that way. She only had two weeks and was determined to learn all she could in that time, so things could continue as they were. However, she didn't let cooking get in the way of looking after the children.

"Terrance," she said with warning. "We walk in the house."

"Yes'um," he answered, slowing his pace considerably.

"Where are the rest of the children?" Stafford asked.

The smile on his face, or perhaps the glint in his eyes, made her heart stutter again. "Beatrice and Charlotte are in the kitchen with Mrs. Baker, we just finished mixing up a batch of bread, and Samuel, Charlie and Weston are up in the window room."

"What are they doing up there?" he asked.

Lowering her voice, for it was a secret game the boys enjoyed wholeheartedly, she whispered, "They are on lookout. For Indians. One never knows when we might come under attack."

Stafford laughed, and she did, too. He was the one that had started the adventure. When they'd asked what that room was for, he'd said precisely those words. He'd assured her he was joking, which had eased her fears. He was good at that, easing her fears, and that was something else she wondered about. As much as his presence riled her at times, it was comforting to know he was nearby.

"Go get your brothers and sisters, Terrance," he said. As the boy walked away—though Marie knew he'd be running as soon as he was out of sight—Stafford asked her, "The things that arrived on the freight wagon the other day, it's all in that room?"

"Yes."

"Come on, then," he said, and to her utter surprise, he took her hand.

His palm was warm as his fingers wrapped around hers.

"I picked some things up for the kids," he said, tugging her into the hallway. "I forgot to tell you about it."

Her heart pounded inside her chest. Gifts for the children had nothing to do with it. Having Stafford hold her hand did. Even with all the things Gertrude said, Marie couldn't find it in herself to dislike him. Neither did she want to be disloyal to him. He'd already provided her and the children with far more than he needed to.

The room was full of evening light, due to the numerous windows, but it held no furniture, just a few boxes and crates sitting along one wall. Gertrude had said this room would make an ideal sewing room, and Marie had agreed, even though she didn't know how to sew. The other woman had picked up on that and offered to teach her as soon as her cooking skills were far enough along. There again, Marie had silently agreed with a nod. Soon she'd have to tell the woman she wouldn't be able to afford her beyond the two-week span of cooking lessons.

Stafford let go of her hand to move across the room toward the supplies, and she stopped near the window, gazing out at the garden in the backyard. That was another thing Gertrude had offered to teach her, how to tend a garden. If she'd known all the things she didn't know, and would need to know, she might have never left Chicago.

No, she would have still left, and she was never going back there. No matter what it took.

Rubbing her hands together, for one in particular was still tingling, she turned. "You really didn't need to purchase anything for the children. They have everything they need for right now."

"They don't have hats," he said. "I noticed that on the trip here."

His grin was back. It was slightly slanted, one side higher than the other. She'd noted that before, and each time she saw it, it became more attractive.

"You noticed it, too," he said. "That's why we needed the covered wagon, remember?"

"Yes, I remember," she said, and then wrinkled her nose at him for making her cheeks feel so flushed.

He laughed and tossed something across the room. She caught it. Well, rather, it sailed directly into her hands. A yellow straw hat with a wide brim and pink silk ribbon.

"That's to keep the sun off your head," he said.

Her heart swelled, but the children rushed into the room before she could respond.

"Really, Stafford? Really? You bought us hats like yours?" Samuel was asking as he scurried across the room.

"Yes, really," Stafford answered. "But girls first." He waved a hand. "Beatrice, Charlotte, these two are for you."

While they oohed and aahed, and thanked him, he settled hats on their heads very similar to the one Marie held between trembling fingers.

"Now these," he said, pointing toward four others he'd laid on the floor, "are for boys. Cowboys. Are there any of those around here?"

"Yep, right here," Terrance answered.

Marie couldn't contain the happiness erupting inside her. The children had been extremely well behaved lately, and she was so very proud of them for that. But this, the way Stafford had them shining brighter than they had in months, made her joyous.

"Are we really cowboys, Stafford?" Samuel asked.

"I am," Weston answered, holding on to the brim of the hat sitting on his head with both hands.

"Me, too," Charlie added.

"There you have it," Stafford said. "We have a room full of cowboys."

"Marie?" Charlotte asked, "Can we go look in the mirror?"

She nodded and watched as all six of them hurried for the door. That's when she spied the scowl on Gertrude's face. The woman's disapproval couldn't be missed. She'd laid out several warnings about allowing the children to become overly attached to Stafford.

"I picked up some other things, too," Stafford said. "Material and such. I thought you might want to—" he shrugged "—sew some things."

The sinking in Marie's stomach prevented an answer from forming.

"Miss Hall may need instruction in that, as well, Mr. Burleson," Gertrude supplied. "But I'll see what we can manage during my time here."

Marie didn't take her eyes off the hat in her hand as a thick silence filled the room. At most times, Gertrude was pleasant, even fun to be around, but when it came to Stafford, she was rather tart.

"Thank you, Mrs. Baker," Stafford said. "Would you mind tending to the children for a few minutes? There are some things I need to discuss with Marie."

This time Marie's stomach hit the floor. His somewhat demanding tone was back. She shifted her gaze slightly, just to see how the other woman reacted.

Gertrude walked farther into the room. "I do not believe it would be appropriate for you and Marie to be alone together."

"We aren't alone," he said. "And even after you leave this room, we won't be alone. You'll be right outside the door."

Marie gulped at the way Gertrude gasped. She certainly didn't want Stafford to dismiss the cook, but being a household employee, she'd learned how one should speak to an employer. Gertrude, as much as she did know, didn't know that.

"I'm not precisely sure what I did to gain your dislike or distrust, Mrs. Baker," Stafford said. "I would like to discuss it with you, because I do appreciate you being here, but right now, there are some things I need to discuss with Marie concerning Mr. Wagner."

Marie's insides were now trembling, and her mouth was so dry she couldn't speak. Things got worse when Stafford crossed the room and took her by the elbow.

"Marie and I will be in my office, Mrs. Baker," he said. "I'd appreciate it if you would mind the children."

Gertrude glared, but nodded.

"Thank you," he said. "When Marie and I are finished, you and I will have a discussion."

Marie didn't dare cast a glance toward the

other woman as Stafford led the way to the door, still holding her elbow. A hundred questions were bouncing inside her head, yet she had an inkling that the answer to all of them included an end to her plan. The one that hadn't worked very well since the beginning.

Chapter Eleven

Stafford waited until Marie was settled in a chair before he pulled the letter out of his pocket. It had still been in his saddlebag in the vestibule. After handing the envelope to her and watching her brows pull down, he walked around his desk and took a seat.

"I'm assuming you recognize that." A part of him wanted to start questioning her, but another part told him to take it slow, let her reveal her story.

"Yes, it's the letter I sent Mr. Wagner." She'd turned it over, was staring at the wax seal on the back.

"I picked it up when I was in town the other day."

"I mailed it a long time ago," she said. "I never imagined it would take that long to arrive."

"It probably didn't. Mrs. Smith had it. Said she was holding on to it until Mick got back."

"So he never saw it?"

Stafford shook his head.

"Did Mrs. Smith put this on it?" She was delicately running a finger over the wax seal.

Stafford figured the woman had resealed it, but it made no sense for her to seal a letter that hadn't been in the first place. "You didn't?"

"No, I used some of Emma Lou's—Mrs. Meeker's—stationery. It was prepasted." Marie laid the envelope on the desk.

Verna Smith had been a burr in his side—everyone's side—since she'd married Henry only six weeks after her second husband had died and the two merged their dry-goods stores. The way she'd raised all of Henry's prices could almost be counted as stealing, and her meddlesome activities irked everyone, but this really irritated him. Stafford lifted the envelope off the desk. "She must not have been able to reseal it, so thought this might fool everyone."

"Are you implying she opened it and read it?"

"Yes."

Marie, looking stunned, glanced from him to the envelope and back again. "That would explain how she knew the children's last name."

Protectiveness as he'd never known it bloomed inside him. "What did she say?"

"Just something along the lines that they were the Meeker children."

Her timidity implied that Verna Smith had said more, but he wasn't going to dwell on that now. "What does the letter say?"

"Open it. Read it. It explains how Emma Lou and John Meeker died in a fire, and since he, Mr. Wagner, that is, was Emma Lou's cousin, he is the only family the children have left." With a wave of her hand, she said, "Go ahead. Open it."

Stafford did, and read it. The letter, in perfect penmanship, explained just that, and how she didn't think Mick would want the children sent to the orphanage so she was bringing them to him. He read it twice before saying, "It doesn't say anything about you being Mick's mail-order bride."

Her grimace was accompanied by red cheeks. "That was my friend Sarah's idea. I didn't have enough money to pay the train fares. Sarah told me about a woman she knew who became a mail-order bride and the husband paid for her travels upon her arrival. When I promised to pay for my ticket, the train agent agreed the children could accompany me, as long as their fares were paid in Huron."

He had to wonder what anyone would have done if he hadn't paid their fares. Arrest her? That was doubtful. "You had enough to pay your way?"

She nodded. "I'd saved most of my salary

since starting to work for the Meekers, and last year for Christmas they gave me a necklace and ear bobs. They weren't overly expensive, but I got enough by selling them to provide meals for the children while traveling." Her sigh echoed across the room. "I waited as long as I could to hear back from Mr. Wagner, but when the man from the bank insisted we had to move out of the house, we had nowhere to go."

"What happened to everyone else? I'm assuming they had other servants." He didn't like using that word when it pertained to her. "Or employees."

"They did. A cook, maids, a gardener. They all found other positions."

"You could have, too."

"The children wouldn't have had anyone if I'd done that."

The one question he really wanted answered couldn't wait any longer. "Are you fully prepared to marry Mick?"

"I won't abandon the children," she said.

"That doesn't answer my question."

She hesitated, but eventually said, "Yes, I'll marry him."

Stafford wasn't exactly sure what that did to his insides. He liked the idea that Mick hadn't ordered her, but knowing she'd marry a complete stranger—she would, he had no doubt, considering all she'd already done—didn't sit well with him.

His thought voiced itself before he could stop it. "What if someone else, another man, was interested in adopting the children, all of them, would you consider marrying him?"

Something unusual shot through Marie. A shiver of sorts. She didn't *want* to marry Mick Wagner, but the children belonged to him. Allowing Stafford to read the letter, to understand what had happened, was one thing, but all this talk of marriage made her nervous. Realization though, when it arrived, wasn't as comforting as it should be.

"No one else can adopt the children," she said. "Emma Lou had a life insurance policy. It lists Mr. Wagner as guardian of the children. He'd have to agree to any adoption." She blew the heavy air out of her chest. "That's what Mr. Phillips said. He was the Meekers' solicitor. He wanted to file an affidavit, one where the courts could put the children in an orphanage until Mr. Wagner contacted him. That's why I brought them here."

She could go on, explain to him what orphanages were like. How she'd spent most of her life in one. How she had been adopted out, twice. Once by a man who insisted upon peace and quiet all the time so that eventually his wife took her back to the orphanage, and a second time by a woman who took her back after two weeks, saying having a child underfoot was too much trouble. An adopted child wasn't always a wanted child, and being returned, proving to everyone you were completely unwanted, made life at the orphanage so much worse.

"But you're willing," Stafford was saying, pulling her mind back to the present. "To stay here at the ranch until Mick arrives, decides what he wants to do?"

"Yes, as long as you are willing to allow us to stay." Fear leaped forward, had her adding, "I have the life insurance policy. It's not a lot of money, but enough to repay the expenses we've accrued." She cringed. "Not the cabin, though."

His slanted grin was back. "You don't need to worry about reimbursement. I— Mick has enough funds to cover it. Including the cabin."

"But that's probably not how he'd choose to spend it," she said aloud, though she hadn't meant to.

He chuckled. "Probably not. But Mick's a good guy. He'll understand. The cabin would have needed to be torn down eventually, so don't waste another thought on that, either."

Once again she was thankful his easy demeanor was so calming. "You seem awfully confident about that."

"I am," he said. "Mick's like a brother to me. I know what he wants almost as well as he does."

"Does he want six children?" she asked.

This time his laugh was so genuine she grinned. Stafford stood then. "We've been closed up in here long enough. Mrs. Baker will soon be knocking upon the door."

Marie allowed him to take her elbow. It seemed so natural, almost as if he was an ally, the first one she'd ever had. "Thank you for not firing Mrs. Baker."

"Firing her?" He shook his head. "I haven't eaten so well in years. And don't worry about her wages, either, I'll pay them. That's what I'm going to discuss with her now."

When Marie opened her mouth to protest, he shook his head. "I'm benefitting from her being here as much as anyone. I pay the wages around here, and I'll pay hers."

He pulled open the door, and Marie couldn't say the words that had formed, not with Gertrude standing right there.

Stafford and Gertrude were still in his office long after she'd put the children to bed, and the next morning, when she and the children walked down the stairs, the kitchen was full of laughter.

Unable to resist, Marie glanced between the two people in the room. Stafford sat at the table, drinking coffee, and Gertrude was at the stove frying pancakes, which thrilled the children. Wondering what had happened to the animosity that usually hung in the air between the other two, Marie walked to the stove. Though her heels clicked steadily upon the floor, her steps were awkward, as unsure as everything else.

Smiling more brightly than usual, Gertrude said, "Good morning. I was just telling Stafford about my George. He was a prankster, my George was. There wasn't a day I knew him that he didn't make me laugh."

Marie lifted an egg out of the bowl Gertrude gestured toward and cracked it against the edge of a pan already sitting upon the stove. Her stomach swirled. She'd been full of pride when Stafford praised her cooking last night, but there was still so much to learn. Of course he'd hire Gertrude over her. Why hadn't she thought of that?

She cracked three more eggs, and retrieved a spatula as the eggs sizzled and spat. Stafford was talking with the children, the boys mainly, about hats, and a hard knot formed in the center of her chest. The children were so happy here, and in an odd way, that hurt. They'd be sad, uprooted again, when Mick Wagner arrived, even if it meant just moving across the bridge.

"You only sleep with your hat on when you're on the trail, ain't that right, Stafford?" Terrance was saying. "Like you did when we traveled out here."

Flipping the eggs, Marie waited for his response.

"Well," he said, "if Weston wants to sleep with his hat on, I don't see how it'll hurt anything."

A yoke on one of the eggs broke when Stafford asked, "What do you think, Marie?"

It wasn't the first yoke she'd broken. And, most likely, it wouldn't be the last. She turned and found Weston's gaze. "I don't believe it will hurt anything," she told the child. "But you might accidently crush it in your sleep."

"That could happen," Stafford agreed. "Maybe we need to put a hook on the wall in your room. That way you can hang it up before going to sleep."

"Can I have a hook, too?" Charlie asked.

"Sure," Stafford answered. "I'm sure there are a few around here somewhere."

"Those are done," Gertrude whispered in Marie's ear, pulling her attention back to the stove.

After placing the eggs on a platter and filling the pan with four more, Marie's gaze once again shot to the table. Stafford was watching her, just as the tingle in her spine had said. There was something different in his gaze this morning. It was more thoughtful than usual. She shivered.

Was he thinking she wasn't needed at all? Not as a nursemaid or a cook, now that he'd hired the other woman?

"I must say," Gertrude whispered, "I wasn't giving credit where credit was due. Stafford is very tolerant when it comes to the children. Charitable, too."

Marie couldn't stop the sting that formed behind her eyes.

Gertrude chuckled and patted Marie's shoulder before carrying the platter of eggs and pancakes to the table.

By that afternoon, Marie could no longer hold her silence. She'd hinted about her curiosity as to why Gertrude changed her opinion of Stafford, but the other woman overlooked each question and simply chatted on about a plethora of other things.

"What did he say to change your mind so completely?" Marie finally asked, bluntly.

"Who?" Gertrude asked as she unfolded a length of material from one of the crates that had also held hats for everyone. "Stafford?"

"Yes, Stafford," Marie answered. Usually the children attended to their studies after lunch, but today Stafford had asked if they could accompany him out to the barn. She'd agreed, knowing the studies wouldn't hold their attention—or hers. The frustration she'd held in all morning came out in a gush. "Yesterday you were warning me to not let the children become too close with him. Today you act like he's your best friend."

"That should make you happy," Gertrude said. "You've been trying to convince me he wasn't as bad as I believed."

"I have not," Marie insisted. "I never said anything." She'd bitten her tongue several times to keep from telling the other woman she was wrong about Stafford. He might have hit it rich in the gold fields, but he wasn't squandering his money, not that she'd noticed, and he wasn't as boorish as Gertrude made him sound. He wasn't attempting to take advantage of her, either—not in the way the other woman had implied he would. Of course, Marie hadn't admitted that he'd kissed her—twice. In a way, she was cherishing those events and didn't want them tarnished. Not even by her own thoughts.

"Exactly," Gertrude said. "If you'd believed me, you'd have agreed with me."

Marie had to take a moment to consider that, but then shook her head. She didn't have time to figure that all out, she just needed to know if he was going to send her away. That couldn't happen. Not again. "What did Stafford say last night?"

"He hired me. Not just for two weeks, but

for as long as I want to stay." Gertrude sighed then. "As if any woman in her right mind would want to leave this place." Smiling, she continued, "And he increased my wage. Twenty-five dollars a month. George didn't even make that much working for the railroad. Furthermore, the more we talked, the more I came to the conclusion most of what I'd heard was nothing more than hearsay. My guess would be rumors started by Verna Smith. That woman has a penchant for sticking her nose in where it doesn't belong. Some folks are like that. Hate to see others happy or prosperous."

Despite the warmth of the room filled with bright sun from the many windows, Marie grew chilled. Verna Smith was the least of her concerns. "Stafford hired you to be his cook?"

"Yes, and to continue teaching you everything I know."

Hope rose. "He said that?"

"Yes, among other things." Gertrude held up thread and buttons, and then walked back to the pretty yellow material with tiny red roses she'd laid out on the floor.

"What other things?" Marie asked, trying not to be too hopeful.

"Sewing for one. I think we'll make you a dress out of this cloth, and one for each of the girls out of the pink striped material," Gertrude said. "Get you out of those blue ones."

Still attempting to hide what had grown into excitement, Marie shook her head. "These blue dresses are my uniforms. I have no need for a new one, but the girls do."

Gertrude smiled. "Verna probably expected some old woman when she read your letter, and I'd guess she's pretty put out that you aren't." Gesturing toward the window, she said, "Now, stand over here, so I can get your measurements."

Stafford stood nearby as each of the children took turns riding Ginger—the gentle mare he'd bought last year—as Shorty led her around the corral. But one eye was on the house. He'd figured Marie would have been out by now. To check on the children, if nothing else, although he'd truly expected her to corner him. She'd noticed the difference between him and Gertrude Baker this morning. It was impossible not to, and it had to be driving Marie crazy. He'd been anticipating a few minutes alone with her. There was a tension between them that he found he thrived on.

Pulling his gaze away from the house, Stafford leaned back against the wooden corral, where five little bodies sat along the top rail like birds on a branch. He thrived on them, too, though in a different way. Having the kids around was fulfilling in a unique sense. All in all, the changes that had happened lately fit him.

Even Gertrude Baker. She'd turned out to be more than a cook. She was smart, and didn't mind telling him exactly what she thought.

It had been an eye-opening conversation—the one the two of them had participated in last night—especially concerning the town of Merryville. Seems Verna Smith was not only exorbitant in her prices, she was quite masterful in starting rumors, too. Mainly about him and Mick. Sure, both of them had visited the saloon in town, but not that many times.

He'd set Gertrude straight, and as they'd talked, about the railroad, her husband and the town of Merryville, they'd both come to the same conclusions. Verna Smith was not only telling tales, she probably was already coming up with a plan to publicly ridicule Marie.

The thought had his jaw tightening. Marie had told Gertrude about the children losing their parents and how Mick was their only living relative. Long after their conversation had ended and Stafford had climbed the stairs to his bedroom, a variety of things circled his mind. Past and present concerns.

He waved to Shorty. "That's enough for now,"

Stafford said. "The kids have lessons this afternoon." And he had things to see to.

Groans sounded, but one by one the children climbed down, with his help, and made their way to the gate. Stafford followed them toward the house, absently answering their supply of never-ending questions. His mind was on another track, wondering what would be the best way to handle Verna Smith, when a plume of dust in the distance caught his attention. Company was a rarity, and he stopped near the steps, watching until a wagon grew close enough for him to make out who it was.

He was biting the inside of his bottom lip when the wagon rolled into the yard. Verna Smith sat on the bench seat, beside a man dressed completely in black, and three other women were in the back of the wagon, the wind tugging at the flowers and feathers on their hats.

"Hello, Mr. Burleson," the man said. "I don't believe we've met. I'm Reverend Saxton."

Stafford had already noted the white collar, and he'd noticed how the three women in the back were shifting their hefty weights to exit the wagon. He supposed he should offer assistance, but since he was already convinced this wasn't a neighborly visit, he wasn't overly concerned about manners.

The preacher assisted Verna Smith, who was

also dressed in black, as usual, and the two of them approached side by side. "It's been brought to my attention, Mr. Burleson," the preacher said, "that you have a young woman living out here, one you aren't married to."

So that was Verna's plan, and she'd wasted no time in putting it in place.

"Hello, Reverend Saxton," a voice said behind him. "How nice of you to visit."

Stafford looked round and found he was very glad he and Gertrude Baker had formed a friendship last night. She cast him a knowing glance as she walked down the steps while Marie ushered the children through the front door.

The Reverend frowned. "Mrs. Baker, I wasn't informed you were living out here."

Gertrude grinned while nodding his way. "Mr. Stafford hired me. He completely understands how some folks might misconstrue Miss Hall and the children staying in his home while he builds Mr. Wagner's new house." She then waved a hand toward the staked-out ground on the other side of the bridge. "Marie and the children attempted to live in the cabin, but it wasn't nearly large enough. Mr. Burleson decided to start from scratch, and that's when I was hired. To keep everything proper."

"Hilda, Wilma, Noreen," Gertrude continued, remaining steadfast as she addressed each of the plump women who looked no worse for wear from their trek in the back of the wagon all the way from town. "I'm glad you came to visit. Do come inside for coffee. Marie just baked a brown-sugar cake. It's fresh from the oven."

Stafford didn't intrude as Gertrude guided the women toward the steps. It was evident she knew how to handle this situation far better than he might. Besides, it allowed him to focus on Marie, who'd walked down the steps and now stood nearby. When the time came—and it would, considering the glare Verna Smith was bestowing upon her—he'd intercept the woman's wrath.

His instincts were to put an arm around Marie, but that would give Verna more ammunition, so he settled for putting himself between the two women by stepping forward. "After you, Mrs. Smith," he said with a wave of one hand.

Nose in the air, and with a huff that folks probably heard in Colorado, the old bag marched up the steps. Stafford wouldn't have minded if she tripped, but she didn't. He chanced a glance toward Marie then, who was chewing on her bottom lip. Unable to verbally offer comfort, or to let her know he wouldn't let the old woman harm her or the children, he winked and then gestured for Marie to precede him. A bashful grin formed as she bowed her head and walked into the house. He grinned, too, liking the fact he could come to her aid when needed, and followed, taking the door the Reverend was holding open when he arrived on the stoop.

Gertrude had stationed herself under the arched opening of the front parlor, directing the flow of women into the room. "Marie," the cook said. "I'll make a fresh pot of coffee while you see our guests are comfortable."

Stafford couldn't help but let his gaze relay his thoughts. Marie was literally trembling in her shoes. He tossed caution to the wind and laid a hand on her shoulder while holding his disapproving glare on Gertrude.

He felt the breath Marie inhaled and squeezed her shoulder as her stance stiffened. "Of course," she said.

There wasn't a tremble in Marie's tone or a stumble in her step, yet Stafford leaned toward Gertrude to harshly inquire, "What are doing? Throwing her to the wolves?"

"No," the woman hissed back. "She'll have to learn how to handle them sooner or later, and I'd say, the sooner the better."

Stafford's gaze followed hers to where Verna's cold stare was still focused on Marie. He held in the desire to shake a shudder off his shoulders and asked himself how he'd ended up in the middle of this. A house full of women, a preacher who was ready to damn his soul and a nurse-maid who mattered more to him than she should.

There were no signs of the children, and as-suming Marie had sent them upstairs as soon as they'd entered the house, Stafford emptied his heavy lungs and walked into the parlor. An after-thought had him removing his hat and setting it on a table near the doorway. Then he crossed the room to where Marie was pulling an additional chair to the edge of the sofa. Thelma (or was it Wilma?) along with Noreen filled the sofa, so the third one, Hilda—she was Doctor Kramer's wife, he recognized that now—needed the chair.

The Reverend and Verna took the end chairs flanking the table. Stafford made his way to the stone fireplace and leaned a hand on the mantel he'd carved himself. There was a vase of flow-ers sitting upon it—an addition that hadn't been there before.

"You certainly have a lovely home, Mr. Bur-leson," Hilda Kramer said.

"Thank you, Mrs. Kramer," he said. Then recalling their reason for visiting, he added, "Mick's will be just as large, once it's completed. Plenty of room for all of the children."

The tension in the room grew noticeably thicker, and he couldn't help but glance over to see how that was affecting Marie. She'd pulled out the piano bench, but hadn't sat yet, as if unsure what to do. So was he. The longing to step closer, just to offer his support, was hard to contain.

After clearing his throat, the Reverend said, "We are glad to see Mrs. Baker lives here, but that's not the only reason we are here, Mr. Burleson."

Stafford gave a single nod, though he had no idea what the other issues truly were. The first one hadn't been an issue to him, either, and in his mind, it shouldn't be to anyone else.

"Miss Hall has no claim to the Meeker children," Verna Smith spouted. "They should not be here at all." Waving a hand toward the three other women, she continued, "Mrs. Kramer, Mrs. Johansson, and Mrs. Waters have all agreed to take the children in."

Marie's legs would no longer hold her up and she collapsed onto the padded bench behind her. This was just as it had been in Chicago, people coming to take the children away. It was all she could do to breathe, yet at the same time, a fierce determination arose inside her. She'd fought then, and she'd fight now.

"The children," Stafford said as sternly as she'd ever heard him, "do not need any one to take them in. They have a home right here."

"But they do, Mr. Burleson," Mrs. Smith insisted with a nasty sneer. "They do not belong to you, either."

Marie had finally found her wits, now she had to make her voice work. "I—" She coughed slightly to chase away the trembling of her vocal chords. "I have an affidavit from the Meekers' solicitor in Chicago, stating I have permission to oversee the children's journey to be joined with their cousin."

The glare from Verna Smith's beady black eyes stung as sharply as any nasty hornet could have. "Mr. Wagner isn't here," the woman said. "And since you are no longer journeying, your affidavit is no longer valid." Smoothing her black skirt over her knees as she sat stiffer in the chair, she demanded, "It is now the community's duty to see to the children's welfare. Call the children so these women can choose the ones they want."

A scuffling sound came from the staircase behind her at the same time a ball of fury ignited in Marie's stomach. "I will not," she exclaimed, coming to her feet. "Those children will not leave this house, or my care."

Verna Smith stood and placed both hands on her hips. Glaring down her elongated nose, she proclaimed, "You are little more than a child yourself, and don't have anything to say in this situation. It's out of your hands."

Stafford had moved forward to stand beside her, and Marie noted the way his nostrils flared. His anger shouldn't please her, but in this situation, it did. He was an ally, and she couldn't help but look to him for support.

"I," he said directly to Mrs. Smith, "have legal authority to oversee any dealings concerning Mick Wagner's property in his absence. In this situation, that includes the children, and I say they aren't going anywhere."

Chapter Twelve

The battle back in Chicago had been a difficult one, but looking back, it had been a simple task compared to the one Mrs. Smith was merciless in creating. Marie had attempted to make the woman, as well as the others, see how uprooting the children yet again would be sinful, but that had backfired. Verna Smith had insisted what was happening—the children living at Stafford's—was sinful. Corrupt, she'd called it, and immoral. Marie had insisted Stafford had been nothing but a perfect gentleman during their stay, but that hadn't helped. Nor had Gertrude's offering of cake and coffee stopped the other woman from spouting accusations.

Relentless, that's what Mrs. Smith was. Marie was just as determined to keep the children, but the woman's accusations, how she kept insinuating there were less than proper activities happening—Marie would have had to have been

blind and deaf not to understand exactly what
the woman was alleging—were draining. She
was close to tears. Not because of the woman's
fabrications, but because she'd never truly feared
losing the children before. Not like this.

Stafford had turned uncommonly quiet, and
that, too, hurt. Marie didn't expect him to completely deny everything the woman said—for
they had kissed—but she couldn't fathom why
he let the woman prattle on.

The others were quiet, too. The three women
were drinking their coffee, having already devoured the cake, and the Reverend had found a
particular spot on the floor he kept his gaze on.
Even Gertrude remained silent.

Marie, though, wasn't about to back down.
"You can spread all the rumors you want, it's
obvious nothing will stop you, but know nothing will stop me from keeping those children
together." She'd never directly challenged someone, and doing so had her insides shaking.
"Now," she continued, willing herself to sound
calm, "if you really believe I've done something
illegal, I suggest you request a lawman to investigate the situation. I'll gladly share how you
held the letter I mailed Mr. Wagner for weeks,
as well as how you read it and resealed it, hoping no one would notice."

Verna Smith turned as red as a freshly shined

apple, and Marie flinched, half expecting the woman to take a swing at her.

Stafford stepped between the two of them. "I completely agree with that suggestion," he said. "Find the territory marshal, Mrs. Smith, and have him investigate who has rights to the Meeker children." Stafford turned to the other women. "If you ladies are finished with your coffee and cake, I'll show you to the door."

The three women jumped to their feet, as did the Reverend. "Yes, yes," the man said. "I do believe it is time for us to leave." He nodded accordingly. "Thank you for the coffee and cake. It was very delicious, and I hope to see all of you in church on Sunday."

"We'll be there," Gertrude replied, eagerly waving a hand toward the door.

Marie hadn't moved. Neither had Mrs. Smith. They were still in a stare down, though they both had leaned slightly, to see around Stafford's broad shoulders.

"This isn't over," Mrs. Smith hissed.

"It most certainly is not," Marie answered. Now that Stafford had intervened, proved he was on her side, the fight inside her had increased. She was ready to go in fists flying, as she had in the backyard of the orphanage when the kids teased her for being returned twice. A returnee they'd called her. Stepping up beside

Stafford, she leveled a hate-filled glare at the other woman. "No one will separate those children. Especially not some crotchety old woman who does nothing but spread lies."

"Why you little—"

"Mrs. Smith!" the Reverend interrupted.

Stafford had grabbed Marie by the waist and was towing her backward. She struggled against his hold, mainly to hold her glare on the other woman. "Do you hear me, Mrs. Smith?"

"She hears you all right," Stafford said. "So does everyone else."

Marie shoved at his shoulder, attempting to see around it as the Reverend led Mrs. Smith from the room by one arm.

"Calm down," Stafford said.

Marie glanced up, barely able to see past the fury inside her. "What are you grinning about?" she asked. "This is not a laughing matter."

"I know that." He let go of her waist and took hold of both shoulders. "Stay here while I go see to our guests' departure."

"Guests," she huffed, trying to ignore the tingling at her waist and now her shoulders where the heat of his hands had her blood pooling. "If those are guests, I'd hate to see what intruders look like."

He grinned again, which only made her insides flip. "Just stay here."

Marie spun around, no longer able to fight the sensations looking upon him created. Focusing on the piano, she took several deep breaths, but it didn't help. Rage pounded in her blood at Mrs. Smith's accusations, and a different type of frenzy had her skin throbbing where Stafford's hands had been. When it was apparent she was too upset to stand still, she paced up and down. The desire to march outside and grab Mrs. Smith by her coiled black hair held strong, yet she knew she couldn't do that. This wasn't the orphanage, and even if it was, fighting had never solved anything. She'd been known as a returnee until she'd left the orphanage for Miss Wentworth's boarding school. There she'd put all her focus into becoming what someone would want. The best nursemaid ever. She'd become that, and no old biddy was going to take her children away from her.

The pent-up energy had her hands shaking as Marie began to gather the cups and plates left on the table.

"I'll do that," Gertrude said, bustling into the room. "The mood you're in, you'll break every one of them."

She was right. Her inability to channel the frustration inside her had the china clattering in her hands. Marie set the things she'd gathered back on the table. "I'm not leaving, and neither are the children."

"Of course you aren't," Gertrude said. She chuckled then. "I knew you had it in you, but I didn't expect it to come out so fiery."

"What are you talking about?"

"You silenced the room when you started in on how distressing separating the children would be after all they've been through."

Marie couldn't remember exactly what she'd said, but she knew that was right. "It would be, and I will not let it happen."

Gertrude held up one hand. "I know that, and I agree with you." She skirted around the table and took Marie's arm. "Go outside. Hoe the garden, get rid of all those bad things inside, then you'll be able to think straight."

Marie wanted to say she didn't know how to hoe the garden, but it really didn't matter. A few moments alone might help. Mrs. Smith had been so vehement, far worse than anyone she'd encountered in Chicago.

"I'll see to the children," Gertrude said. "Go."

Once outside, Marie made her way across the backyard to the fenced-in garden. A hoe was balanced against the gate, from when Gertrude had inspected the area. The woman had been overjoyed by the garden, and Marie had once again realized her lack of knowledge when it came to

managing a household. Her abilities to manage
children had been sorely tested, too, ever since
Emma Lou and John Meeker had died. As she
picked up the hoe, she wondered again if she'd
been wrong in bringing the children west. What
if the future turned out to be as complicated and
difficult as the past few months had been? Could
she handle it? Would everyone have been better
off if she'd let the children go with the families
in Chicago?

Entering the garden, she began turning the
soil with the hoe. No, they wouldn't have been
better off. She'd seen kids separated from their
siblings, heard them cry themselves to sleep at
night. Maybe she was the part that didn't fit in.
Mrs. Smith seemed to be the most disturbed
by her, and the fact she was living at Stafford's
house.

Anger flared in her stomach again, followed
by a touch of shame. If Stafford hadn't stopped
her, she might have attacked the woman. It had
been years since she'd resorted to such acts.

"Have you ever hoed a garden before?"

Marie spun around, and the pitching of her
stomach had her planting the sharp edge of the
tool in the ground. She was mad at him, too.

"No," she snapped.

"It shows." Stafford pushed open the gate.
"You just dug up a row of potatoes."

"That wasn't a row," she explained. "They were little hills."

"That's how you plant potatoes. In mounds."

An overwhelming hollowness filled her. "Well, I guess that proves it, doesn't it?" She released the hoe handle, letting the tool fall to the ground. "I don't belong here."

"In the garden?" he asked, picking up the hoe and carrying it to the fence.

"Yes. No." She walked to the gate. Not belonging wasn't new, she'd felt it most of her life. Living with the Meekers, before Emma Lou and her husband had died, had been the first time she truly felt she belonged somewhere—an integral part of a family—but none of this should ever have been based on what *she* wanted. Turning, her gaze went from Stafford's house, to the trees lining the creek that wound around the backyard and the garden. She couldn't see the barns or Mick's place from here, but really didn't need to. Sighing, she said, "Here in general."

"Well, you can't leave now." Stafford shut the gate and hooked a wire around the pole next to it.

She pulled her eyes away before he turned, not wanting to be caught staring. He was so tall and broad and handsome, and she'd truly wanted him to stand up for her with Mrs. Smith. Another reason she shouldn't be here. "Yes, I can. I can

leave whenever I want." It was a lie. She didn't
have enough money to get back to Chicago.

"And let Mrs. Smith win?"

Fury bubbled inside her all over again. "As if
you'd care. You didn't even try to stop her from
spouting lies."

He lifted a brow. Just one, and along with his
slanted grin, it made her insides flip.

"I didn't have to," he said. "You were doing
a good job of it yourself. Putting Verna in her
place. If I'd stepped in, she wouldn't have understood just who she was going up against."

Marie didn't completely understand what he
meant, and didn't take the time to try. She already knew why he hadn't stopped the other
woman. "You never wanted us here."

"Maybe not in the beginning." He lifted a
hand and softly ran a knuckle over her left cheek-
bone. The touch was as soft as a feather and had
her holding her breath. "But I do now."

Her eyes smarted. "You do?"

"Yes, I do. And I was very proud of you. The
way you stood up to her. The way you stood up
for the children. She now knows you aren't afraid
of her, and that you won't back down. That she
may have just met her match."

Warmth was pooling in her stomach, spread-
ing through her veins. Not sure what was hap-

pening, she shook her head. "Y-you were proud of me?"

"Very."

His whisper locked the air in her lungs. A transformation was taking place. Not just inside her, but between them. She'd sensed it before, both times he'd kissed her, but hadn't explored it or tried to understand why. This time she would. Had to. Stafford had to like her in order to be proud of her. Didn't he? "Why? Why would you be proud of me?"

Stafford had never fought the things he was fighting right now, but a piece of that battle included pulling her against him, kissing her. The confusion on her face mirrored his own. "How could I not be proud of you?" he asked, voicing his own bewilderment. "From the moment I met you, you've been full of determination. Thinking of no one but the children. You've taken on things unimaginable to others. Bringing the kids out here, a place completely foreign to you." As he spoke, something inside him, as foreign as the ranch was to her, was opening. He shook his head at the disbelief he couldn't quite grasp. "Living in the cabin, learning how to cook. Hiring Mrs. Baker. You haven't let anything stop you."

"I haven't had a choice."

"That's where you're wrong, Marie. You could

have walked away. The day the Meekers died, you could have walked away."

"No," she said softly. "I couldn't. The children needed me. They didn't have anyone else."

At that moment it dawned on him, something he'd never expected to happen. He'd fallen in love with her. Stafford took a step back, needing a moment to process that. His first instinct was to deny it. She'd irritated him, more than once, yet even then, she'd been endearing, and he'd kept coming back for more. In the past, when someone annoyed him, he'd simply stayed clear of them. That hadn't been possible this time. Even that first day, he'd been ready to go back for more. Had been thrilled by the idea of goading her by taking a bath, getting a shave, having his hair cut.

"That's not completely true."

Her whisper had him pulling his gaze off the fencepost he'd used as a focal point while examining his internal revelations. The tear on her cheek had more things coming to the surface inside him. He reached up and gently wiped it away. "What's not true?"

"The children didn't need me." She sniffed and wiped at her nose with the back of her hand. "Not as much as I needed them. I'd never had a family before, and I wasn't ready to give it up." She shook her head. "That was completely selfish."

Stafford framed her face, combing his fingers into her hair as he lifted her face to look at him. The tears pooled in the bottom of her luminescent eyes, her puckered brows, her sad frown, all made her more endearing. He had to pinch his lips together to keep from voicing a question he'd never planned on asking any woman ever again. When she blinked, and a tear dropped off her long lashes, he bowed his head and pressed his lips to hers.

Her tiny gasp, barely noticeable, was rewarding, and he tilted her head to move his mouth over hers, using his tongue to encourage her lips to part. Even as her sweetness filled him, as her tongue gently met with his, Stafford kept telling himself he couldn't ask her to marry him. The idea, though, continued to grow, as did the strength of his kiss. She completed him in a way he'd never known possible. Not just with passion, but with inspiration, showing him a future he'd never imagined before.

She grasped the shirt at his waist, and Stafford tugged her closer, pulling her graceful curves against him. This, the connection, the bonding, was exactly what he needed. He was no different from her. From the time he'd left home, he'd been searching for one thing, fearing one thing.

As much as he'd denied it, he, too, was afraid of being alone.

That's why he'd partnered up with Mick.

Mick.

Stafford backed out of the kiss, slowly, because he really didn't want to. Ultimately, knowing he had to, he pulled away and took a step back. "I—uh—I think we need to go to town."

"Town?" she asked with bewilderment.

"Yes, town. Ralph Peterson, he's the banker, but he's also the closest thing we have to a lawyer in these parts." His mind was miles ahead, or days, leastwise. Mick might not be home until next spring, and living with Marie all those months, feeling the way he did right now, would be impossible.

"What do we need a lawyer for?"

Stafford slid his hand to the middle of her back to guide her toward the house. "Because," he said, once they started walking. "We need to find out exactly what rights we both have concerning the children. Mick may not be back until spring, and we can't have Verna Smith breathing down our necks that entire time."

A plan was forming, yet he needed time for it to settle. Or maybe he needed time to justify it. Mick hadn't ordered her, so it wasn't as though he was taking her away from his friend. The children were Mick's, but if he was responsible for them until Mick's return, that meant he had to do whatever was in his power to keep them safe, which meant preventing Verna Smith from convincing the authorities to pass them out like a litter of puppies. If that meant marrying Marie so she and the children remained right here until Mick returned, so be it. And if that wasn't his only reason, then that was his business.

"Stafford, I—"

"Go get your paperwork," he said. His rationalizing wasn't working as well as he wanted it to. A hard lump had formed in his stomach, but still, he said, "I'll go get the wagon."

Marie was balancing somewhere between a dream and reality, thanks to Stafford's kiss. Her thoughts were still lingering in a wonderfully misty place, making anything he said incomprehensible. Going to town, where they could very possibly encounter Mrs. Smith, made absolutely no sense.

Stafford patted her back before he turned and jogged around the house. Jogged. Why would he be in such a hurry to go to town? She'd just told him things that should have left her completely vulnerable, yet she didn't feel that way. His kiss had made her feel wanted in a way she'd never imagined. His other kisses hadn't done that. Maybe because then—when he'd kissed her before—she hadn't understood other things.

Such as the fact she liked Stafford. Really, really, liked him. In a way that made her heart beat faster, and recalling he'd said he did want her here—all of them, her and the children—still had her head in the clouds. He hadn't said he liked her, but he was proud of her.

She drew in a deep breath and climbed the back porch steps. It was silly—wrong even—the way she wanted Stafford to care about her, to like her. Her focus should be on the children. Yet what she'd told him was the truth. She'd been using the children since the beginning. Her true fear had been being returned again. This time it would have been to Miss Wentworth's instead of the orphanage, but a return, nonetheless. Now, however, she couldn't return to Miss Wentworth's school. Not after kissing Stafford.

Sounds drew her down the hall, and she took a moment to find a smile to plant on her face before she turned the corner to step into the kitchen. Charlotte and Beatrice rushed forward, wrapping their arms around her waist.

"You sure told that Mrs. Smith," Terrance said, stepping up behind the girls.

Marie grimaced. "That was not something you should have been listening to."

"I made the rest of the kids go up to the window room," he said, as if that justified his actions.

Since she had her own mistakes to live with, Marie chose not to chastise him. "There's nothing to worry about." She lifted her gaze to include Gertrude. "Stafford and I are going to town." A thrill shot through her, which she tried to ignore.

Gertrude nodded. "Don't fret about anything here, we'll be fine." Her gaze roamed over Marie from head to toe. "Children, clean up the table. I'll be back in a moment." Curling a finger, she added, "Come with me."

Marie planted a kiss on several foreheads before she followed the other woman up the stairway. Gertrude hadn't been shy about voicing her opinion, and wouldn't be now. Listening was Marie's only choice, so she braced herself for what was to come.

Once in the other woman's bedroom, Gertrude lifted a lid off a rounded trunk she'd brought with her from town. After setting several things on the floor, she said, "Here it is." With a flip of her wrist, she unfolded a dress.

It was a soft shade of orange—peach, really— with white that formed a tiny plaid pattern. A row of pearl buttons went from the waist to the lace collar. "That's very pretty," Marie said.

Gertrude turned the gown around. "There's barely a wrinkle. Seersucker is like that. Doesn't wrinkle, and wears well, along with being cool. I made this when George and I were first married and I was a bit thinner." The woman laughed. "That was years ago, and I kept this dress all these years just to treasure the memories."

"It is a treasure," Marie agreed.

"And ready to be worn again." Gertrude held the dress in front of Marie. "I'm sure it will fit you."

"Me?"

"Yes, you." Checking the length by leaning over, Gertrude continued, "You can't be going to town, meeting the banker, dressed in a uniform." Rising her head, she asked, "That's who you're meeting, isn't it?"

Marie nodded.

"Thought so. Ralph Peterson and his wife are good people. You'll like them, and they'll help you." Without pausing, she laid the dress on the bed. "Take off that uniform, and be sure to wear your new hat."

That was how Marie ended up wearing the lovely gown and the new hat Stafford had bought for her. Sitting next to him on the wagon's bouncing bench reminded her of the trip from Huron and all that had happened since. Life-changing things, and despite how challenging they may have been, she still didn't want to go back to Chicago. Not just because she didn't want to start over again, but because she wanted to stay here.

Stafford seemed as lost in his thoughts as she was, and Marie didn't mind the silence. He did, however, reach over and fold his fingers around hers. Her heart flipped in her chest, but there wasn't a single part of her that wanted to pull her hand away. They stayed that way until Merryville appeared on the horizon. During the trip she came to a conclusion. She was more than a nursemaid here. Something she'd never imagined, and she wanted that. Wanted to be more.

He gave her hand a squeeze before letting it loose. "There's nothing to worry about," he said. "Ralph Peterson's a good man. His wife's nice, too. You'll like her."

"Gertrude said as much," Marie answered, but had to admit, "I'm still not sure what we hope to accomplish by speaking with Mr. Peterson." The banker in Chicago had been no help at all. Then again, she hadn't had Stafford at her side. That filled her with a sense of safety she'd never known.

His answer, "A solution we can all live with," did create more questions, though.

Stafford was full of questions himself, and more than a little frustrated he couldn't come up with satisfying answers. The ride to town had given him plenty of time to contemplate his actions, and ultimately, he found himself thinking of his brother. Taking Marie away from Mick was relatively close to how Sterling had taken Francine away from him, and deep down, Stafford doubted that was something he could live with.

They arrived at the bank just as Ralph was exiting the building, and he didn't seem surprised to see them. With a nod, Ralph said, "I'd appreciate a ride home."

Stafford scooted closer to the edge, giving Marie more space as Ralph climbed onto the seat beside her.

"Hello. Miss Hall, I believe it is?" Ralph extended a hand once he'd sat.

"Hello, Mr. Peterson," she greeted. "It's nice to meet you."

"Please call me Ralph." Leaning forward, to look around Marie, he explained, "Hilda Kramer was over to see Becca this afternoon. Right after returning from your place, I believe."

Stafford nodded, already assuming that word of what had taken place at the house would spread like typhoid fever.

"I told Becca to expect company for supper," the banker continued. "She'll be especially glad that includes you, Miss Hall."

"Thank you, but we wouldn't want to intrude," Marie answered.

"It's no intrusion," he said. "Stafford's like family."

Stafford frowned at that, yet inside he smiled. He hadn't considered just how deeply he'd already planted himself in his life here, but considering everything else he'd unearthed in himself, he could admit to liking it.

Becca was not only welcoming, she insisted everyone eat before discussing business, and watching how Marie so readily offered assistance, and provided it, had pride once again glowing inside Stafford. The two women seemed to form an immediate friendship, the way they giggled, and that, too, delighted Stafford. Marie had been alone too long. It was time for her to know what it felt like to really belong. Not just with a family but a community.

The meal was tasty, though he hardly noticed what it was. Sitting next to Marie stole his attention. Watching her interact with the Petersons and include the Peterson children in the conversation might have some believing her nursemaid skills were top-notch, but he was thinking how perfect a wife and mother she would be.

He and Ralph stayed at the dining room table, talking about the sawmill, the bank and other topics that didn't relate to his visit while the women cleared the table. Once the kitchen chores had been seen to, both Marie and Becca returned.

"Shall we go into the parlor?" Ralph suggested. "We'll be more comfortable there."

Stafford rested a hand on Marie's back as they followed their hosts into the other room. Becca suggested he and Marie sit on the sofa, while she and Ralph took seats in the nearby chairs.

"I hope you don't mind if I join you," Becca said. "I suggested it, because sometimes a woman needs another woman's support."

Marie looked toward him, and Stafford could see that she wanted the other woman to stay, but she also wanted his approval.

"No, we don't mind," he answered.

"I often seek Becca's advice," Ralph said, unfolding the papers Stafford had given him before supper. He shuffled the sheets, briefly glancing at each one. "I'm not a lawyer, I want to emphasize that, but I've read many legal documents, and these seem completely genuine. Before I explain my understanding of them, tell me what's happening."

This time it was Stafford who waited for Marie to nod. He'd let her explain things if she wanted to. Her grin was a bit unsure as she gave her permission to go ahead.

He made the story brief, starting with the deaths of the children's parents and ending with

Mrs. Smith's departure, promising to have the law investigate who had rights to the children.

Ralph remained silent, and in those heavy moments, Stafford leaned back and stretched an arm along the top of the sofa back trying to hide how his nerves were ticking. Marie's were, too, judging by the way she was fiddling with the buttons near the collar of her dress. He patted her far shoulder while turning his gaze back to the banker.

"From what I've read," Ralph said, "Mrs. Smith is right as far as Miss Hall is concerned. This paper states she has permission to oversee the children during their travels west. Once she reached Mick's—and your—property, all rights were relinquished."

"But Mr. Wagner isn't there," Marie said.

"I know, but these other papers, Stafford's papers, give Stafford permission to manage all of Mick's affairs in his absence. In this instance, that would include the children." Ralph turned toward him. "Since those kids arrived, they've been Stafford's responsibility."

It's what he'd expected. The news didn't bother him at all; however, Marie was a different story. She was blinking and nibbling on her bottom lip, and refusing to glance his way.

Ralph, noticing her reaction no doubt, offered,

"Of course you could hire Miss Hall to continue being the children's nursemaid."

Stafford nodded, but hiring her was not something he wanted to do. It was too shallow. "What if I adopted the children?"

Marie's gasp couldn't be missed. His arm was still stretched along the sofa behind her and he squeezed her shoulder again as she turned to look up at him with bewilderment in her eyes.

"You can't," Ralph said. "No more than you could buy out Mick's half of the ranch without his permission. If he was deceased, that would be one thing, but he's not, he's just out of town."

Stafford was disappointed, even though he'd expected as much. "I just thought that would put an end to Mrs. Smith," he said, trying to hide his regret. He wanted to marry Marie, was no longer kidding himself that he didn't. Mick didn't know her and wasn't in love with her, so it wasn't really as if Stafford was stealing her from his best friend.

"There really isn't anything Mrs. Smith can do," Ralph said. "The Meeker children are your responsibility until Mick arrives. With Miss Hall hired as their nursemaid and Mrs. Baker hired as your cook or housekeeper, there isn't anything illegal happening."

"Or unethical," Becca said. "I'll see the community understands that."

Stafford nodded and voiced his thanks. Becca would see word was spread and people would listen to her, but that wouldn't solve his dilemma.

Chapter Thirteen

The stars seemed almost close enough to touch. Their shining brilliance, along with the full moon, gave plenty of light for the horses to find their way home, the same two that had pulled the wagon from Huron.

Marie emptied her lungs. The ride home was as quiet as the ride to Merryville had been, but she wasn't as content with it as she'd been earlier. Ralph and Becca Peterson were friendly and kind people. She did wonder about Mr. Peterson's long sideburns. Black and bushy, they came way down to his chin. She much preferred Stafford's clean-shaven face, which was such a silly thing to be thinking about right now. Truth was, she was trying to hold her silence and forcing her mind to think of anything but the suggestion Stafford had made—that of adopting the children.

He hadn't agreed to hire her to continue on

as their nursemaid, either, and she couldn't help but wonder if he was considering adoption so her services would no longer be needed. That wasn't really probable. He didn't need to adopt the children to send her back to Chicago.

She sighed again, shifted her weight on the hard seat and once more tried counting stars. The sheer number of them made that impossible.

"What are you trying so hard not to say?"

Wondering if she'd heard a hint of humor in his tone, Marie turned slowly, hoping to sneak a peek before coming eye to eye. There was more than enough light to see his slanted grin, and when he reached over and took her hand in one of his, her heart jumped.

"Well?" he asked.

"I was just wondering why you wanted to adopt the children."

"Like I said, to put a stop to Mrs. Smith."

Even though she didn't completely believe him, she nodded. "Becca says Mrs. Smith sticks her nose in everyone's business. She said Mrs. Smith will soon find something else to worry about. That's what usually happens."

"I hope so," he answered.

"You sound like you don't believe it."

He shrugged. "Do you?"

"I don't know," she answered.

A thoughtful silence settled between the two

of them. Nothing more than the steady clop of the horses trudging onward echoed through the night until Stafford said, "Look, a shooting star."

She glanced up, but saw little more than a fading streak of light. When he pulled on the reins, she asked, "Why are we stopping?"

"So you can make a wish."

She shook her head. "I didn't really see it."

His smile rose slowly as he laid the reins over his thigh and twisted slightly so they were angled toward each other. "I did, and I'm giving you my wish."

He wasn't giving her anything tangible, so why did she feel as if he was? "I don't think it works that way."

"Why not?"

"I don't know, it just—"

"Close your eyes and make a wish, Marie."

His breath brushed her lips as he said her name. An inexplicable and blissful sensation rushed over her. She closed her eyes and wished he'd kiss her.

"Did you make a wish?"

She nodded, just barely, trying to hold her lips perfectly still. His breath was mingling with hers, making the bliss filling her more intense and creating a pool of warmth deep in her belly.

"Have you ever had a wish come true?"

His lips had brushed hers as he spoke, leaving

her unable to answer. Her mind however, was wishing beyond eternity her wish would come true. With the dozen other things she should be thinking about, should be wishing for, it seemed trite, but it was the one thing she wanted above all else at that moment.

The next second, when his mouth covered hers, his hands slid around her waist, and she'd never known such completion. That's what being in his arms was like. As if she miraculously grew into the person she'd been born to be. When his hold pulled her closer she went willingly. The kiss was so tender and precious her hands went to the sides of his face. Smooth skin filled her palms and she held on, not wanting him to ever move.

Other than to keep kissing her. That was her wish, that Stafford would never stop kissing her.

He shifted slightly, pulling her closer yet and moving his mouth across hers, licking her lips with the tip of his tongue. It wasn't a gasp, but more of a pleasure-filled sigh that made her lips part, and when his tongue entered her mouth she grasped his face more firmly. An inner desire took over, had her swirling her tongue with his until she grew dizzy and remarkably clear-headed at the same time. Her focus had crystallized. Stafford. He filled every single thought and sensation.

They kissed until her lungs could no longer hold air. He pulled his lips from hers and kissed the side of her face, her eyelids and brows, while she struggled for a full breath. The air refueled her, and as if he sensed the exact moment it happened, his lips returned to hers.

This happened several times, each kiss more perfect than the last. She'd never felt so alive. Every part of her throbbed and tingled. Stafford's hands showed her just how sensitive some areas were. Her back, her shoulders, her sides, and as shocking as it was, her breasts. He was fondling one right now, and it was the most amazing thing. Half of her said she shouldn't let him do that, the other half was disappointed he wasn't caressing the other one the same way. His whispers were addictive, too. Even while kissing her he kept saying how beautiful she was, how soft and that she smelled wonderful. No one had ever said such things to her, and they must be going to her head for she'd certainly never felt so dizzy.

He shifted again, easing her back against the seat, and she couldn't think beyond how wonderful he made her feel. His kisses roamed down her neck, his breath hot and his lips moist. Eyes closed, fully enthralled by the sensations, she leaned her head back. His mouth went lower, licking the skin exposed by the neckline of Gertrude's seersucker dress.

Her breasts were throbbing now, and her back arched, straining her upward toward him. Stafford's kisses went lower and the heat of his mouth penetrated the material of her dress and underclothes. It was wicked, but so fascinating she prayed he wouldn't stop.

To her shock, he mouthed her nipples, which had grown hard, and the sensation had a sharp effect on her lower body. Her most private region was burning with a remarkable heat that was as pleasurable as it was torturous.

"Stafford," she whispered, unsure what she should do.

He mumbled and brushed each nipple with his lips again before his kisses trailed up her neck and settled over her mouth again. When that kiss ended, she was as weak as an infant, yet full of unexpected cravings that had her catching glimpses of paradise. At least that's what she assumed the flashes were.

Images of Stafford kissing and caressing her, and laughing and loving, kept flashing behind her closed lids. Each one was like a miniature promise and she wished there were a million falling stars, so she could cast wishes and have every one of them come true.

"We need to start rolling," Stafford said, his voice husky.

Her head was resting against his chest, where

she could hear his heart thudding. That was as remarkable as kissing him. She'd never been this close to someone, almost as if they were a pair, like shoes, that belonged together. That, too, was a silly thought. She seemed to be full of them— silly thoughts—and unable to comprehend what he'd meant, she asked, "Rolling?"

"Yes," he said, kissing the top of her head. "It's late. Mrs. Baker and the children will be wondering where we are."

Almost like a clock chiming the hour something clanged inside her head. How had she forgotten the children? How had she—

"Marie." Stafford had leaned back, was now forcing her to look up at him by holding her chin with one hand.

"What?"

"I won't let anyone take you or the kids away." He leaned forward and kissed her softly, which shattered her thoughts all over again.

She was still trying to gather the pieces when the wagon started to move. He must have taken the reins, but one arm was still around her, holding her close to his side. Unable to make sense of all the things still going on inside her, all the silly notions and images still flashing, she laid her head on his shoulder. She'd be able to think again when everything slowed down.

That did finally happen. In an almost vicious

way the world returned. The one where she had
six children to take care of and those children
belonged to Mick, not Stafford.

The air in her lungs turned stale, and Marie
sat up to let it out and take a new breath, which
didn't ease the emptiness rising inside her. Nothing made sense. How could she be so full one
minute and so empty the next? It was as though
someone was playing a cruel trick on her.

"We have some decisions to make," Stafford
said.

She nodded, but a short time later, when his
words sank in, she asked, "Decisions about
what?"

Stafford bit his tongue. He was jumping the
gun. One kiss, well, several, hot and rather life-
changing kisses, didn't guarantee she felt the
same way he did. He wasn't so sure he felt *that
way*. His mind was miles ahead. Or weeks ahead.
Thinking of the life he now wanted. Marriage.
A wife. A family.

Marie.

He eased his arm over her head and took the
reins in both hands. Then he flipped the leather
over the horses' backs, making the animals put
a bit more speed in their steps.

"The children," he said. "Mrs. Smith."

"Oh, yes," she said. "Mrs. Smith."

Regret sprinkled over him like a mist of

spring rain. Inside, where he was still hot and craving her the way he'd never craved anything, he'd wanted her to understand he was speaking about them. Him and her. Not the children. And not some old nosey-nosed merchant.

A transformation had happened inside him. Or, now that his mind was open, lending clarity to his thoughts and emotions, maybe it wasn't so much of a transformation as a revelation of just how deeply he'd been lying to himself. He did want all he'd had as a child. Not just the house.

Stafford twisted his lips, trying to hold back a grin. The image of her lily-white backside still shot into his mind on a regular basis, and it never failed to affect him.

It might be easier, everything that was happening, if she wasn't living in his house. Then he could separate himself, take the time to figure out if he really was in love with her or simply pondering a future that was different from what he'd set up for himself. As it was, seeing her every day, watching her take care of the children and now his home, he couldn't imagine a future that didn't include her.

A coil of heat let loose inside him, and he took the reins in one hand again, placing the other around her shoulders to pull her back against his side. That's where she belonged. Nothing had felt this right in a very long time.

The trepidation in her eyes had him wanting to slay dragons for her. There were no dragons in this part of the country, or anywhere else in the world, just nosy old women. "Don't worry about Mrs. Smith," he said, kissing the top of her head. "She's just an old busybody."

Unease still filled her gaze. "Gertrude says Mrs. Smith may have had something to do with the deaths of her first two husbands."

"I've heard the rumors," he said, rubbing his hand up and down her upper arm. Marie's beauty had enticed him since the beginning. The blue dresses she normally wore gave a hint of the curves beneath, but the peach one she had on today molded to her form perfectly. Pride had filled him as he'd watched her interact with Ralph's wife, Becca. He was smart enough to know it wasn't just the dress, and vain enough to know he wanted to claim what was beneath that dress for himself.

"You don't believe it?"

"The rumors?" he asked, getting his mind back on the right track.

"Yes. That Mrs. Smith killed her husbands."

Stafford took time to ponder what he did believe. He'd never jumped to conclusions about people in the past, had just let things that didn't concern him roll off his back. It wasn't quite so easy this time. Mrs. Smith's actions might truly be endangering things he held dear. Yet, when it came to protecting those people he considered his own, he needed to think with a clear head so he didn't put them in more danger.

"Well," he finally said, grasping for the correct response. "I can't say that whether I believe them or not has much bearing."

"What do you mean?"

"I'm not the law. I'm not a judge and jury. But—" He gave her a gentle squeeze to emphasize his answer. "I won't let her hurt you or the children. I guarantee that."

Her smile was tender and the way she bowed her head bashful. He kissed the top of her head again. The action offered little release, considering the desire he had to ravish that delectable body, lily-white backside and all.

"Why?"

"Why?" he repeated her question, astounded she didn't know. "Because you're mi—" His mind, clear enough to understand most things caught him in time. "My responsibility."

"Because you're Mick Wagner's partner." It wasn't a question, just a statement that held weight with the way she said it.

That was the one thing he hadn't quite worked through. Mick hadn't ordered her as a bride, had no real claim on her, but a small portion of Stafford still held on to an uneasy feeling he was stealing her out from beneath his partner. Having been on the end of such an event once made his behavior hard to justify.

"Yeah," he answered, struggling to take a breath.

They traveled the remaining miles in silence. The ranch was dark and quiet upon their arrival, everyone already settled in for the night. Stafford lifted her from the wagon and bid her a soft good-night, fighting the urge to kiss her one last time.

Her responding good-night was just as soft, just as lonesome sounding. Stafford waited until she entered the house before leading the horses toward the barn. He had decisions to make, all right. Figuring out if he could live with them was the hardest part. Either way, life was going to be hellish. Having her as his wife was what he wanted, but doing that to Mick…the air lodged in his lungs. There were things a man couldn't live with, and betraying his best friend was one of them.

Marie watched Stafford through the window of the front door. Something had happened on the way home. Not just the incredible kisses and caresses that left a deep longing inside her. Actually, that longing had grown bittersweet and stronger. Stafford's later silence had chilled her as poignantly as his embrace had warmed her.

She had some serious thinking to do, and afraid of encountering anyone, especially Gertrude who'd want to know what had happened in town, Marie tiptoed away from the door and, as stealthily as possible, made her way up the stairs and into her room.

There, she plopped onto the bed. She'd used the ruse she was Mick Wagner's mail-order bride, but only because of the children. She'd never wanted marriage. Yes, she had wanted to be part of a family, but an outside part was all she'd hoped for. A nursemaid. That's what she was. Although she'd once thought differently, she now knew she wasn't the best nursemaid on Earth. Her behavior of late proved that. Her mind had grown so fickle that the children were rarely her first thought.

The environment in which they now lived had altered her priorities. Academics and manners—the two subjects Miss Wentworth's training had focused on—had been overtaken by more basic needs. She still took care of the children's studies and behavior, but ensuring they had food and shelter, and that they were safe, had overridden other needs ever since leaving Chicago. None of her training had prepared her for that, and life in general hadn't prepared her for Stafford.

She'd come to think of him constantly, as well as her wants. Things she hadn't known she did want—would ever want—were wholly wrapped up with him. Becoming his bride, sharing a life with him—a life she'd caught a glimpse of tonight at the Petersons—was consuming her right now. That and being a proper family. Not just an addition to one.

Marie bent over to unfasten and remove her shoes and the borrowed dress. Besides being lovely, and as comfortable as Gertrude had claimed it to be, the dress also had a magical quality. It had made her feel pretty and self-assured. Although maybe that hadn't come from the dress, but from the way Stafford had looked at her when she was wearing it. Several times since leaving the ranch today, when his gaze settled on her, wonderful things had happened inside her. It was as if he admired her, and that allowed her to respect herself in a way she never had before. Had her wanting things for herself, too.

Wanting him.

Stepping out of the dress, she hung it on a hook in the wardrobe and inwardly laughed at herself. Respect. No self-respecting woman—nursemaid or not—would have let a man do the things she'd let Stafford do. Marie closed her eyes as her hands went to her breasts. He must think she was nothing short of a trollop. How would she ever face him tomorrow? How would she face herself? Miss Wentworth's training had dedicated an entire quarter to appropriate behavior—nursemaid conduct—and actions that should never be entertained. Though she couldn't recall what she'd done tonight being mentioned, it surely had been part of what Miss Wentworth referred to.

Moonlight filled the room so brightly that she hadn't lit a lamp, and as she stared out the window, toward the million stars she'd cast wishes upon a short time ago, she chastised herself for failing so miserably. When it came right down to it, she'd failed everyone—Miss Wentworth, Emma Lou, the children, Gertrude Baker—the way she'd hired her under false pretenses—herself, Mick Wagner and Stafford. There wasn't a single person she hadn't failed. And she had the horrible feeling it wasn't over. Mrs. Smith might still win. Especially if she learned about the kissing she and Stafford had done on the way home.

Marie pulled on her nightgown and got into bed but sleep was slow in coming, and when sunlight eventually filtered through the window Marie wondered if she had slept. Exhausted, inside and out, she climbed from the bed, dragged on one of her blue uniforms and left her room to wake the children.

Stafford wasn't in the kitchen, which didn't provide the relief it should, and he didn't join them for breakfast. Cooking was becoming second nature and she no longer relied on Gertrude's watchful eye. That didn't mean the woman wasn't as vigilant as ever.

"What happened yesterday?" Gertrude asked, as they stood side by side washing and drying dishes. "Both you and Stafford are as gray as winter skies this morning."

Marie wanted to assure Gertrude that nothing had happened, but the lie formed a lump in her throat. She shrugged and wrung out a cloth to wipe the table.

"It's a hard thing," Gertrude said, "what life does to us. One minute we're walking along just fine, and then in little more than an instant, we're tossed into a whirlwind so fierce we fear we'll never get out."

Marie paused in midswipe, letting her hand and the rag rest in the center of the table as she turned to the other woman.

Gertrude's expression was a combination of thoughtfulness and confusion. With a shrug, she lifted a stack of dry plates and carried them to the buffet cupboard. "That's what happened when George died. It took the very definition of who I was away from me." She shut the glass door and walked back to the sink. "Mrs. George

Baker. How I loved being her." With her eyes closed and a smile on her lips, she said, "It was all I ever wanted."

Marie wasn't exactly sure what caused goose bumps to stand out on her arms, empathy for Gertrude or the flashing images of herself and Stafford that were still plaguing her.

Opening her eyes, Gertrude sighed audibly. "We didn't have a lot of money, but we had a good life together."

"You still miss him very much, don't you?" Marie asked, wondering if she'd ever stop missing Stafford in the same situation. He was merely outside and she missed him.

"Not a day goes by where I don't miss him," Gertrude said. "But the pain isn't as sharp. It's still there, a dull ache, but I can live with it. Remember him now with joy instead of sorrow." She crossed the room then, laid both hands on the other end of the table. "Sometimes life pitches us into whirlwinds of good things, too. Like when you hired me."

The sincerity in the other woman's face was so real Marie had to coax up a smile, if for no reason other than to show appreciation. "I'm glad you like it here."

"I surely do." Gertrude reached across the long table and took the rag from beneath Marie's hand. "I'd gone to work for Chris Striker in order not to starve to death, but here…here I feel whole again."

Marie wanted to close her eyes, achieve the same kind of harmony Gertrude showed, but the knot in her stomach, or maybe it was in her heart, wouldn't let her.

"Enough of this," Gertrude said, tossing the rag on the counter. "Come, I want you to try on your new dress so I can make adjustments before finishing it."

"Finishing it?" Marie shook her head at being tossed from one subject to the next. "When did you start it?"

"Yesterday." Hooking her arm around Marie's elbow, Gertrude continued as they walked toward the arched doorway. "I stayed up half the night sewing so you can wear it to church tomorrow."

Chapter Fourteen

By sheer will, Stafford found ways to stay clear of the house. Odd jobs kept his hands occupied, but not his mind. That was harder to control. So were his eyes. If they weren't on the house, hoping to catch a glimpse of Marie, they were looking across the creek.

The lumber hadn't arrived yet, but there were things he could do to be ready once the order was delivered. Building Mick's house, though— a new place for Marie to live—sat badly with him. As did most everything else he thought of, in one way or another.

Pushing the air from his lungs, he dragged his gaze away from Mick's place and refused to let it wander as he planted the post-hole digger into the ground. The new enclosure was needed. He'd planned on building it this summer. Half— if not all—of the town of Merryville would survive on beef from the Dakota Cattle Company this winter and they'd need this pen to hold the animals they'd deliver on a regular basis. It was a deal Mick had made with Wayne Orson while Stafford had been south. Chris Striker's hotel was serving cuts of beef from their herd right now. The hands had delivered half a dozen head to Orson's butcher shop while Stafford had gone to Huron to fetch Marie and the children.

He'd overlooked that aspect of things. How would Striker feel about serving up Dakota Cattle Company beef while his former cook now resided at and worked for the ranch? Not that it mattered. Ultimately it was Orson selling the beef to Striker. The butcher was creating quite a thriving business for himself, and Striker wasn't his only customer.

"Company coming in."

Stafford caught the direction Red was looking and let his gaze go to the single rider stirring up dust on the long driveway.

"Time to call it a day, anyway," Shorty said. "I've got supper on the table."

Noting the sun was sinking in the western sky, Stafford nodded. The day was coming to an end, and though he'd had plenty of hours to contemplate things, he hadn't made any headway.

There was no reason he couldn't tell Shorty to save a plate for him—that he'd join them for a meal in the bunkhouse after seeing who was

approaching on the brown-and-white paint—
other than the fact he didn't want to. He used
to do that more often than not, but he'd become
accustomed to eating with Marie and the kids,
and he liked it.

"If it's someone looking for work or just pass-
ing through," Shorty said, squinting toward the
rider, "I can scrounge up another plate."

Stafford acknowledged the man's offer with a
nod as he pulled off his gloves and left Mike and
Red to carry the tools to the shed. He rounded
the barn as the rider slowed his horse to a walk.
It was a good-looking animal, well cared for, and
Stafford understood why once he noted the star
pinned to the man's leather vest.

"Stafford Burleson?"

"Yes."

"I'm Marshal Abel Crane."

Verna Smith hadn't wasted any time. Merryville didn't have a sheriff, or any other type of
lawman. Crane, the territory marshal, patrolled
the area that included most everything west of
Huron. The man must have been close by to have
arrived so quickly.

"I know we haven't met," Crane said, swing-
ing out of his saddle. "But I met your partner,
Mick, while making my rounds last winter."

"Mick said as much," Stafford said, holding

out a hand. "It's nice to meet you." He hoped he wasn't wrong in that respect.

Tall and broad shouldered, with a grip that said he was as strong as he looked, Crane let out a chuckle as they shook hands. "Yes, I'm here because of Verna Smith."

The marshal's voice was low and scratchy, the kind that probably stopped outlaws in their tracks, yet Stafford didn't miss the humor he spoke with or the grin in the man's eyes. He took that as a good sign. "How's Jenkins?" Stafford asked, referring to the past territorial marshal who'd taken a bullet while apprehending several members of a notorious gang of outlaws the previous summer.

"Good," Crane said. "He's all healed up and settled himself down in Yankton as the town's sheriff."

"I hadn't heard that." Stafford gestured for the man to bring his horse to the barn.

"Then you probably haven't heard he got himself married, either," Crane said, walking alongside him.

"Married?"

"Yep, the woman that patched him up. Guess he figured since she'd saved his life, he might as well stick with her."

Stafford joined the other man in a short laugh, even though his spine was tingling.

They entered the barn and Stafford opened a stall gate. Doug Jenkins had spent nights at the ranch several times when traveling through, and Crane would receive the same hospitality no matter who'd sent him.

Most men prefer to unsaddle their own horses, so Stafford stood back and let Crane see to his animal.

"Verna Smith caught me as I rode into town last night," Crane said while unbuckling his cinch. "And Chris Striker filled my ear while I was eating breakfast this morning."

"I assumed as much," Stafford admitted.

"So you've got yourself a half-dozen kids and a nursemaid from Chicago, and Gertrude Baker is now your cook," the man said as he flopped his saddle over the side of the stall.

"That about sums it up," Stafford said, gathering a bucket of grain for the horse.

"There's no law against irritating people," Crane said, leading the animal into the stall. "And, though some folks like to claim there is, there's no law about men and women who aren't married living in the same house."

Stafford's spine was tingling again. His expression must have given away more, too, because Crane held up a hand.

"Don't be jumping to conclusions," the marshal said. "I'm on your side. You haven't done anything illegal, and I already told Verna Smith and Striker that." He took the offered grain bucket and held it out to the paint. "I just wanted to ride out here, let you know my thoughts."

Stafford attempted to keep his assumptions from becoming apparent this time. He must have succeeded because Crane didn't bat an eye.

"I don't know what Jenkins was thinking, though."

Now, wondering when the conversation had flipped to the past marshal, Stafford frowned.

"Give me rough-riding, gun-slinging outlaws over a town full of persnickety people any day," Crane continued. "They're the dangerous ones."

Still wondering what he'd missed, Stafford gave a single nod when the marshal looked over, as if to see if he was still following the conversation. He was. Sort of.

"Town folks are like that," Crane said. "Get along about as well as a den full of rattlers and water moccasins." Shaking his head, the man added, "They'll eat each other, you know? Snakes that is."

Yep, the mention of snakes had a lily-white backside flashing before Stafford's eyes, and not even a quick shake of his head dispelled it.

"They will," Crane said. "I've seen it." Dropping the feed bucket near the barrel of grain, the marshal nodded toward the door.

Stafford waved a hand as he pushed off the opposite stall to follow the other man.

"Anyway," Crane said, once they left the barn. "I listened to what they had to say, Verna Smith and Striker." With a perplexed grin, he added, "When I told Striker no laws have been broken, he claimed Gertrude Baker stole from him."

Crane waved a hand at that, as if it held no consequence, and the action did quell the bout of ire that had sprung forth inside Stafford. She hadn't been here long, but he'd bet his last cow Gertrude had never stolen anything in her lifetime.

"I also visited Ralph Peterson at the bank, mainly because I'd told both Striker and Smith I'd investigate their complaints. From what Peterson said, especially concerning the paperwork you have in your possession, I'd say everything is about as right as rain. What do you think?"

Stafford didn't know what he thought, that was part of his problem. At least, believing what he thought was. Furthermore, his mind was still flashing images. Lily-white ones. "I'd say my thoughts are right next to yours," he said.

"Good. I'm glad that's settled."

Nothing had been settled, yet Stafford once again nodded.

Crane pointed his chin toward the bridge.

"Heard about the fire, too, but in all honesty, Mick's gonna need a bigger house."

Stafford might have responded if he hadn't picked up the sound of the front door opening. His mouth went dry at the sight of Marie standing there. He hadn't left the ranch all day, yet he'd missed her as if he'd been on the other side of the world.

"Since I've met Gertrude Baker before, I'm assuming that is Miss Hall."

Unable to tear his gaze from her, Stafford once again gave a brief nod. This time he didn't care what the other man read in his expression. Lawman or not, it was best every male for miles around understood Stafford had staked a claim. Marie was his.

Air locked itself in Marie's lungs, and even as the men approached, it wouldn't let loose. Stafford was a tall man, but the one with a badge pinned to his chest was taller yet. He had a booming voice, too, and the only thing that kept her from jumping out of her shoes upon their introduction was the way Stafford settled a hand in the small of her back.

He kept it there as he explained the marshal would be joining them for supper and spending the night. She attempted to be affable, but Stafford's penetrating gaze made it difficult. Her heart took to beating so fiercely she was afraid it might leap right out of her chest. The children were just as skittish, squirming in their seats as if their pants were on fire. Only Gertrude seemed at ease. She and the marshal carried on conversations as if the rest of them were barely there.

After the meal, however, the marshal sent a pointed stare her way. "Miss Hall," he said in that rough voice. "I do need to speak with you."

"Go into the parlor," Gertrude said, as brightly as ever. "The children will help me clean the kitchen, and afterward we can all have a piece of cobbler."

Not a single one of them made a peep, yet every child at the table turned toward Stafford. Marie couldn't blame them. She was waiting for his approval, too.

His smile was reassuring, to the children anyway. They took his permission to leave their seats, taking their plates with them. He rose and walked around the table, pulling her chair out upon arriving at her side.

"There's nothing to worry about," he said reassuringly.

She still had to swallow hard as he guided her, with his hand on her back again, out of the dining room and down the hall to the parlor. Marshal Crane followed and the solid thud of his footsteps on the wooden floor had her nerves running amok.

Stafford sat down next to her on the sofa, and Marie found she was more thankful for his nearness than she'd been for anything before in her life. But as her gaze met his, all she could think about was how they'd kissed last night. The shame—that which she'd acquired last night while convincing herself she was a trollop—was nowhere to be found. Instead, warmth spread across her stomach and lower, in the exact spot it had last night. Marriage flashed across her mind again. Marrying Stafford, not Mick Wagner.

"Miss Hall."

Marshal Crane's booming voice shattered her thoughts, and though Stafford took her hand and gave it a gentle squeeze, she accepted that marrying him wasn't an option. She had no rights to the children, no reason for being here, and the marshal could send her back to Chicago faster than a hummingbird flies.

"I just wanted to talk with you," the marshal said. "I know Mrs. Smith can be a bit frightening. I'm sure the rumors about the deaths of her husbands, both of them, have something to do with her attitude. Those events were thoroughly investigated, and Verna Smith was found completely innocent in both cases." The man glanced toward Stafford. "Privately, because it's really no one else's business, the evidence suggests both men may have taken their own lives. Verna, of course, knows that, and that, too, most likely has a bearing on her disposition. Knowing your husband would rather be dead than married to you probably isn't easy to live with."

Having never considered such a tragic thought, Marie whispered, "How dreadful. The poor woman."

"Yes," Marshal Crane responded. "It is dreadful. But it doesn't give her the right to unjustly accuse others of wrongdoing when no crimes have been committed. Neither she, nor anyone in the community of Merryville, has the authority to remove the Meeker children from Stafford's home, so rest assured the children are safe and will remain right where they are."

In view of the fact her thoughts had been more focused on herself than the children, a large lump of guilt formed in Marie's stomach. "Thank you, Marshal Crane," she said. "I've told the children as much, but it will be nice to reassure them you said the same thing."

"Go right ahead and tell them the territory marshal says they don't have anything to worry about."

His kindhearted smile suddenly made the large man seem much more approachable. "Thank you," she replied.

"Now," he said. "I'm sure Stafford has already told you this, but let me reiterate it. Mrs. Smith is, well, she's a bit crotchety. Her goal seems to be to find something people can gossip about in order to make her past not matter as much. I believe that's how most people are. They like to have others talk about them when it comes to good deeds, but don't want to be the center of attention when it comes to bad ones. I've seen it in all the towns I patrol. I'm sure before Mick arrives home she'll find something else to focus on. Something else to file a complaint about."

Marie tried to nod, but couldn't quite manage it. Mick Wagner's return was something she was not looking forward to.

"It's too bad," the marshal said. "If Verna would just realize it's not doing herself or her past any good to stir up trouble she'd be much better off. Some folks just don't understand that, though."

This time Marie was able to nod. She had firsthand knowledge of causing trouble.

"So, rest assured," Marshal Crane said. "You and the children aren't going anywhere."

Stafford's hold on her hand tightened, and she couldn't help but sigh. He and the marshal started talking about other things then. The weather, the price of cattle and other such concerns she let float in and out of her ears. An easy comfort had settled in the room, and it increased when Stafford leaned back. His fingers had laced between hers in a more relaxed way, too, and that had other thoughts springing into her mind.

What Gertrude had said earlier was making more sense. How life throws people into whirlwinds, good ones at times. It was happening to her. She'd defined herself as a nursemaid, but that had changed. Now she just had to figure out what to do about it.

"I wonder where Mrs. Baker is with that cobbler," the marshal said. "If it's anything like the meal she just cooked, I may need two helpings."

Marie's gaze went to the doorway, where the woman stood, tray in hand.

"I'm right here," Gertrude said. "But, I didn't make the meal, Marie did. She made the cobbler, too."

Marie doubted her cheeks had ever burned so hotly, not with the way Stafford was smiling down at her.

Gertrude set the tray on the table. "But trust me, Marshal, you're going to want two servings."

Squirming under such praise, Marie scooted to the edge of the sofa. "I best go see to the children."

"There's no need for that," Gertrude declared. "Weston was listening at the doorway. He's already explained that the territory marshal said there's nothing to worry about."

Everyone chuckled as Gertrude handed Stafford a plate, which meant he had to let go of Marie's hand. She formed a fist then, just to contain the warmth left behind.

"The children are eating their cobbler in the kitchen," Gertrude said. "And then they will see to Polly's needs." Handing Marie a plate, she added, "Terrance put himself in charge, as usual."

That was something else that had changed. Terrance. He'd matured lately. Instead of teasing his siblings and causing never-ending disturbances, as he had on the train and even while back in Chicago, he was now growing into a responsible young man. Actually, some of his behavior put her in mind of Stafford. Samuel was following in his brother's footsteps, as always, but this time it was encouraging. It seemed Stafford was a positive influence on all of them.

The cobbler—which had turned out remarkably well—and coffee—which she now also knew how to make—were consumed as the four of them conversed on a variety of subjects. Marie hadn't participated in many social gatherings and found it stimulating. It was very pleasant, and well, it fit her. She liked it.

Not until the clock on the mantel, the one she

enjoyed winding each day, struck the hour did Marie realize how late it was. "Excuse me," she said, once again moving to the edge of the sofa to stand. "I need to see the children to bed."

"I need to stretch my legs," Marshal Crane said. "But first I have to say, I haven't enjoyed an evening so much in a very long time."

Marie started to make a reply, but noted how the marshal was looking at Gertrude, who was blushing brightly.

Stafford had stood, as well, and was also noticing the other two. "I'll help you with the children," he said, rather hushed, as his hand slid down her arm to catch her hand.

As they left the room, she heard Marshal Crane ask Gertrude if she'd like to step out onto the porch, just to stretch her legs.

"It's a good thing you are such a fast learner," Stafford whispered. "It looks like we may lose our cook faster than anticipated."

Marie frowned, but as his meaning settled she bit her lips to contain a giggle. All sorts of things happened then. Several inside her. They'd entered the kitchen, and as she started toward the stairway, he stopped her with a tug on her hand, spinning her round and bringing her entire body up against his. At almost the same instant, his mouth covered hers.

Not a single part of her protested. The opposite happened. She wound her arms around his waist and participated in the kiss she'd been dreaming of all day.

Stafford was the one to draw back, all too soon to her way of thinking, but his hug was as wonderful as his kiss had been. Nothing had ever felt so right. So real.

"I've wanted to do that all day," he whispered.

She couldn't very well admit she'd wanted the same thing. Not aloud, anyway. Inside was a different story. There she let bliss completely fill her heart.

"Come on," he said. "Let's get the kids in their beds."

He kept one arm around her while the other carried the lamp. They climbed the steps all the way to the window room, where the children were busy making cards stand on top of one another.

"Where did you learn to do that?" she asked, entering the room and already missing Stafford's arm.

Terrance, whose structure resembled a castle, glanced toward Stafford.

"Guilty," Stafford said. "I taught them."

"While you were leaning to cook," Samuel said. "It's fun. You should try it."

"Cooking or stacking cards?" she asked, pretending to be serious. It had been a long time since she'd been able to partake in a bout of teasing with the children. The seriousness of their situation hadn't allowed time for that. Actually, it hadn't been in her heart, not the way it was now.

"Stacking cards," Terrance said. "You've turned into a right fine cook."

"Oh, I have, have I?" The ability not to smile evaded her. "Should I make you scrambled eggs for breakfast tomorrow?"

"Uh, no," Terrance answered.

The sparkle had returned to his eyes, the one he used to have back in Chicago. She took a moment to examine each child, see the healthy glow they now had. While her gaze was on Charlie, it fell to his shirt collar. Usually twisted and wet from him sucking on it throughout the day, it was lying as flat as it had that morning. A moment before happiness totally overtook her, Marie asked, "None of you want scrambled eggs for breakfast?"

One by one, doing their best to hide grins, each of the children shook their heads. It was nothing really, yet the moment was so poignant Marie's eyes smarted. Then, as if they all comprehended what was happening at the same time, the air filled with laughter. There were hugs, too, disguised as tickling sessions, before they all set to straightening up the room.

When Stafford finally held a wiggling twin

under each arm as if they were bags of flour, Marie told Charlotte to retrieve the lamp from the table while Terrance picked up the one Stafford had carried up the stairs.

"Follow me, Terrance my boy," Stafford said teasingly. "You and Sam can help me get these two scalawags into bed while Marie helps the girls."

Still caught up in the silliness of it all, Marie mockingly whispered to Charlotte and Beatrice, "He doesn't know what he's in for."

Both girls giggled and nodded in agreement.

"I think I can handle it," Stafford replied.

"Yeah, we can handle it," Terrance piped in as conceited as Stafford had sounded.

"They're going to be shouting for help in no time," Charlotte said, with a smug expression.

"Let's hurry," Marie whispered, "so we're ready when they call for help."

"We won't be calling for help," Samuel insisted.

"Yeah," Terrance said. "I bet us boys are in bed while you girls are still brushing your hair."

Marie caught Stafford's gaze.

What have we gotten ourselves into?

She laughed, realizing she'd just read his mind.

He lifted a brow. "So the race is on?"

She bit her lip, tried hard not to answer.

Beatrice, on the other hand, was up for the challenge. "Yes," the girl said. "The race is on."

What a race it was. Marie could barely keep up with the clothes flying around. She ran from room to room, seeing to one of Charlotte's tasks, only to sprint out the door at Beatrice's yell for assistance.

Stafford was doing the same, and they side-stepped each other in the hallway, laughing as loudly as the children. She was too slow one time, darted left instead of right, and they collided. Stafford took her by the shoulders and held her until she had her feet beneath her again.

"It's a good thing the marshal and Gertrude are outside," he said. "Otherwise they'd be wondering if the roof was going to cave in."

"Not in this house," she answered. "It's too well built."

Time froze for a moment as they stood gazing into each other's eyes, but the trance was soon broken by the shouts echoing out of the bedrooms.

Laughing, Stafford let her go, and this time her feet were rather wobbly as she hurried into Beatrice's room. Or was it Charlotte's? Either way, she buttoned up the back of the nightgown, before saying, "Say your prayers then jump into to bed," and rushing down the hall to repeat the process.

Two trips later, she blew out the light beside Beatrice's bed. "I know we won," the girl said.

"I'll go see," Marie whispered. "It's awfully quiet out there."

"Yeah, it is," Beatrice whispered in return. "I still hope we won."

"I'll tell you in the morning," Marie answered as she pulled the door shut.

Stafford was directly across the hall, closing Samuel's door. She glanced left and right, noting all the doors were closed.

"A tie?" The lamp in his hand was shining up into his face, making his grin more charming than ever.

Still lost in the game, Marie tilted her head. "I don't know? What do the rooms look like? Are there clothes strewn about?"

Tiny flashes of light, like miniature stars, danced in his eyes as he took a step forward. "The condition of their rooms wasn't part of the race."

A click sounded down the hall. Then another, and another, followed by two more, one behind him and one behind her. Marie didn't look in any direction. Neither did Stafford. However, he said rather loud, "It's been declared a tie."

Groans sounded and Marie bit her lip.

"Hop into bed," he continued. "The first ones asleep win. I'll be checking in five minutes."

Giggles faded as the doors snapped shut, and Marie covered her mouth, muffling her own.

"You do this every night?" Stafford said incredulously.

"Yes," she answered. "Although it's usually at a slower pace and takes much longer."

He took her elbow and turned her to walk beside him down the hall. "One of Charlie's socks flew out the window."

She let out a chuckle.

"I'm glad it wasn't him."

Even while laughing, she said, "You wouldn't have let that happen."

"No," he said. "I wouldn't have. And I'm glad you know it."

The bedtime commotion was over, but her insides were still aflutter. "Of course I know that," she said. He turned, and in order to stay beside him, she did, too, following him up the staircase to the top floor. "Why are we going up here?"

"To return the lamp you're carrying."

"Oh." Her grip was so tight—just to make sure she didn't drop it—it would seem impossible she'd forgotten about the lamp, but she had. Stafford made it hard to remember anything. Even how to breathe. Each breath she took snagged in the back of her throat before tumbling its way into her lungs.

Once in the window room she walked to

the far side, to set the lamp on the table beside the chair she sat in to read to the children each day. Stafford had given permission to furnish the room with whatever was needed. Gertrude had helped her carry the chair up the stairs— it had been in the back parlor, as had the table. The only other thing they'd carried up was a large rug, giving the children something to sit on while playing with the toys they'd stacked in the room.

Stafford had paused by the door and she turned around. "The children love playing up here."

He shut the door, set down the lamp and slowly walked toward her, which caused her heart to skip several needed beats. Every movement he made was full of determination, and his stroll across the room was no different. His legs, long and lean, carried him smoothly, and his shoulders, broad and square, moved in time with each foot. He'd left his hat on the table near the front door before supper, and though he was handsome while wearing it, she liked how his hair fell across his forehead.

"I'm glad they like it."

"What child wouldn't?" she asked, waving a hand as she took a step forward.

"Don't move," he said, still approaching.

"Why?" There was nothing in her way, no

chance she might trip, or— The lamp. She hadn't blown it out.

He arrived as she started to turn and grasped both of her shoulders. "Don't move," he repeated.

"Why?" she asked again, though no longer caring what his reason might be.

"Because, earlier, when we were up here, you were standing right here, with the windows behind you and I wondered if I'd ever seen anything like it."

"Like what?"

"The stars reflecting against the glass, and you, standing among them, took my breath away."

His whisper, let alone the words, took her breath away. She didn't need air anyway. Did she? No. Not with the way his breath entered her mouth as his lips settled on hers. Her hands found his hard, powerful upper arms, and she held on, knowing this kiss would once again take her to that place where promises and wishes came true.

Stafford wasn't exactly sure when he'd made up his mind. It could have been at several points during the evening. He was going to marry her. Make her his wife for all time.

"You have no idea how badly I want you," he announced, somewhat surprised he'd allowed the words to escape and that he'd stopped kissing her long enough to say them.

The next time he pulled his lips from hers, he admitted, "I've got this fire in my belly that doesn't go away unless I'm kissing you."

"Me, too," she gasped with such tender sentiment his thoughts spun.

They kissed again, longer this time, more feverishly, and Stafford couldn't deny the need to feel her. As relentless as his lips and tongue, his hands moved up and down her back, and lower, to caress the firm behind he dreamed about seeing again. He explored her waist too, before shifting slightly so one hand could cup her breast. The perfect weight filling his hand aroused him in ways he'd have never imagined possible. He'd kissed those breasts last night, through the material of her dress, and wanted to do so again, but without any barriers.

Chapter Fifteen

Moments before he lowered her to the rug, Stafford regained a fleeting ounce of common sense. He couldn't take her here, not the way he wanted to. When they came together in the ultimate act of love, it would be in a soft bed, where they both could rest afterward, and repeat their actions over and over again until they were too exhausted to keep their eyes open. Then they'd sleep, and when a new day dawned, they'd start the loving process all over again.

He wasn't exactly sure where he found the ability to stop, but did, and he wrapped both arms around Marie to hold her against his chest. The fires of passion burned so hotly in his loins the room was probably as smoke filled as Mick's cabin had been right before bursting into flames.

The decision he'd made didn't come with all the answers he needed, but the way he loved

Marie, with an intensity that couldn't exist otherwise, he believed those answers would appear.

Stafford had set the lamp he'd carried up the stairs near the door, and once his and Marie's breathing returned to normal, somewhat, he took her hand. After blowing out the lamp on the table, he led her to the door and picked up the other lamp.

They descended the steps in silence, nothing more than the faint clip of her heels and the louder clop of his boots stepping on and off each stair. The idea of repeating tonight appealed to him profoundly, and he'd admit to anyone who questioned him that he'd changed. The things he now wanted couldn't be bought by striking it rich or even by working from sunup to sundown. Perhaps he'd simply come full circle, as his father had once told him he would, right before he left home, when he'd hated the world and all that lived in it.

It was hard to believe he'd held such wrath, and someday soon he'd tell Sterling he did understand. That some things, especially love, did just happen.

As they stepped onto the landing of the second floor, he let go of Marie's hand to press a finger against his lips and nod toward the closed doors lining the hall. Her smile was so precious, like a sunrise, full of promise and enchantment.

They peeked into the rooms, one by one, taking quiet moments to check on each sleeping child. In the room the twins shared she shook her head at him with a teasing grin and picked two pairs of britches, two shirts and three socks off the floor and laid them on a chair near the wardrobe as they exited.

Down the hall, Terrance was the only one awake. "Are the girls sleeping?" he asked.

"Yes," Stafford answered.

"Aw, shucks," he grumbled, while grinning from ear to ear. "That sure was fun."

"Yes, it was," Marie agreed, tucking the covers beneath his chin. "And if you go to sleep right now, we'll still declare it a tie in the morning."

"All right." He closed his eyes. "Good night."

Marie kissed his forehead while wishing him sweet dreams, and Stafford ruffled the boy's hair when she stepped aside. He would never claim a favorite, for each of the children were special in their own way, but Terrance was the first one he'd formed a bond with, and because of that, Stafford felt a strong kinship with the boy.

"Night, Stafford," Terrance said.

"Night," he replied as he pulled the door closed. Once in the hallway, the desire to kiss Marie flared inside him. Stopping once was something he'd been able to manage. Twice might not happen. He led her to her door. "I'll see you in the morning."

"But Marshal Crane and—"

He put a finger against her moving lips, absorbing the warmth of her mouth. "If Gertrude hasn't shown him to the guest room downstairs, I will." He held up the lamp. "I'll put this back and make sure the rest are extinguished."

She nodded, and he couldn't help but read the want in her eyes. He compromised by kissing her forehead.

"Good night."

"Good night," she said. "Thank you for—"

Pressing a finger to her lips again, he shook his head. He wasn't made of stone, and standing here, whispering with her, was wearing down his defenses. "Go to bed."

Marie opened her door and he thought about following her in, just to provide light for her, strike a match to the lamp beside her bed. It wouldn't be smart. Leaving would be hard.

She giggled then, and whispered, "Good night, Stafford," before closing the door.

He took a deep breath and thought about banging his head against the door just to jostle his mind, but instead he grinned and let the joy inside him break free. It had been a good night, and tomorrow would be a good day.

The day started out that way. Good. Everyone,

including Marshal Crane, ate a hearty breakfast before leaving for church. Stafford hadn't gone to church in years. Not because he didn't believe, but because he hadn't made the time to do so. Today, though, as Marie sat next to him in a dress made out of the fabric he'd purchased in town—he truly had never seen a more beautiful woman—he was looking forward to the event. Thanking the Lord for all the blessings bestowed upon him lately was more than fitting.

Marshal Crane rode alongside the wagon on the right, where he and Gertrude talked nonstop. The children were as full of spice and vinegar as ever, but there was no arguing or whining, and no one complained of their small bladders. The remembrance made him grin, and when he glanced toward Marie, she was smiling, too, and blushing, which was very becoming.

The service was likely thought provoking. Stafford sat through it, but didn't hear much of what the preacher said. He was too busy intercepting stares, mainly from men—married and not. Marie seemed to have captured everyone's attention. Thanks to Mrs. Smith, no doubt, who, with nose in the air, marched out of the building as soon as services ended.

Most folks were pleasant, including a tall young woman who introduced herself as the schoolmarm—she had a name, he just couldn't recall it—and asked if the children would be attending school when classes resumed in September.

Marie said she hoped it would be possible, but would need to discuss alternative options for the children with their guardian since the distance was too far to walk.

Stafford saw no problem. By then, the older ones would know how to ride well enough, and the twins were too young for school, yet he held his silence. That was one of the answers that hadn't come to him yet. Unlike Marie, the kids were legally Mick's.

Marshal Crane bid his farewells in the churchyard, promising—mainly Gertrude—that he'd be in these parts again soon. The Peterson family also said their goodbyes, with Becca insisting that next Sunday everyone was invited to their home for dinner after church.

The ride home was just as pleasurable as the one to town had been, and as Stafford put away the wagon, with help from Terrance and Samuel, he wondered exactly how he should go about asking Marie to marry him. It had to be soon. He'd never been a patient man.

"Could we go fishing after lunch, Stafford?" Samuel asked stepping out of the tack room where he and Terrance must have noticed the fishing poles.

"I don't see why not," Stafford answered. "We'll need some worms, though."

"We can dig some right now," Terrance answered.

"There's a shovel and pail in the tool shed," Stafford answered, liking the idea of stretching out on the grass near the stream. With Marie at his side, they could talk while the kids fished and played. Maybe he'd ask her then. Noting the white shirt he'd donned for church that morning, he stopped the boys before they reached the barn door. "Go change your clothes first."

"Yes, sir!" they chorused.

He chuckled while crossing the yard. This was a good life and was only going to get better. He certainly was one lucky man. A happy tune entered his head and he started whistling it as he bounded up the porch steps.

"Fishing?" Marie asked, standing near the front door the boys had dashed through.

"Sounds good to me," he said. "How about you?"

"I've never gone fishing."

"Never gone fishing?" he asked, as if appalled.

She laughed. "No." Holding out a glass she said, "Here. I just carried some apple cider up from the cellar. It's nice and cool after that long ride from church."

He took the glass and was about to take a

drink when he noticed a frown forming above her brows. Slowly, since an eerie sensation was inching its way up his spine, he turned in the direction of her gaze.

"That can't be Marshal Crane returning, can it?"

The cider almost slipped from his hand. Stafford tightened his hold, and then wishing it was whiskey, he downed the entire glass. "No," he said, fighting the regret filling his system. "That's not Marshal Crane."

Only one man he knew of rode a solid black horse. Had for years. As long as Stafford had known him. The rider, coming closer, would soon slow to a trot, then a walk to keep the dust down.

Stafford handed Marie the glass. "Thanks."

"Who is it? Do you know him?"

It wasn't as though he could put off the inevitable. "That," he said gravely, "is Mick Wagner."

There had been times in Marie's life that she'd wanted to run and hide, but never so much as now. It was impossible, though; her feet had frozen to the porch boards. The rest of her started to tremble and shake. A thud told her the glass had slipped from her fingers. It didn't break, just rolled until it stopped between two rungs of the white-painted railing that edged the porch. Marie gripped the column supporting the porch roof.

The rider had slowed his horse to a walk. It was a big animal, as black as the coal so many homes in Chicago burned for heat. The man was big, too, or appeared to be. Probably the same size as Stafford. That was the only similarity. Where Stafford was clean-shaven, this man had a full beard and mustache, the same sand color as the hair hanging well past his shoulders.

"You look almost surprised to see me," Mick said, as he kicked one leg behind him to swing out of his saddle.

Marie held on tighter to the column.

"I'm always surprised to see you," Stafford answered.

A tiny sigh escaped her lips. Of course he'd been talking to Stafford, not her. Actually, Mick Wagner may not have seen her yet, with the size of the column. She eased closer, hiding herself for a bit longer. It wasn't that she was afraid to meet him. She just didn't know if she was ready. If she'd ever be ready.

"I couldn't make heads or tails out of those messages you kept sending me, Staff," Mick said. "Then my ma returned home. I was stuck in Austin waiting on her. Knew I couldn't go on to Mexico until I said hi to her. Well, you ain't gonna believe this, but..."

Marie's skin grew chilled. Had Stafford sent messages about her?

Mick was still talking and she tried to clear her mind to listen.

"Ma had gone up to Chicago. Some lawyer had sent a wire asking about my whereabouts. Ma had wired back, told him I was out this way, and asked why. He wired again saying my cousin Emma Lou—we grew up together, she was my Pa's sister's daughter—and her husband were killed in a fire and they had six kids. Now orphans. Ma went up there to claim them, but they were gone. Seems some nursemaid left with the kids. Said she was bringing them out here to me. Have you seen them? Ma wants me to bring them down to Texas. Said she'll raise them."

Marie's heart stopped in her chest.

"Yeah," Stafford answered. "I've seen them. They're here."

"Where?" Mick asked.

Marie peeked around the column in time to see the man spin around, glancing toward his property.

"Hey," he said. "Where's my house?"

If only the column was big enough for her climb into. It was big enough, but it would also need a door. It wasn't as if she could just magically seep through the wood. It would be nice, though. To just disappear.

A hand grasped one of her elbows and tugged.

Having no choice, for Stafford was much stronger, Marie stepped out from behind the column.

"Mick, meet Miss Marie Hall. Your cousin's nursemaid." Stafford glanced toward her then. It would help if his smile didn't look so cynical. "Marie, meet Mick Wagner."

The man's eyes grew as round as egg yolks. "You're—" He turned toward Stafford. "That's the nursemaid?"

Where the children were concerned, she'd never been cowardly and couldn't start now. What was done was done, and what had to be, had to be. The coolness vibrating off Stafford increased her determination. He was acting remarkably close to how he had when they first met. Rather standoffish and boorish.

"Yes, Mr. Wagner, I'm the children's nursemaid." She held out one hand. "It's a pleasure to meet you."

Mick was staring at her again, all wide-eyed and open-mouthed. He clamped his lips shut and shook her hand with one of his gloved ones. "I…uh…well, I was expecting someone…older." He shot a glance toward Stafford. "You know, all gray haired and frumpy."

The only movement Stafford made was the tiniest hitch in his chin. That irritated Marie even more, but when she tried to tug her arm from his grasp, his grip tightened.

"I'll go find the children," she said, hoping that would make Stafford let loose. "So you can make their acquaintance."

Mick stopped his head mid-nod. "First, what happened to my house?"

Marie almost gagged on the lump that shot into her throat.

"That worn-out stove of yours," Stafford said. "We're lucky Marie and the children weren't hurt when it blew up."

"I should have guessed," Mick said, eyeing his property. "It was bound to happen sooner or later."

"I've staked out a new foundation," Stafford said. "And ordered lumber. It should arrive within a couple weeks."

"It ain't gonna be as big as yours, is it?"

Marie did note the humor in Mick's eyes, but it did little to calm her jittery nerves.

"You'll need a house this big," Stafford said. "You now have six kids."

Mick frowned and shook his head. "Didn't you hear me, Staff? I'm taking those kids to Texas."

"Texas?" Marie wasn't sure if she said the word or simply thought it.

She must have said it aloud because Mick answered, "Yeah, to my ma. She'll take them all. The lawyer in Chicago said the nursemaid wouldn't let them be put in the orphanage." He paused long enough to narrow his eyes, which were the same blue as Emma Lou's. "That would have been you, huh?"

"Yes, that would have been me," she answered. "Your cousin would not have wanted the children separated."

"That's what Ma said," he replied. "She arrived in Chicago a week or so after you'd left." He laughed then, as if the entire situation was rather comical. "I gotta tell ya, the telegraph lines were on fire. She wired her husband in Texas to say she was coming out here after the children and he wired back saying no, that she had to come home because I'd just wired them saying I was in Texas."

Marie didn't find anything funny right now, and was working out exactly how to say that when Mick's laughter stopped rather abruptly.

He was frowning again, and looking at Stafford. "Why were you wiring me about a bride?"

Marie wanted to hide all over again. Especially when Mick seemed to put everything together. His gaze returned to her and his expression wasn't joyous or irate, it was more as though he wanted to run and hide as much as she did.

"I think you should meet the children," Stafford said. "We can discuss the other details later."

Mick continued looking at her while he reached out and grabbed Stafford's free arm. "Will you excuse us, Miss—uh—"

"Hall," she supplied.

"Yeah, Miss Hall. Would you excuse us?"

Glad to do so, in part because Stafford would have to let her loose, she nodded. "Of course. The children will be in the front parlor when you're ready to meet them." She turned then, and kept her chin up even as the rest of her quaked. Why, oh, why had she pretended to be Mick Wagner's mail-order bride? That's right. It had been her only choice.

Stafford waited until the door closed behind Marie, cursing himself up one side and down the other for sending those stupid telegrams. He wasn't overly impressed with the whole Texas idea, either.

"You know I was always joking about the whole getting-a-wife idea, don't you, Staff? Neither one of us really wants that."

Stafford sighed. At one time he had known they were joking. The joke was on him, though, because now he did want it. He chose to put off that conversation for a short time. "You can't send the kids to Texas, Mick."

"I sure as hell can't keep them," Mick answered, speaking more freely now that Marie wasn't around. "I don't know a thing about having kids. Well, I know how they come to be, but I don't know about raising them. I don't want to know, either. My ma will take care of them. Be happy to. What's wrong with Texas anyhow?"

"There's nothing wrong with Texas," Stafford said. "But those kids already lost their parents, had to move away from one home. They've just gotten settled here. They shouldn't be uprooted again."

Mick took off his hat and slapped it against his thigh, sending out a cloud of dust that had no doubt been gathered in several states. "You don't expect me to keep them, do you?"

Stafford wasn't exactly sure what he wanted Mick to do, other than not send the kids away. "Marie has a life insurance policy from your cousin, naming you as the benefactor. The money is for the children."

"Marie? Oh, Miss Hall." Mick wiggled one brow. "I truly expected some old gray-haired nag." Frowning, he continued, "Why'd you say she was my bride?"

"She didn't have enough money for the tickets for all of them to travel out here, so she claimed to be your mail-order bride, telling the railroad you'd pay for their passages once they arrived."

Mick was scratching his head, so Stafford continued his tale, "Walt Darter rode out and told me her and the kids were in Huron. I picked them up, paid their fares, and brought them home."

"But if you knew she wasn't, why'd you wire me?"

"I didn't know she wasn't. Not in the beginning." It was too complicated to explain easily, and he couldn't very well tell his partner he'd fallen in love with her, so Stafford switched subjects and tried using a bit of subtlety. "Your ma's getting up in years, Mick. She's already raised her family. Weston and Charlie, the youngest of your cousin's children, are only four. They'd be a lot for your Ma to take on."

Mick squirmed, shuffling his feet and shaking his head. "But, Staff, me? Married? With six kids?"

"That's not what I'm telling you do to, Mick," Stafford quickly corrected him.

"What else can I do? I can't raise them alone." Mick was now rubbing his mustache. "At least the nursemaid's a looker."

Jolted into a reaction, Stafford held up one hand. "Mick—"

The door behind them opened. "Mr. Wagner, are you ready to meet the children?" Marie's gaze landed on Stafford then. "I'm sorry to interrupt, but lunch is getting cold."

It was Mick who replied, or at least spoke. "You know how to cook, Miss Hall?"

"Yes, Mr. Wagner, I do."

Now. Stafford bit his lip.

"Really? I didn't think they taught nursemaids how to cook," Mick said as he shouldered his way toward the door.

Where would you have ever gained that insight? Stafford wanted to ask as he followed. Mick had never had a nursemaid, and he was a terrible cook, but meals meant a lot to him. He ate each one as if it might be his last.

"Well, let's see the little tykes," Mick said.

Stafford grinned. Small bladders had come to mind.

Twenty minutes later all Stafford's humor had given way to a red haze of ire. The kids were so well behaved he wanted to puke, and the way Mick was flirting with Marie—yes, flirting—with dazzling grins and oozing charm, Stafford wanted to punch something. For the first time ever, that something might just be his partner's nose.

Marie was lapping it up as though she were Polly going after a bowl of leftover gravy. She was rhapsodizing about how well the children behaved, completed chores, recited poems and ciphered numbers. Which was all true, of course, but what about fighting in the back of the wagon and small bladders? Or hiding pregnant dogs?

Mick should know about all those things, too, if he was considering taking them on.

The only other person frowning was Gertrude, but that was probably because she was missing Marshal Crane. The two of them had hit it off. They'd met before, the marshal had explained this morning while helping harness the horses. He'd investigated her husband's death and stopped to check on her whenever he came this way.

"Stafford?"

Stafford looked across the table, at Mick. He didn't say a word, just waited to hear what his partner wanted.

"Have you drawn up a house plan for me?"

"Not completely. I have the general idea in my head. Why?"

"Because I think Marie should help you design it," Mick said. "She knows what the kids will need, what she'll need."

He wasn't exactly sure if it was fire or ice that entered his veins. The table grew exceedingly quiet and the only one not looking at their plate was Mick. His gaze was expectant.

"I'll draw something up." Stafford laid his napkin down and pushed away from the table.

"Are we still going fishing, Stafford?"

He stopped near the dining room door. Terrance had never sounded quite so forlorn. It almost gutted Stafford to say, "Sorry, Terrance. Maybe another day."

Leaving the house he cursed himself all over again. There was no reason he couldn't go fishing, other than that he needed to distance himself from everyone, everything, until he could get his thinking back in order. He loved Marie, still wanted her, but that wasn't it. He'd forgotten one thing. Marie was committed to those kids. He loved that about her, but where they went she went. Whether that might be across the creek or Texas.

Chapter Sixteen

So this is what it felt like. Love. Marie couldn't say the exact moment it had happened, but she knew it was real. It wasn't something she'd thought about—falling in love—but now that it had happened, she couldn't imagine life without it.

She glanced up to meet the gaze reflected back at her in the mirror. The image in the silvered glass looked the same as the one she'd seen for years, but inside she was different. She was no longer just a nursemaid and wasn't going to live the rest of her life as one.

Reaching such a revelation hadn't come easily. A broken heart is rather painful, especially to someone who didn't know such a thing could happen. That, too, she'd rectify, but first things first. Today, instead of wondering what the day might bring, she was going to make something happen.

Upon leaving her room, she saw to the morning tasks, helping the children dress and comb their hair, and then prepared breakfast. Mick joined them for the meal, since he was living in Stafford's house, too, and would until his was built.

Looking across the table, Marie drew a deep breath, willing her nerves to remain in check.

Mick was nice and funny, and the children liked him, but they liked him for the wrong reasons. In her mind, anyway. Though he was close to the same age as Stafford, Mick was annoyingly immature. Right now, he was teaching the children how to make spoons stick to the ends of their noses by blowing on them.

She cast a warning gaze around the table, which caused the children to set their spoons down and resume eating the meal. If Stafford had been here, they'd all be talking. The subjects would be varied, and there'd be laughter, but not the uncouth kind instigated by Mick. In the week that had passed, the boys, particularly Terrance and Samuel, had become almost as unruly as they'd been on the train ride west.

A moment rarely passed when she didn't miss Stafford, and during his absence she'd come to realize the little things he'd done that she'd taken for granted. How he'd helped Weston or Charlie cut their food, or refilled their glasses with milk, and those were just mealtime things.

In order to stay calm, Marie had to chase all thoughts of Stafford from her mind. He'd cast her aside easily enough. No, she wasn't going to think like that. Gertrude was right. Men were like children. They had to be told things.

She had a few things to tell him, all right, and he'd listen. He wouldn't have a choice. Neither would Mick. This had all gone on long enough.

"Mick." She waited for him to pull the spoon from his nose. "I'd like to speak with you after breakfast."

"Sure," he said, waggling an eyebrow toward Terrance.

She chose not to chastise the boy for his smirk. Mick's silliness wasn't harmful, just tiresome—to her, not the children.

It was close to an hour later when Marie finally settled in the front parlor. Gertrude had taken the children outside as requested. The other woman was far more than a cook, she'd become the best friend Marie had ever had, and had taught her about several other things.

Mick strolled in, the spurs always attached to his boots jingling as he walked. "So," he said slowly. "Have you set a date?"

Marie honestly didn't know if he was teasing when it came to her marrying him or not. "No," she answered as he sat in the chair on the other side of the small table. "That's one of the things we need to discuss."

If only there was a way to chase aside the nervous energy inside her. Her trembling hands made her stomach queasy and that made concentrating difficult. She was about to be rather bold, assuming things, but she had to believe she was right. Starting with an explanation might help. "I've explained that the Meekers hired me over a year ago, and how I've been with the children every day since."

He held up a hand. "I've already decided I'm not taking them to Texas. Stafford was right. It would be too much for my mother."

Marie couldn't stop the way her mind shot off. "Stafford? When have you spoken to him?"

"Just that first day I was home, before he went to town. Red saw him yesterday, though, said he's almost done designing the plans for those precut houses for Otis."

She nodded, having heard all about how Stafford was staying out at the lumber company on the other side of Merryville, helping the man who owned the mill design houses that people just had to hammer together. Everyone at church had talked about it on Sunday. As had Ralph Peterson when she, Gertrude and the children had joined him and his family for dinner that day. That had been two days ago, and she'd once again seen flashes of the future she wanted.

Stafford hadn't been kissing her that time, but he'd been in the images, and that night, when they arrived home, Gertrude had helped her to understand all the things happening inside her and to figure out a way her wishes could come true.

Wrestling her thoughts back to the children, Marie said, "I'm glad you're no longer considering sending them to Texas."

Mick twirled his hat around and around by the brim. "Marie," he said somberly. "I...uh... well, I rightly don't know how to tell you, other than to flat-out say I'm not cut out for marriage."

That was the understatement of the year. She did her best to refrain from letting him know how deeply she agreed by offering a small nod.

"But I can't raise those kids on my own." His blue eyes reminded her a lot of Terrance's when he'd been attempting to decipher the ins and outs of his parents' deaths. "I don't want them adopted out, either," Mick said. "So the only thing I can think of is for you to continue on as their nursemaid. I'll pay you anything you ask."

His offer was sincere, and at one time that was exactly what she'd wanted, yet she had to shake her head.

He slumped in his chair.

"I do have another idea," she said.

"What's that?"

She took a deep breath before answering, "You could let me adopt them."

Stafford stared at the can of beans he'd planned on opening for supper. There were also half a jar of pickles and two biscuits left over from the lunch that Ralph had delivered that day. The three of them, him, Ralph and Otis, had eaten right here in the lumberyard office he was staying in, talking about the number of orders already coming in.

It had been what he needed, a diversion, a place to stay away from his house for a while. Let Marie get to know Mick, see if she was still willing to become his partner's bride.

His stomach revolted at the thought, and he turned from the shelf where the can of beans sat. The sun was just about to disappear, ending yet another long day, and he walked to the open doorway.

The big water wheel was still but the paddles continued to drip, having grown motionless only a short time ago when all the workers left. Otis and his family lived a short distance away, in a nice two-story home, and the shouts of children not yet being called in for the night filtered down the hill.

Stafford couldn't help but smile, thinking of the kids back at his ranch. Grasping the doorframe overhead with both hands, he stood there, just listening. This wasn't where he'd planned on going when he rode away from the ranch nine days ago. It's just where he'd ended up. The excuse of checking on his lumber order made one thing lead to another and here he was, drawing up plans that specified exactly how many boards, and their exact size, were needed for each home. Everyone liked the idea, and with the orders they already had, real homes would soon replace a good number of tents in Merryville. That was a good thing, considering winter wasn't too far off.

Dropping his arms, he turned, glancing toward the extra set of clothes sitting on a small table in the corner. Otis's wife had washed them for him. Once he'd agreed to stay here to draw up the plans, he'd sent word to the ranch, asking Shorty to see that a few things were delivered to him.

The small office was like an oven, and left him smelling about as ripe as an old man who only came to town once a year. Stafford gathered the clothes and headed for the river. He'd stretched out this stay as long as he could. Tomorrow he'd go home. Back to the ranch. Marie should have made her mind up by now.

At the riverbank, he stripped to his skivvies

and then dove into the flowing water. When he surfaced, filling his lungs, he flipped onto his back and relaxed, letting the current carry him downstream.

It felt good to let something else be in control for a moment. Every part of him had been strung tight the past few days. Not from work. From worry. He wasn't exactly sure what he'd do if Marie and Mick chose to marry.

When that had happened before, with Sterling and Francine, he'd been angry, but not hurt. He understood the difference now. He also understood this wasn't Marie's doing. She wasn't breaking an engagement with him. He'd never asked her to marry him, and he worked hard to remember that.

He flipped over and started swimming upstream, working against the current with every stroke. The exertion felt good, and once he'd reached the spot where his clothes lay on the bank, he flipped onto his back again, catching his breath as he once more started floating in the opposite direction.

His heart was thudding from the swim, and he closed his eyes to let everything relax again. That didn't happen. Instead something snapped in his mind. What on earth was he doing? He'd rather swim upstream than float downstream any day.

He dropped his feet to sink below the water, and when he came up, he started swimming again. He'd walked away from something he'd wanted once and wasn't about to do it again. Mick might be his best friend, and an all-around good guy, but he wasn't responsible enough to take on six kids.

A rather sarcastic laugh sputtered out of Stafford's lips. Sterling had said practically the same thing about him at one time. Said he wasn't responsible enough for marriage.

He hadn't been then, but he was now. Furthermore, Marie needed to know just what her choices were. He loved her in a way he'd never loved Francine. Couldn't have. He hadn't known something this powerful existed.

Stafford shed his wet underclothes and pulled on his britches, socks and boots. He flipped his dry shirt over one shoulder and bundled his dirty clothes along with his wet ones. He'd shove them all in his saddlebags in a few minutes. He was heading home. Tonight rather than tomorrow.

Walking between the big water wheel and the office, he paused, seeing a horse and rider coming up the road. He'd heard of mirages, but had never experienced one. Several blinks later it was still there. It was the murky time of evening, where day hadn't yet given in to night, yet he made out the image. Clearly. The horse was Ginger and Marie was the rider.

She didn't even know how to ride a horse.

He barely paused long enough to throw his soggy bundle toward the platform the office sat upon while marching forward. The need to pull her out of the saddle, make sure she was all right and then kiss the daylights out of her had his hands balling at his sides.

She was wearing that peach-colored dress again and the hat he'd given her. Breathtaking, that's what she was. More so even than he remembered.

Keeping his breathing even was harder now than when he'd been swimming. He did it though, even managed to voice a question.

"When did you learn to ride?" he asked as she brought the horse to a stop.

Her grin was adorable. "I don't know that I have," she answered. "I've just held on, hoping I wouldn't fall off." Tilting her head to one side, she added, "Terrance gave me instructions before I left the ranch. He said they were the exact ones you gave him on how to ride." She glanced toward the ground. "However, I didn't ask how to get down."

Stafford reached up, took her waist and held his breath as a bolt of heat almost split him in two. "What are you doing here? Is something wrong at the ranch?"

She placed both hands on his shoulders. "Everyone is fine. The children asked me to tell you hello. They miss you."

He lifted her out of the saddle and not pulling her close was difficult. His shirt must have fallen from his shoulder because his skin burned from the touch of her palms and fingertips.

Her feet touched the ground, but he didn't let go of her waist. Couldn't just yet. Not with the way she looked at him.

"I've missed them, too," he said, unable to come up with anything else. His throat felt as though it was coated with sand.

She bit the corner of her bottom lip, blinked once and then said, "I've missed you."

The physical ache in his chest, the one that had kept him awake every night since he'd left the ranch disappeared, leaving nothing in its wake except profound joy. He bent his head, ready, so very ready, to take her lips.

A hand, well, the tips of four fingers, intercepted his action.

"No, Stafford," she whispered. "If you start kissing me, I won't be able to say what I have to tell you."

Half afraid he'd imagined she'd said she missed him, he took a step back and dropped his hands from her waist. Something he could only compare to fear clutched his guts and clung there. "Tell me what?"

Regret instantly formed. His bark had startled both Marie and Ginger. He reached around her and took Ginger's reins to lead the animal toward the paddock holding Stamper.

"So this is where you've been staying?" Marie asked, walking beside him.

Not in the mood for small talk, he nodded.

"Are you almost finished?"

Not bothering to unsaddle the animal, he simply knotted the reins so Ginger wouldn't stumble on them, looped them over her neck and opened the gate. Once he'd latched it closed, he turned to Marie. It was close to being dark now, but he could see her as plainly as if the sun was shining. "What do you want to tell me?"

Marie had never been so lightheaded. It could have been from the long ride—the sun had been fierce—or it could be from seeing Stafford. He must have been swimming. His hair was still wet. A water droplet fell from a strand every now and again, and his glistening skin took her breath away.

That could be why her head was spinning. No air. Then again, it could be because she'd stopped his kiss. That had taken all the strength

she'd ever possessed for she had wanted it so
badly. His lips against hers. His tongue inside
her mouth. His hands touching her in the most
wonderful and scandalous places.

"Marie?"

Stafford wasn't an overly patient man. She
knew that about him. She liked it, too. There really wasn't anything she didn't like about him.

He had that look in his eye right now, the one
that said he didn't have all day to wait for her
to say what she had to say. It made her want to
smile, and she bit her lips together, trying not to.

The way he cocked his head said his tolerance
was slipping. It was just as well. She could think
until she was blue and not have a clever way of
saying it, so she simply took a breath and asked,
"Will you marry me, Stafford?"

He took a step backward, a slight stumble
actually, and her instinct was to reach out and
grab his arm.

Snapping shut the jaw that had gone slack, he
said, "What?"

It wasn't the exact reaction she'd hoped for, so
she started the explanation she'd rehearsed while
traveling upon the horse's back mile after mile.
"I asked Mick if I could adopt the children, and
they don't want to leave your ranch, your house.
If you were to marry me, we could stay right

where we are. Mick would be next door. He is their only living relative and—"

"You want me to marry you so the kids don't have to leave my house?"

"I just can't uproot them again and—"

He grabbed both of her arms. "The children? This is only about the children?"

The annoyance in his voice forced her to snap her mouth shut. He cared so much about the children, was so wonderful with them, she'd thought that would be the part he'd understand, accept. It didn't feel that way though, and she couldn't help but wonder if she and Gertrude had been wrong.

Glancing up, refusing to let the burning in her throat make speaking impossible, she said, "No, it's not only about the children. It's about me. I tried, Stafford, I truly did, to obey all the rules, to not…to not want certain things, but I want—" The burning was growing stronger, as was the sting in her eyes. She swallowed and pressed on. "I want you. I want to be your wife."

His features had softened, or maybe it was the shadows of night, the mist in her eyes.

"Why?" he asked quietly.

She didn't exactly know for sure, since it had never been in her life, yet it was the only explanation she had. With a shrug, she posed it as a question, "Because I love you?"

He lifted a brow. "Do you or don't you?"

Explaining her past might have been a better way to approach all this. "I was left in the hallway at the orphanage in Chicago as a baby. That's where I got my last name. Hall. I was adopted twice, but neither one worked out. So I lived at the orphanage until I was old enough to go to Miss Wentworth's school, and—"

Frowning, he held up one hand. "What do you mean, didn't work out? People can't return an adopted child."

"Yes, they can," she told him. "People get rid of things that aren't needed." Refusing to let that take hold, she continued, "A rule at Miss Wentworth's school included servitude of seven years to those who couldn't pay their tuition upon acceptance. I only had a little over a year left when I was assigned to the Meekers. It was to be short term, just until they could find someone else. When Emma Lou wanted to hire me permanently, Miss Wentworth said the only way that could happen was for them to pay off my debt."

He smoothed back the hair on one side of her head. "That's all interesting, but I believe my question was whether you love me or not."

"I'm getting to that part." She wanted him to understand why it had taken her so long to figure out what was happening. How she'd fallen in love with him. "When the Meekers died, I still owed them, and if I didn't find a way to keep the children all together, I'd have to return to Miss Wentworth's. Start all over."

His other hand was on the other side of her face, holding it still. "That's why you brought them out here?"

"No. Yes." This wasn't going as she'd planned. How could it, with him touching her and looking upon her so tenderly? "I thought the life insurance policy and Mick, was the answer. I didn't want to see the children separated. They'd already lost so much." She had to close her eyes, break connection with his penetrating gaze in order to think straight. Lifting her lids, she said, "But there was more to it. I love them. I didn't realize that until you left. Mainly because I didn't know what love was."

"And you do now?"

She nodded.

"You love the children?"

"Yes, and I love you."

She couldn't say he grinned, for his lips didn't curl upward, but his eyes sparked. "What about Mick?" he asked.

Moving, even her head, was impossible with his hold, the way his fingertips were combing her hair. "He's nice enough, and the children like him, but…" Mick did have many redeeming characteristics and she didn't want to sell him short. "I can't marry him."

Stafford cocked his head to one side. "I make a good second choice, huh?"

That sent Marie right off the cliff. "Oh, for goodness' sake." He'd frustrated her before, but not to this extent. "I just told you I love you."

Laughter rang out. "You are so adorable when flustered."

Before she had a chance to respond Stafford's lips met hers, and everything else ceased to exist. She clung to him, working her fingers into his warm, firm flesh, while his tongue danced with hers.

He ended the kiss by tilting her head back slightly. "I love you, too," he said. "And I was going to ask you to marry me."

The moon was out, the sky dark, yet it was as if sunshine was being poured over her, filling her very soul. Gertrude had insisted Stafford loved her, yet Marie had to ask, "You do?"

After kissing the tip of her nose, he said, "Yes, I do. I was going to ask you to marry me before Mick arrived home, and as soon as I arrived home tonight. I even contemplated asking you while lifting you out of the saddle a few minutes ago."

Too full of elation to think straight, she asked, "Why didn't you?"

"Hell if I know," he said, moments before kissing her again.

Chapter Seventeen

"You still can," Marie whispered. "Ask me. If you want to."

Stafford wanted a lot of things. Such as her wearing fewer clothes than she was, a comfortable bed, big enough for the two of them, and to never stop kissing her. He brushed his lips over both of her cheeks before taking a step back. "Marie Hall, will you marry me?"

Her giggle was just one of the sounds he'd missed so much the past week. "Yes."

"When?"

"Whenever you want." The smile dropped from her lips as she whispered, "I'm serious about adopting the children, Stafford. We all come together."

"I wouldn't have it any other way," he answered.

She took another deep breath. As she let it

out, she whispered, "Mick told me about your brother's wife."

Stafford had told himself he was over all that, and the fact nothing erupted inside him proved it. "I never loved her," he said. "Not like I love you."

"I promise to do anything, everything I can to make you happy. I'll learn—"

He stopped her by whispering, "I've no doubt you will. Your determination is just one of the things I love about you." Knowing himself as well as he did, Stafford kissed her one last time and then took her hand. "Come on."

"Where are we going?" she asked.

"Home," he answered.

"But it's dark, and it's a long ride."

"I know. But we can't stay here."

It took Stafford a matter of five minutes to gather his shirt, grab his other belongings and saddle Stamper. While helping Marie onto Ginger, he commended himself on his fortitude. He would not kiss her again tonight. Would not.

He failed. It was a long ride home. His stamina was sorely tested several times the following week, as well. She'd become the center of his universe, and it delighted him to no end to realize he'd become the center of hers, too. They couldn't be in the same room without touching, and the glimmer in her eyes drove him to the very edge of endurance at times. He held strong, though, and slept in the bunkhouse until the following Sunday.

That afternoon he discovered that his house, as big as it was, wasn't big enough. Not for the wedding. There weren't enough chairs, either, so people sat in the backs of their wagons lining the creek bed on both sides, with the children right up front, as he and Marie stood on the bridge. It had been Gertrude's idea. She said that way everyone could see them. The woman had also put her needle to work again, sewing him a new white shirt and Marie a shimmering gold gown that made her shine as brightly as the sun overhead when they exchanged their vows.

Shortly after the ceremony ended, Stafford's patience evaporated. The food—enough to feed the entire town, most of whom had shown up, including Verna Smith—was set up in Mick's bunkhouse. His partner was playing host and doing a great job of it. He even had Verna blushing and giggling like a schoolgirl.

"Come on," Stafford whispered in his bride's ear.

"Where are we going?" she asked.

"Home."

"We are home," she insisted, even while walking beside him. She did glance over her shoulder, at the people entering the building for a plate of food or cup of punch. "Aren't you hungry?"

"Not for food."

"Won't we be missed?"

He scooped her into his arms while walking across the bridge. "No. Mick and Gertrude have everything under control, and what they don't catch, Marshal Crane will."

"But it's our wedding. Surely we should…" She pinched her lips together having caught his gaze. Then, smiling, she finished, "Go home now."

Stafford carried her all the way to his—no, their—bedroom. Once inside, he kicked the door shut and, with her still in his arms, fell onto the bed. He groaned, or maybe it was more of a growl. "I didn't think this moment would ever come."

Laughing, Marie rolled off him and scooted into the center of the bed, resting her head on a pillow with her hair cascading around her face. He'd asked her to leave it down today. Crawling up to lean over her, he ran his fingers through the long, lush strands. "You are so beautiful."

"You're only saying that because you love me," she said.

"You sound awfully sure of yourself," he teased.

"I graduated at the top of my class," she replied tartly.

He laughed. "Yes, you did, and I do love you,

but even before I knew I loved you, I thought you were beautiful."

Her cheeks turned a soft shade of pink as she cupped his face with both hands. "I keep pinching myself to make sure I'm not dreaming."

"We aren't dreaming." It did amaze him, how much he loved her, but it completely astonished him how much she loved him. He'd questioned it, a few times anyway, but that was only because of his past, which he'd let go. Completely. This was now his life. Marie and all six of the children they were adopting.

"I'm going to show you," he whispered, "for hours, that this is no dream."

"Just hours?" she asked coyly.

"All right, years."

Years were what Marie wanted, and she pulled Stafford's face down, captured his mouth with the kind of kiss she'd wanted to initiate for days. She may not have ever been loved before, but that no longer mattered. Stafford's love made up for it.

The kiss had the fire inside her flaring hotter than ever. Or maybe it was the fact this kiss would lead to the ultimate union. The one Gertrude had told her about, assured her it was nothing to fear. As if she could ever fear Stafford.

Love him. Want him. Support him. Cherish him. But never fear him.

When his lips left hers, started kissing her nose and eyelids and forehead, her fingers found the string tie at his neck. After removing it, she started on the buttons of his shirt. Ever since seeing his bare chest, weeks ago while traveling out here, she'd dreamed about it, wanted to explore it at leisure, feel every curve, every inch of skin.

She parted his shirt and leaned forward to kiss the hollow of his throat and nuzzle his neck.

His hands had already roamed along her sides and were working their way up her torso. "Where are the buttons on this dress?" his whispered. The question tickled her ear.

"They run up the back."

He growled. She laughed.

Grasping both shoulders, he pressed her deeper into the pillows. "Fine, I'll start somewhere else."

He sat up, and when she reached for him, wanting him back, he grabbed both of her wrists with one hand. Placing them on her stomach, he said, "Keep your hands right there."

"Why?"

"Because you won't need them for a while."

"What? Why not?"

His grin was the most charming she'd ever seen, and the way he lifted a brow and then winked had a surge of fire bursting inside her, much like the one that had blown apart the stove in the cabin.

Starting with her shoes, he removed the clothes covering her legs, article by article, inch by inch. He told her what he was doing the entire time, and explained how he was going to kiss her. Her ankles, her shins, her knees. Each one made her sink deeper into the mattress and several times she had to close her eyes, she was so overcome with pleasure. Her skirt was flared out across the bed, with his hands beneath it, slowly tugging her pantaloons down. The sensation was unfathomable, and had her giggling.

"Ticklish, are you?" he asked.

She shook her head. "Just excited." A flash of embarrassment heated her cheeks. "I always giggle when excited."

"Then I'll have to excite you more often," he said. Leaning forward he kissed the tip of one of her breasts, right through the material.

"Stop that," she said teasingly, while truly hoping he'd do it again.

"Not on your life, darling."

She giggled again. "All right."

He pushed her skirt up, exposing her now-bare thighs. His hands rested on her knees, and then with firm, warm pressure, he moved them upward, toward her hips, his thumbs pressing into her inner thighs. Short of reaching her very center, his hands reversed, went back to her knees, slow, steady and firm. He repeated the action several times and created a mass of turbulence in the spot that, up until now, had been seen by no one but her. Now it wanted to be set free, exposed fully to him, and she experienced no embarrassment about it. In truth, she could barely contain her want, and she lifted her hips, trying to encourage his hands not to stop. Not to return to her knees.

"Hmm," he groaned huskily. "I almost can't believe I'm about to see it again."

Trying to think beyond the misty, wonderful fog his touch created, she asked, "What? See what again?"

He leaned down, kissed the underside of her chin and then her neck. "Your lily-white backside. The little glimpse I caught on the trail wasn't nearly enough."

Not an ounce of the humiliation she'd felt that day returned. "Ah, yes," she said, sighing at how wonderful life had become. "The day you became my hero."

"Your hero?" His hands were on her knees again, and he wrapped his fingers beneath them, lifting until her heels dug into the mattress so she could hold her legs up herself. "All this time I thought I was the wrong cowboy."

She couldn't help but laugh, and then assure him, "You could never be the wrong cowboy, Stafford."

Starting at her knees, he kissed the entire length of her thigh, and when the warmth of his breath caressed her juncture, Marie lost all ability to think. She could feel though, the tender caress of his mouth, the undemanding brush of his tongue. Each foray, no matter how soft and gentle, had her responding. Her body needed no mental command to react. Her hips rose, her legs parted further, begging him to continue.

He caught her bottom with both hands and lifted her, kissing her there as he did her mouth, with his tongue twisting and curling, exploring every inch.

A fiery straining grew at her point of entry, and an urgent need had her legs trembling. Powerless, Marie was unable to protest, not that she wanted to. Not to Stafford, not at what he was doing, but she wasn't able to encourage him, either. The sensation was so overpowering she couldn't speak, tell him how glorious he made her feel.

Marie flung an arm across her face, bit into her forearm to muffle the cry of absolute perfection building beneath his mouth. But there was more. Much, much more. Desire—she had no idea what else it might be—red hot and maddening in an utterly pleasing way, filled her very being until she was so full there was nowhere for it to go.

She closed her eyes, only to wrench them open as the turmoil, the marvelous chaos inside her, let loose. A current of unimaginable satisfaction flowed throughout her body, making her heart hammer so hard she felt it clear to her toes.

"Oh, my," she mumbled, running a hand over the sweat beading on her forehead.

Stafford lowered her trembling legs to the bed and, hands on both sides of her, leaned over and kissed her. As if she wasn't already senseless enough.

He chuckled, his breath filling her mouth. "Did you like that?"

She managed to open one eye. "What do you think?"

"Want more?"

The exhaustion that had left her limp disappeared. The promise in his eyes replaced it with excitement, and she giggled.

"Excited?"

"Yes," she admitted.

"Good." He pulled her into sitting position. "Then let's get rid of this dress."

Completely forgetting the satisfaction that had just consumed her, she pushed the shirt off his shoulders. "You have a few clothes we need to get rid of, too."

In its own right, undressing Stafford filled her with a new kind of excitement, and when all was said and done, when they were once again on the bed, the throbbing in her breasts, which he'd kissed thoroughly without any material separating the heat of his mouth from her nipples, told her that the mind-stealing sensation he'd created before was on the way again.

More powerfully than before, because she knew what to expect, her body took over again. Reacting to each touch Stafford provided, her blood rushed from point to point. She explored him, too, and relished the way he assured her that he liked her touching him, tasting him.

He was a large man, in all areas, and though she anticipated the final act, the coming together, she did harbor a touch of alarm. How *that* would fit *there,* it seemed impossible.

"Don't fear," he whispered, as if she'd expressed her uncertainties aloud. "I promise it will be all right."

His gaze was so sincere, and so loving, she had to believe him. "I know."

"I love you," he whispered.

"I know that, too."

"Then hold that thought," he said, guiding the tip of himself toward her.

His movements were slow, and Marie felt herself welcoming him, as if she'd waited her entire life just for him. She had, and remembering that had her pleasure increasing as Stafford entered her. Instinct made her hips arch upward again, as they had earlier, but Stafford wouldn't allow that. With steady pressure he held her still while he moved into her.

A quick, shocking slice of pain had her stiffening, and he kissed her then, deeply, wholly. Marie wasn't sure if she'd relaxed, or if her body had expanded more during their kiss, but the sensation of his hips meeting hers, of him totally inside her, increased her pleasure tenfold.

Stafford starting moving then, and kissing her, and the combination was as wondrous as it was commanding. That straining sensation was back, the one that said desire would soon overcome her, and this time, she accepted it fully, let it take her away.

When she was beyond holding on anymore, the riot that let loose and fanned throughout her body was full of love. Stafford was holding her just as tightly, and his body was quaking, too, telling her they'd just shared the most intimate, profound act possible. True love fully united.

"Are you all right?" he asked, after they'd both stopped gasping. He rolled off her but hugged her against his side.

"All right?" she asked, propping her chin on his shoulder to gaze into his handsome face. The one she'd wake up to every morning and fall asleep beside every night. "Of course I'm all right. I'm married to you. Life couldn't be more all right in any possible way."

They'd been married at three in the afternoon, so sunlight still shone through the windows, bathing them in its evening glow, and she wondered if others thought their disappearance scandalous. Too happy, too content to care, she twirled a fingertip in a few of the fascinating hairs covering Stafford's chest. "Except," she finally said, slowly.

He laid a hand over hers. "Except what?"

"Well, how would you feel about seven children?"

One brow arched, and she grinned. He always looked so charming when he did that.

"Six aren't enough?"

She shrugged. "For you?"

He flipped around so she was flat on her back with him leaning over her again. "No. I was thinking eight."

"Eight?" She waited a moment, just until a tiny frown formed between his brows, and then she laughed. "I could live with that. After all, I am an excellent nursemaid."

* * *

When all was said and done, Marie and Stafford raised nine children and had twenty-seven grandchildren, fifty six great-grandchildren and…

* * * * *

MILLS & BOON®

Want to get more from Mills & Boon?

Here's what's available to you if you join the
exclusive **Mills & Boon eBook Club** today:

✦ *Convenience – choose your books each month*
✦ *Exclusive – receive your books a month before
  anywhere else*
✦ *Flexibility – change your subscription at any time*
✦ *Variety – gain access to eBook-only series*
✦ *Value – subscriptions from just £1.99 a month*

So visit **www.millsandboon.co.uk/esubs** today
to be a part of this exclusive eBook Club!